AN

The blue h   the marigolds were in place, even a few of the stakes had been left in the ground, pieces of twine dangling like forlorn windsocks from where they had been tied, but the tomato plants themselves were missing. Pile after pile of dark rich soil sat upturned in what had once been neat rows. Whoever had done this had grabbed the plants and ripped them out of the ground, roots and all. A few tomatoes, both red and green, lay scattered about, most trampled, no doubt, by the bootheel of the plant burglar.

The ground under their feet was soggy, and a garden hose continued to leak water out onto the churned-up earth, nearly drowning the bright yellow marigolds. By all appearances, it looked as if the crop had been ripped up and carted away while someone was watering the plants.

And that someone was lying face down in front of the high-topped wooden planting table that sat in one corner, stacked with supplies necessary for the growing side of the business.

"Is that—" Sissy started. From where she stood, she couldn't see the face of the person, but the industrial-blue pants and the mud-caked work boots seemed to indicate the person was male.

"Walt Summers," Bethel reported. "He's dead . . ."

Books by Amy Lillard

The Wells Landing Series
CAROLINE'S SECRET
COURTING EMILY
LORIE'S HEART
JUST PLAIN SADIE
TITUS RETURNS
MARRYING JONAH
THE QUILTING CIRCLE
A WELLS LANDING CHRISTMAS
LOVING JENNA
ROMANCING NADINE
A NEW LOVE FOR CHARLOTTE

The Pontotoc Mississippi Series
A HOME FOR HANNAH
A LOVE FOR LEAH
A FAMILY FOR GRACIE
AN AMISH HUSBAND FOR TILLIE

The Paradise Valley Series
MARRY ME, MILLIE
THE AMISH MATCHMAKER
ONE MORE TIME FOR JOY

Amish Mysteries
KAPPY KING AND THE PUPPY KAPER
KAPPY KING AND THE PICKLE KAPER
KAPPY KING AND THE PIE KAPER

Sunflower Café Mysteries
DAIRY, DAIRY, QUITE CONTRARY
A MURDER OF ASPIC PROPORTIONS

Published by Kensington Publishing Corp.

A
MURDER OF ASPIC
PROPORTIONS

AMY LILLARD

Kensington Publishing Corp.
www.kensingtonbooks.com

KENSINGTON BOOKS are published by

Kensington Publishing Corp.
119 West 40th Street
New York, NY 10018

All Kensington titles, imprints, and distributed lines are available at special quantity discounts for bulk purchases for sales promotion, premiums, fund-raising, educational, or institutional use.

Special book excerpts or customized printings can also be created to fit specific needs. For details, write or phone the office of the Kensington Sales Manager: Attn.: Sales Department. Kensington Publishing Corp., 119 West 40th Street, New York, NY 10018. Phone: 1-800-221-2647.

The K and Teapot logo is a trademark of Kensington Publishing Corp.

First Printing: July 2023
ISBN: 978-1-4967-3347-4

ISBN: 978-1-4967-3348-1 (ebook)

10 9 8 7 6 5 4 3 2 1

Printed in the United States of America

To Mom. Always.

ACKNOWLEDGMENTS

There are always a million people to thank once a book has been published. My editor, my agent, my husband who wears the dirty clothes and doesn't (hardly ever) fuss about it. At least not *much*. But with this book, I have a couple of readers to thank.

It's always more fun to get readers involved in books before they are finished. Mainly because while I'm writing a new book, my readers are reading something else. Maybe something I wrote a year ago, maybe something from another writer. Truth be told, it gets to be a challenge to talk about one book—already written, edited, and in print—while working on a different book. Holding little contests for readers to participate in the writing of the book—say naming puppies or restaurants—is a fun way to stay involved and current. Meaning the reader is involved and I'm current. And that's exactly what I've done with this book.

I would like to thank reader Tina Oliver for submitting the "Aunt Bessism" from the beginning of Chapter Two. "Never argue with a goof; people passing by won't know which is which."

And thank you to Syble Ditzler for naming the twins: Joshua Albert and Maudie Rose. So much fun to have you two involved.

If you would like to get more involved as a reader, be sure to sign up for my Facebook reader's group and/or for my newsletter. Both can also be accessed from my website: https://amywrites romance. com/for-readers-2/

Thanks for reading!

Amy

CHAPTER ONE

Apparently there's nothing that can't happen today.
—Aunt Bess

" 'To Die For Tomatoes One Quarter Mile Ahead.' " Sissy read the sign as she and her aunt, Bethel Yoder, passed by. Usually, Sissy was hard pressed to get her aunt to ride around in her "little car," as Bethel called the convertible Fiat, but today she didn't have a choice. Not since Sissy offered to drive Bethel to her doctor appointment to have her cast removed in front of witnesses. The offer, that was: Sissy had made *the offer* in front of witnesses. No one but the tech and Sissy witnessed the removal of the cast. The cast that had brought Sissy to Yoder in the first place.

And if she wanted that cast off, what could Bethel do but hang onto her prayer *kapp* and frown at Sissy as they zoomed along?

Though Sissy's parents had left the Amish and moved to Oklahoma before Sissy was born, the

rest of the family had remained in Kansas and kept
to the Plain lifestyle. Bethel and her family being
some of the ones who remained.

"That's a bold statement to make," Sissy continued.

Her aunt shot her a look, which happened a lot,
though Sissy had a difficult time figuring out what
some of the looks meant. It might be that Sissy was
bothering her aunt by chattering on or that Bethel
had to go to the bathroom. These looks could go
either way. "I don't know about bold, but I'd say a
quarter mile is understating it a bit."

"I was talking about the 'to die for' part," Sissy
clarified. Honestly, her aunt could be so literal.

"They are pretty tasty."

"To die for tasty?" Sissy pressed.

"Maybe." Perhaps the biggest compliment she
had ever heard her aunt deliver.

Sissy had decided that since she and Bethel
were already going to be away from the café today,
it was the perfect time to check out the local
tomato crop. Now that the cast had been removed,
they were on their way to the Summers' Tomato
Farm, the pride of Yoder, Kansas, owned and oper-
ated by Walt Summers, most hated man in the
area. Or, at least, that's what her cousin Lizzie had
told her. But Bethel's daughter hadn't had time to
finish the juicy tidbit before Bethel herself shushed
Lizzie for gossiping. Honestly, poor Lizzie was
trapped in the house, spending most of her time
in one bedroom, on bed rest, as she awaited the
birth of her boy-girl twins. What else did the sweet-
but-bored *mamm*-to-be have to do but gossip? Still,

when Bethel spoke, most everyone in her vicinity listened. She just had that way about her.

"If they're as good as everyone says they are, then we're going to have a great summer at the café." Sissy smiled, pleased with her plan.

The Sunflower Café was one of the five places to eat in Yoder, including the Carriage House Restaurant, the Bull in Your Eye Diner, the deli at the Yoder Meat Market, and home.

Sissy supposed it was more accurate to say that the café was the real reason that she had made the temporary move from Tulsa to Yoder, Kansas. So she could help.

When Bethel had broken her leg and Lizzie had been prescribed immediate bed rest, it was Sissy to the rescue. Of course, it didn't hurt that she had just caught her boyfriend cheating, and he just happened to be her roommate's brother, and . . . sigh. Some things were better left in the past.

Sissy pulled her shiny red convertible into the gravel drive. The large white sign next to the road declared that she had indeed arrived at the correct place, but it seemed deserted.

"Not many people around for the best tomatoes in three counties," she commented as she cut the engine.

Bethel removed her hand from the top of her head, where it had been holding her prayer covering to keep it from blowing away in the wind and harrumphed, her favorite vocalization, Sissy was certain. She made another disapproving noise in the back of her throat. "I don't know why we're even here."

Sissy got out of the car, and Bethel grudgingly followed suit. Her aunt was nothing if not testy, but the woman worked so hard every day, Sissy had determined that her grouchy attitude was merely one of focus and determination. At least, that's what she wanted it to be. See in the weeks that she had been in Kansas, Sissy had reluctantly grown fond of her aunt, and she didn't want the woman to be as unhappy as she appeared. She couldn't be, Sissy decided. Not with a thriving business, two new grandbabies on the way, and a solid, white two-story on the edge of Yoder. Focus and determination, that was all.

From the back seat, Duke, her precious Yorkie, barked as if to say, *Don't forget me!*

Sissy turned back to the car and retrieved the dog, who had been usurped from the coveted front-seat position since Bethel was traveling with them.

"We're here because we need to add a few new items to the café's menu," Sissy reminded Bethel. She hooked Duke's leash to his harness and set him on the ground in front of her.

"So you say," her aunt grumbled.

"And Josie agrees." Though Sissy still wasn't a hundred percent sure of Josie's on-the-levelness, she and the café's main cook had grown into a kind of uneasy truce these days. Sissy supposed Josie was just as skeptical of her as she was of the cook. But they had teamed up to broaden the menu while adding a few healthier choices for the diners.

The idea had come to Sissy a few weeks ago when she was talking to town legend Howard

Yoder. Howard was a disabled Vietnam vet who rode around town on a purple Jazzy scooter and conked people with his cane if they didn't move out of his way fast enough. Howard had recently stopped eating at the Sunflower Café because Bethel had stopped serving chili dogs. He had lamented the fact to Sissy, saying that her aunt had gotten on a health kick and taken his favorite lunch item off the menu.

In truth, Bethel was unhappy with the changes the meat company she used had made in the hot dogs themselves and decided they weren't worth the hassle. But the seed had been planted for Sissy. And since the tomatoes were red, ripe, and delicious, it seemed the perfect place to start.

"We can make caprese salad, tomato aspic, bruschetta." Sissy ticked off the new dishes, one by one, on her fingers.

"I don't even know what those are," Bethel grumped. She shut the car door and looked around, her mouth turned down at the corners in her signature frown. "Where is everybody?"

For a place that sold "to die for tomatoes," it certainly was dead. Pun completely intended.

"I don't know," Sissy replied. It was better to acknowledge the question, which wouldn't bring a whole host of queries about tomato dishes, and just focus on the lack of workers at the tomato farm. "He doesn't work on the honor system, does he?"

Several of the Amish houses had little shops out front and sold everything from home-canned goods to tasty baked items. Some left a box or a jar for the customers to put money in if there was no one around to help them. But this didn't look like the same sort of setup, and Walt Summers, owner of the Summers' Tomato Farm, was not Amish.

"Not that I've heard." Bethel walked toward the wooden stand, where several baskets of tomatoes sat, just waiting to be sold. As she lumbered along, Sissy noted that she limped a bit, no doubt the muscles in her recently de-casted leg getting used to working once again without their fiberglass support.

Sissy never had found out how Bethel broke her leg, though she had heard many wild variations of the story. So many that she wasn't sure if anyone other than Bethel herself knew the truth.

Sissy glanced toward the house, but there was no fluttering at a window or any movement to make her think someone was inside watching and waiting for customers, as sometimes was the case.

"He's around here somewhere."

Sissy wished she had the same confidence she heard in Bethel's voice. And she never thought that this idea would ever cross her mind, but a deserted tomato farm was a bit eerie. "Maybe he's in the growing shed."

Growing shed was not the best term for the structure that sat halfway between the end of the drive, where Sissy had parked, and the house itself, where Walt Summers lived. The shed was a four-sided building with walls formed of a light-filtering mesh. The top was made of screening, no doubt to keep out the bugs and other vermin and still allow more than enough of the Kansas sun to come through. And even though all five sides were covered, she could see enough to know that no one was inside.

"You don't think—" Sissy couldn't finish the thought. Mainly because there were too many thoughts hitting her brain all at once. She didn't know how old or healthy Walt Summers was, but she had heard of people younger than their teens having heart attacks and dying. Or perhaps he had been robbed, conked on the head, and left for dead. Or tied to a chair like in the *Die Hard* movie. Or kidnapped for ransom. Or perhaps she was just being a bit dramatic.

Bethel started toward the entrance of the growing shed, a modified screen door covered in the same light-filtering mesh as everything else. "Be careful," she told her aunt. "There's a lot of standing water around here."

Ripple upon ripple of water seeped from under the walls of the growing shed and reached out in all directions. The wetness spread even farther the longer they stood there.

Duke happily started through one of the patches of water, until Sissy scooped him up in her arms. In addition to not wanting wet, muddy feet in the back of her car, she couldn't be certain how deep the puddles were, and Duke, for all of his fierceness, was a very tiny dog.

"Sissy," Bethel called. Her aunt stood, one foot inside the growing shed and one foot out, the screen door propped open on one ample hip.

"Is he in there?" Sissy asked, but she could tell from the sound of her aunt's voice that something was wrong. She minced her way through the puddles, which seemed to be getting deeper, and lamented that she had picked today, of all days, to wear new white canvas shoes.

"He's in here," Bethel replied.

Sissy pushed past her aunt but stopped after taking one giant step into the growing shed. From the inside, the place looked even larger and even more impressive. Given any other time and any other day, Sissy would've stopped in that same position in awe.

She could almost imagine what the place should have looked like.

Rows upon rows of beautiful tomato plants propped up lovingly with wooden stakes and pieces of twine. Marigolds planted painstakingly in short rows between the cash crop, no doubt there to keep the insects away from the fruit-bearing plants. It was a trick her mother swore by. Buckets of Walt's own Special Blend of fertilizer sat along the perimeter, stacked three high. They looked like the buckets the pickles came in for the café, but these were blue, with a logo consisting of a fat tomato intertwined with the *SF* of Summers' Farm.

That's what it should have looked like. But not today.

Oh, the blue buckets of not-pickles and the marigolds were in place; even a few of the stakes had been left in the ground, pieces of twine dangling like forlorn windsocks from where they had been tied, but the tomato plants themselves were missing. Pile after pile of dark rich soil sat upturned in what had once been neat rows. Whoever had done this had grabbed the plants and ripped them out of the ground, roots and all. A few tomatoes, both red and green, lay scattered about, most trampled, no doubt, by the bootheel of the plant burglar.

The ground under their feet was soggy, and a garden hose continued to leak water onto the churned-up earth, nearly drowning the bright yellow marigolds. By all appearances, it looked as if the crop had been ripped up and carted away while someone was watering the plants.

And that someone was lying face down in front of the high-topped wooden planting table that sat in one corner, stacked with supplies necessary for the growing side of the business—starter trays, small pots, and stakes, along with twine and other gardening equipment.

"Is that—" Sissy started.

It seemed to take a great deal of effort, but Bethel started her feet into motion and made her way over to the man. At least, Sissy thought it was a man. From where she stood, she couldn't see the face of the person, but the industrial-blue pants and the mud-caked work boots seemed to indicate the person was male.

"Walt Summers," Bethel reported.

Sissy waited for her aunt to continue, though she had an overwhelming feeling that she didn't want to hear what Bethel had to say next.

"He's dead."

"He can't be dead," Sissy protested.

"Well, he is."

Why was this happening again?

"Are you sure?" Sissy inched closer. She didn't want to be closer, but she felt pulled toward the prone figure.

"Come see for yourself."

That was probably the last thing she wanted to do, and yet she found herself standing next to her aunt, looking down into the vacant eyes of Walt Summers. Well, eye. His head was turned to the side, one arm under him, the other stretched wide. In his hand, he clutched a pink piece of paper that looked like an invoice. Sissy could barely make out the letters PIP in bold across the top. He was lying on the garden hose, which gushed water out and around him. The ground had been turned into a muddy, soupy mess.

"He wasn't stabbed," Sissy whispered in awe. But even as she said the words, she knew that not all dead people were stabbed. Somehow, though, that's exactly what she had been expecting. Yet just because he was dead didn't mean that he had been murdered. He could have had a stroke or a heart attack or—

"Looks like someone conked him on the head." Bethel gestured toward him.

"I think you're right." Details started to rise through the fog of shock at finding the tomato farmer dead. Blood had trickled from the ear they could see, and a lump the size of a goose egg had begun to take shape in his thinning gray hair. A baseball cap advertising YODER SOD AND FEED lay off to one side. It was splattered with blood, making her think that perhaps he had been wearing it when he had been attacked. A shovel rested on the ground a few feet away as if it had been tossed there by a careless hand.

Duke barked and squirmed to get down. Until

that moment, Sissy hadn't realized that she had been tightly clutching the poor pooch to her chest. "Shush," she told him, but kissed him on the top of his tiny head. "You have to stay with me."

He barked in response.

Bethel shook her head at the two of them and turned her attention back to the scene at their feet. "Whoever did this must have taken the tomato plants."

It was only logical.

"Do you suppose they hit him to knock him out so they could take the plants and accidentally killed him in the process?"

Bethel grumped. "How am I supposed to know?"

"We should turn off the water," Sissy said.

"We should call the police," Bethel countered.

"The police!" Her aunt was right: The police needed to be there. Sissy hadn't thought about that. Honestly, finding another dead body in such a short period of time had her head a bit muddled. "I should call 9-1-1."

"*Jah.*" Bethel shot her a pointed look.

"Oh." Sissy shuffled Duke from her right arm to her left and felt her pocket. Keys, but no phone. "I must have left it in the car."

"Then go get it." Bethel's patience was beginning to run thin.

"Right," Sissy said. She started backing out of the growing shed as if she couldn't turn away from the body or . . . something; it didn't matter. She couldn't just ignore its presence. Another dead body and another possible murder. A farm of tomatoes vandalized and most likely destroyed. It seemed Walt Summers's tomatoes really were to die for.

As Sissy and Duke backed out of the growing shed, Bethel tsked, and Sissy thought she heard her say, "What's this town coming to?"

CHAPTER TWO

*Never argue with a goof; people passing by won't
know which one is which.*
            —Aunt Bess

Sissy called the emergency number, and Bethel
turned off the water. Now all they had to do was
wait for the deputy to show up. Surely, a dead man
at a tomato farm trumped traffic tickets and bar
fights. Not that there were many bar fights in
Yoder. There weren't many bars, come to think of
it. And it was just after noon, a fact Sissy's stomach
reminded her of with an empty growl. She should
have swung by a McDonald's or something while
they were in Hutchinson. As it was, they would be
lucky to get out of here before dark.

Still, she couldn't help reminding herself that
her problems were nothing compared to those of
Walt Summers.

"Is he married?" Sissy asked with a small nod toward the growing shed.

She and Bethel had moved back into the yard to wait for the police. Since she couldn't have Duke ruining a crime scene, on top of running around in the mud and getting filthy, she was still holding him close. Now her arms were beginning to grow tired from carrying him around. He didn't weigh much at all, but it was enough that, after a while, she could feel the extra strain.

"Walt?" Bethel asked. "*Jah.*"

Sissy looked back to the house. "Should we see if his wife is home?"

How strange would that be, to knock on her door and have her answer, not knowing that her husband had just been killed sometime before.

Bethel shrugged. "I suppose."

Together, they started toward the back door.

"Should we go to the front?" Sissy asked. Her footsteps were slowing of their own accord. Honestly, she didn't actually tell her feet to slow down, but it was happening all the same. The last thing she wanted to do was tell a stranger that her husband was dead. Or tell anyone that anyone was dead, for that matter.

"Bah," Bethel said.

Sissy took that as a no.

"You knock." She held back and waited for her aunt to climb the small stoop that led to the back entrance, with its glass and screen storm door. Just two layers between them and telling a woman her husband was gone.

Bethel knocked on the door loud enough to wake Walt himself, but no one came to the summons. Sissy took a step back and looked toward the windows. The house was still, eerily quiet. Sissy didn't know if Walt and his wife had a pet, but if they had a dog, he surely would've started barking at the commotion they were making outside. Then again, he might be used to people coming and going at all times, seeing as how this was their place of business as well as their residence. The truth of it was she didn't want Walt Summers's wife to be home. She didn't know the woman, and she surely didn't want to tell her that the police were on their way. Yet there was no getting around the consideration aspect of the situation. If the wife was in the house, then she surely should be notified the police were coming before Earl Berry just showed up on her doorstep. Then another, more horrible thought seared through Sissy's imagination. "What if—what if she's dead too?"

For the first time since Sissy had met her, Bethel Yoder appeared shaken. Her aunt took a step back from the door, as if standing too close to it would somehow bring a bad omen onto herself. "No," Bethel whispered.

Perhaps that was why the house was so still. Perhaps that was why no curtains moved, no pet barked, no one was answering. A helter-skelter image of blood-smeared walls flitted through Sissy's overactive imagination before she put the brakes on her own thoughts. Still, she managed to choke out, "Maybe we should just wait for Berry to get here."

Bethel took another small step back. "*Jah.*"

"She's not home."

Sissy and Bethel whirled around as a man came striding up from the house next door.

"That's Weaver Justice," Bethel said.

The name sounded vaguely familiar, but in a town the size of Yoder, it wasn't hard to meet everyone in a short period of time. Seeing as how Sissy worked in the café, she saw most of the citizens of Yoder on a weekly basis, if not more often. Though she hadn't been there long enough to remember everyone's name just yet.

"I thought your uncle lived next door," Sissy replied.

"He's my nephew," Bethel explained. "He's not much younger than me, but he's my brother's son."

Such was the way with Amish families. They tended to be large, larger than average, as the Amish believed in God's will. If it was God's will that they had a child, then they had a child. They didn't take birth control and didn't try to stop the natural order of life. They accepted what gifts God gave them. And since most married young and started having children right away, it was fairly common to have aunts and uncles near the same age as nieces and nephews.

"So he doesn't live there?" Sissy pointed to the house to the west of the tomato farm.

Bethel jerked a thumb over one shoulder. "He lives on the other side."

One look and Sissy could tell that this man was not Amish. It was just another reason why she questioned where Amos Yoder and his family lived. They had come to supper a couple of Fridays since she had been in Yoder. That was when Bethel held a family dinner at her house. It was open-invitation potluck, and no one knew who was going to show up and what they would bring to eat. As far as Sissy was concerned, it was always a great time.

Duke barked and growled as Weaver grew closer to them. Sissy shushed the dog. He hadn't taken to many people here in Yoder—her aunt Bethel, her cousin Lizzie, and the reporter Gavin Wainwright were among the exceptions—and he was vocal in his displeasure, though Sissy had never seen him act on those feelings.

"Where is she?" Bethel asked.

Weaver stopped when he got close. He eyed Duke with a wariness that was almost laughable. The dog talked a big game, but Duke weighed only three and a quarter pounds soaking wet. "Mary Ann's gone to Wichita to visit her mama."

Bethel nodded, and Sissy got the idea that perhaps Mary Ann Summers going to Wichita to visit her mama was a regular occurrence.

"Is Walt not in the growing shed?" Weaver asked.

Duke started to growl again, and Sissy shushed him once more. "He's in the shed all right," she replied.

"He's dead," Bethel said, without preamble.

The agonizing look of horror washed over Weaver Justice's expression with such force that Sissy was afraid the man might pass out.

"What?" His voice trembled, and he shook his head. "What are you talking about? Dead?"

"Dead," Bethel repeated.

He continued to shake his head. "No, no, no, I just saw him."

Sissy half-expected Bethel to say that one thing

had nothing to do with the other, but for once her undiplomatic aunt kept her mouth shut.

"This morning . . . this morning we were talking about the weather. He was telling me what a fine day it was going to be."

Sissy glanced back at the growing shed. She couldn't see him from where she was, but she knew Walt Summers was still lying there in the mud, one eye staring blankly at nothing. She wondered how he felt about the weather now.

The crunch of tires against gravel met her ears. Sissy turned just as her aunt said, "And that would be the chief."

Sissy managed to contain her smile at her aunt's words. Even in such a somber time, her aunt wasn't giving an inch toward the deputy who enforced the laws in Yoder. And Sissy couldn't blame her. Earl Berry was . . . Earl Berry. She felt that, at his heart, he was a good man, but he had a tendency to rub her the wrong way. He was a know-it-all from the good-old-boy generation of chauvinists who called women "little lady" yet didn't hold the door open for them. He was too much the quintessential small-town law enforcement officer who wouldn't make it anyplace larger than Yoder. So there he stayed.

Lucky them.

He parked his car, the red and blue lights still flashing as he got out and looked at the three of them.

"Well," he drawled. "What have we here?"

* * *

"So you walked all over my crime scene and contaminated it," Berry said sometime later, looking from Sissy to Bethel and back again.

Shortly after the deputy arrived, a firetruck showed up, along with an ambulance. She supposed it must be a slow day in Yoder, for they continued to hang around, even though now they were waiting on the coroner to take away the body.

"We didn't know it was a crime scene until we were already inside the growing shed," Bethel explained not so patiently.

"Uh-huh." He took a pen from his breast pocket and made a note in his tiny spiral-bound notepad. "And you turned off the water."

"*Jah.*" Bethel lifted her chin as if daring him to say more.

"It was my idea." Sissy took a helpful step forward. At least, she thought she was being helpful. Based on the scathing look he shot her, she decided she wasn't helping anyone at all—especially not herself—and stepped back to her original spot. Duke growled.

Berry continued to glare at her. "Why did that seem like a good thing to do?"

"It was just running," she said by way of explanation. "His water bill is going to be outrageous."

Berry used the clicky end of his pen to point to Summers's body. "His water bill is the least of his worries."

He was right, but no way was Sissy going to admit that to him. Not now.

"Who could have done this?" Weaver Justice asked. His words wavered, and his voice sounded as if he had a sob lodged in his throat. Sissy wondered if the men had been friends for a long time. Or perhaps just friendly neighbors for decades.

Earl Berry looked to Weaver and gave him one of those know-it-all nods. "That's just what I'm gonna find out." He shot a pointed look back at Sissy.

"What?" she asked. Though she didn't need him to answer to know what he was getting at.

Perfect.

Another dead body, and she just happened to be the one to find it. Now he was going to try to pin this murder on her, like he had another.

She'd spent her first two weeks in Yoder trying to prove her innocence in the death of Kevin the milkman. Now it seemed she was targeting tomato farmers.

"You don't think I had anything to do with this?" She tried to make it sound more like a statement, but her voice turned up on the end.

"Just funny to me how you come to town and dead bodies start showing up." He shot her another look and jotted something else down in his notebook.

Great. Up for murder one yet again. At least, they had moved farther away from the growing shed and were now standing in the Summers's yard proper. Sissy had set Duke on his feet and let her arms have a rest from holding him. Still, she was glad that she had put his harness on him. He kept pulling at the leash, barking and demanding to be turned loose on the action.

"I didn't see any puppy prints inside the shed," Berry continued.

"I was holding him," Sissy explained.

"Uh-huh." Berry didn't sound convinced. Though Sissy wasn't sure how puppy prints or the lack of puppy prints had anything to do with her innocence or guilt. Or the murder at all, for that matter.

Beside her, Bethel widened her stance and crossed her arms over her thick chest. "Now why would we kill the man, then call the police and not immediately flee the scene?"

"I suppose that doesn't seem like a logical thing to do," Berry grudgingly admitted.

"Precisely," Bethel said. "And I turned off the water because it was running. We've had enough times of drought in this county. You yourself know better than to let water run unnecessarily, even at a crime scene."

Berry grunted but didn't comment. He just looked at them each in turn, examined their faces, then shot pointed glances at their feet. "Don't go anywhere. We're going to need shoe impressions from the both of you."

"But not me?" Weaver asked.

"Did you go inside the growing shed?" Berry asked in return.

Weaver shook his head.

"Then you can go on home." The deputy gave a dismissive wave. "But I may be by to talk to you later this afternoon."

"I think I'd rather stay," Weaver said. Again, Sissy had to wonder about the relationship between the two men, though she supposed having your neighbor turn up dead, whether you liked him or not, had to be a shock. She tried not to stare as Weaver moved to one side and sat in the lawn chair positioned just behind the wooden vegetable shack. The way he collapsed into the seat made Sissy wonder if it was his nerves or his arthritis that was getting the best of him.

"If you ask me," Bethel said in a low voice, "if anybody around here is guilty, it's old Justice over there."

Sissy took a step to one side and turned back to her aunt. "What?"

Bethel shrugged. "The two of them had a falling out years ago over some special variety of tomato. The 'to die for' one."

Sissy closed her eyes, as if somehow that would bring everything back into focus. "I'm not even sure what any of that means," she returned, her tone matching the low timbre of her aunt's.

"I'm just saying," Bethel said. "There was a lot of money to be made with that tomato. Talk around town was that they came up with the idea for the hybrid together, then, when push came to shove, Walt took all the fame for himself."

"And the money?" Sissy asked.

Bethel nodded. "That too."

Sissy allowed those words to sink in as she turned so she could see Weaver once again. He was all but wringing his hands as he stood next to the lawn chair where he had previously been sitting. He was talking to Earl Berry, explaining how he hadn't heard any commotion that morning and had no idea that his neighbor was in any sort of peril. As distraught as Weaver looked, Sissy couldn't help but believe that he, at least, must've learned to let bygones be bygones.

Beside her, Bethel harrumphed, drawing Sissy's

attention away from Weaver and back to the gang of first responders milling around the scene.

"I wondered when the press was gonna show up." Bethel's words were so jaded that Sissy had to wonder about her aunt's run-ins with reporters. Of course, Bethel knew that Sissy herself had "once worked for the paper." But she, like the rest of the world (her editor aside), had no idea that Sissy was indeed still writing for "the paper" as the infamous Aunt Bess. She wrote a weekly column that appeared in a number of regional newspapers, kind of an Ann Landers meets Grumpy Cat, wherein "Aunt Bess" gave out advice like your own Aunt Bess would. She was straight shooting, rarely sugar-coated anything, and was reportedly in her seventies. Even Sissy's parents didn't know that she wrote that particular column. They knew she had worked at the paper and supported herself with her journalism degree for a while now, even bought her saucy little convertible. But Sissy didn't want word getting out that her alter ego was a grandmother of eight. It was hard enough to find a date without everyone knowing that. No one knew, and that's just how she wanted to keep it.

"I wouldn't exactly call the *Sunflower Express* the press," Sissy said. The weekly newspaper was more apt to cover the birth of cow twins than it was anything of real importance. When a paper only came out once a week, news had to be carefully sorted in order to get the most accurate and up-to-date account. And six days was a long time for news to go cold.

Still, Sissy made her way toward the blond, cute, but nerdy reporter, stopping only momentarily to scoop Duke into her arms before mincing her way through the muddy yard.

"Hey!" Earl Berry hollered. But the rest of his words were lost on Sissy. Honestly, the whole yard couldn't be considered part of the crime scene, could it? She had seen enough episodes of *CSI* to figure out that Walt was watering his tomatoes when somebody decided to clobber him on the back of the head. That meant the mud in the yard wasn't there when the killer ran back through to get into his car and go wherever. And seriously. She had had enough of Earl Berry trying to intimidate her.

"What are you doing here?" Instead of the deputy, she centered her attention on Gavin Wainwright, ace reporter and junior editor for the *Sunflower Express*, Yoder's weekly newspaper. It served the greater Yoder area, including Haven and Buhler, but not Hutchinson, which had its own paper.

"This is big news," Gavin said. He reached out a hand and stroked Duke's silky ears. The dog rewarded him with a lick and a welcoming bark. She had said it before and she would say it again: Duke didn't take to just anyone, and Gavin Wainwright had passed muster.

Sissy shifted the dog in her arms. He was getting restless, being held so much. But she couldn't put him down in the mud, and she wanted to talk to Gavin for just a minute. "How did you know about this?"

"Reporter," Gavin said. "How did you know about this?"

Sissy shook her head sadly. "We found the body."

"We?" Gavin asked. He jotted notes in his little notebook. A Nikon camera hung around his neck, and once again his black-rimmed glasses had slipped a little down his patrician nose. He pushed them up again with one finger, and Sissy couldn't help but notice he had a Band-Aid on that digit. Flashes of Les Nessman from *WKRP in Cincinnati* flitted through her thoughts before she pushed them aside. Now was not the time to relive eighties television.

Sissy made a gesture back toward where her aunt still stood in the middle of Walt Summers's backyard. "Bethel's here."

Gavin jotted a few more notes in his notepad before glancing back at Sissy. "Nice," he said. "Is there anything you'd like to tell me about the scene when you got here?"

The journalist in Sissy wanted to tell Gavin all, so he would have the best story for his newspaper article, but she had a feeling Earl Berry wouldn't appreciate that. A feeling that was reinforced as the deputy stomped over to where they stood.

"What are you doing here, Wainwright?"

"Reporter," Gavin said in a singsong voice. As far as he was concerned, it seemed his reason for being at a crime scene was understandable. According to Berry, it wasn't.

"You need to get yourself on out of here," Earl Berry said. "We haven't opened this up to the press yet."

"First Amendment, Deputy Berry. Ever hear of it?" Gavin propped his hands on his hips and lifted his chin at a stubborn angle. She'd seen that be-

fore. Gavin appeared to be as mild-mannered as
Clark Kent, but he had a streak in him that was as
determined as Lex Luthor.

Berry shook his head. "Stay out of the way."

"I'm not in the way," Gavin protested.

Sissy shook her head, grabbed Gavin by the
elbow, and pulled him a little farther from the
growing shed. "Don't you know? Never argue with
a goof; people passing by won't know who is who."

Gavin stopped and stared at Sissy, as Earl Berry
stomped back to his precious crime scene.

"What?" Sissy asked, as Gavin continued to eye
her, somewhat suspiciously.

"I've heard that before," he said.

Heat started somewhere in Sissy's middle and
crept up into her neck. "What?" She asked the
question, though she knew what he was talking
about.

"That phrase. Never argue with a goof. I've
heard that somewhere before."

Sissy peeshawed and waved a hand as if it was no
big deal. "Of course you have. Everyone's grandmother says that." Okay, so she didn't know that
for a fact, but *her* grandmother sure said it often
enough. That was how it had found its way to the
lips, or rather the pen, of Aunt Bess. But if her
memory served her correctly, that article hadn't
been printed yet. Which meant if Gavin had read
it in her queued Aunt Bess column and managed
to put two and two together, then her cover was
blown. Stupid mistake. She was going to have to be
more careful.

"No, that's not it," he said. "It was somewhere
else."

Sissy shook her head. "I'm sure it was your grandmother. Or one of your crazy aunts," she said, then resisted the urge to clamp her hand over her mouth to keep from explaining further. The last thing she wanted to do was overexplain and have Gavin realize that Aunt Bess was the one who was going to say those words in next Sunday's newspaper. From there it wasn't too far of a jump from Sissy's journalism career to quoting Aunt Bess to the truth. The last thing Sissy wanted was to have to explain how she had become Aunt Bess in the first place.

"Speaking of my family," he continued, "my cousin is supposed to come over this week and fix something at Edith's house."

Edith Jones lived across the street from the Chicken Coop, the tiny house that Sissy had rented for her extended stay in Yoder. Yes, it really had been a chicken coop once upon a time but had been renovated to become a charming one-room—plus bathroom—flat with kitchenette and everything one person and a tiny dog could need. Especially since Edith's flower beds were so entertaining. Each one held a collection of unique items, ranging from window frames to classic toys, to plastic flowers and greenery. And, every day, the arrangement was changed—added to, shifted, and taken away from. It was a constant flow of interesting.

"Thanks for letting me know," she said. "I'll be watching for him. What does he look like?"

Gavin shoved his free hand into his pocket and tucked his notebook against his chest. He shrugged. "I dunno. He's my cousin."

Like that explained anything.

About that time, Earl Berry came striding over to where the two of them stood. "Okay, folks, time to move on."

"So we're free to go?" Sissy asked. She might be able to get a bite to eat after all. Except not at the café, since it was afternoon and the Sunflower was closed. And she didn't want to get too much, since it was Friday and family-supper night.

"Yes," Berry said. "And you need to be . . . going, that is."

"Like we want to hang around here." Bethel approached them from behind.

"I'm clearing this scene," the deputy said. "Everybody needs to get."

True enough, the first responders were climbing back into their sturdy vehicles and preparing to go. While she had been talking to Gavin, the coroner had come in a hearse to take the body away. MOORE FUNERAL HOME was written across the darkened rear windows in elegant white lettering.

"I guess it's time to go," Sissy said.

"What about Mary Ann?" Bethel piped up. "She doesn't know about . . ." She flicked her hand in the direction of the growing shed instead of saying the actual words. Somewhere along the way, her good manners had caught up with her.

"I'll call her," Weaver said.

"Not so fast," Berry cut in. "Notifying the next of kin is police business."

"So you'll call her?" Sissy asked.

"You know it. Now everybody go on about your business," Berry said.

Sissy opened her mouth to say they were doing just that since they had come to the farm to buy tomatoes. But Berry saw the action and cut her short. "Somewhere else," he reiterated. "Take your business somewhere else."

CHAPTER THREE

*Of course we don't all think alike; it's the difference
of opinion that makes horse races.*
—Aunt Bess

"You too, Wainwright." Berry shot Gavin a scathing look.

"No problem," Gavin replied. "I have enough for my story." Then he turned to Sissy. "Want to go get a piece of pie at the Carriage House?"

She shook her head.

"Don't tell me you're not hungry. I can hear your stomach growling from here."

Sissy gestured toward her aunt. "I would love to," she lied, "but I have to get Bethel home. Maybe some other time." *Like when you've forgotten all about my slipup and don't want to question me about old sayings that belong to my alter ego.*

"Another time," Gavin said. "Sure." He nodded once, then headed over to his bike. Sissy still couldn't believe that he rode the thing almost everywhere he went in town. Seriously . . . even the Amish used tractors for everyday transportation. Well, every day but Sunday. But Gavin Wainwright didn't even own a car. He claimed they were bad for the environment, and she supposed that they were, but she was in love with her little convertible and probably always would be. She'd rather give up aerosol sprays and plastic straws for the rest of her life than turn loose her car.

Sissy and Bethel got into the little Fiat without a word spoken between them. It was almost as if they both had so much to tell the other that they didn't know where to begin.

A thousand questions flitted around Sissy's thoughts. Was Walt Summers really murdered? Were the murderer and the tomato plant thief one and the same? Was Mary Ann Summers really in Wichita visiting her mother? Could she have swung a shovel hard enough to hit and kill a man? Was that the killer's intent? What if they just wanted the tomato plants and killed Walt accidentally? And if the tomatoes were that valuable, then why was he working alone?

"I know what you're thinking," Bethel said.

Surprised by the words, Sissy turned slightly to face her aunt. Bethel was staring straight ahead, right elbow braced in the open window, hand securely on top of her prayer covering to keep it in place. Pretty much the same way she had looked the entire time they had been driving before they'd stopped for tomatoes. She shifted her attention back to the road. "You do?"

"And he's not going to try to make you out to be the guilty party this time. I was with you, and he knows better than to mess with me that way."

"Actually," Sissy started, then closed her mouth up tight. She had been about to tell Bethel what she had really been thinking about but decided this was too good of a bonding moment to allow it to pass. Her aunt had acted nothing but put out that Sissy had come up from Oklahoma to help her in the café. Sissy had promised her mother, who had promised Lizzie, that someone in their family would be there. So she had come, and she had stayed, despite her aunt's protests.

It had been luck or fate that th~~...~~
fallen to Sissy. Aside from h~~...~~
recently fallen ~~...~~
anywh~~...~~

n~~...~~
wl~~...~~
frie~~...~~

A~~...~~
now. ~~...~~
about ~~...~~
Chicken ~~...~~
plus was ~~...~~
tiny dog. B~~...~~
time. It gave~~...~~
You know, be~~...~~

A book, oka~~...~~

book, but the more she thought about that, the more daunting it became. So she would barely allow the thought to cross her mind.

"I'm glad you're out here too."

"Hey, anyone home?" a sweet voice asked from the direction of the door.

Sissy had been about to tell Lizzie the unbelievable tale of this afternoon. What were the chances that she would find two dead bodies in the short time that she had been in Yoder? But her anecdote was cut short by the newcomer.

"Sissy, you know Emma, right?"

"I do." She turned toward the young girl, dressed in a wine-colored dress and sensible black walking shoes. Emma Yoder was a little on the plump side, with pale blond hair and a touch of rosacea, the kind that made her look like she was blushing at something someone had just said. She ducked her head a bit as she came through the living room toting a large carry bag, the contents of which smelled amazing. Sissy couldn't discern if the nod was in greeting or more in bashfulness. Emma was a quiet one, but Sissy figured in a house with twelve kids total, quiet was a rare event.

"You didn't have to bring anything," Lizzie called behind her. "But whatever it is smells delicious."

"Chicken alfredo casserole," Emma called behind her.

"She came by this morning too. Before going to work on her classroom." Lizzie looked back to Sissy and shook her head. "That girl works way too hard."

Sissy nodded. She had heard the story of how Emma's mother, Sarah, had suffered greatly after the birth of the triplets, now a year old. As it was told, she just never seemed to recover. Then one day, when the babies were four months old, Emma found her mother in the bathroom, collapsed and dead on the floor. The doctors said she had a brain aneurysm, but to hear some folks tell it, she died from sheer exhaustion.

"I'm surprised she didn't bring one of the triplets with her," Lizzie continued. "Sarah and Sheba must be at home."

Emma's house was filled to the brim with siblings. There were twelve in all, including Emma, and boasted two pairs of fraternal twins and a set of triplets—two girls and a boy. Sissy could not imagine having that many people in one house at the same time. She and her brother, Owen, were something like oil and water. (He would probably say that he was the oil because that was somehow better.) If there had been more just like them in their house, it would have been utter chaos.

Sarah and Sheba, Sissy knew, had recently turned sixteen and were more than ready to start running around. But they still had a lot of responsibilities at home. It had to be hard to watch all your friends going out while you had to stay home and babysit. Maybe she should go over and offer to take a weekend night from the girls to allow them some time to themselves.

"Now," Lizzie said, turning her attention fully back to Sissy. "Tell me about your week."

"Well, we found a dead body today. That's why we were late getting home."

"What?" Lizzie screeched so loudly that she almost knocked poor Duke onto the floor. "You found a dead body, and you're just now telling me about it?"

"Who found a dead body?" Some other members of the extended Yoder clan had come into the house and were staring at her, jaws wide open: Daniel's cousin Marvin, who was a Yoder but not kin to Bethel and her bunch, along with Gideon Yoder, a cousin, Sissy thought, and his girlfriend, Mary, who was a Chupp.

"A dead body?" This from Emma. "Where?"

"At the tomato farm," Sissy said as patiently as she could. She had finally settled down from all their earlier excitement, but now the hubbub around her was gearing her up again.

"Who?" a chorus of Yoders asked.

"Walt Summers," Sissy told them. "He'd been hit on the back of the head with a shovel while he was tending his tomatoes."

"He was murdered?" someone asked, Sissy wasn't sure who.

Bethel picked that moment to come back into the room. She took one look at everyone's faces and spun around to return to the kitchen.

"Mamm, wait!" Lizzie cried. "You have to tell us what you saw at Walt Summers's."

"Bah," Bethel said with a shake of her head. "It was a mess. And I don't want to go around retelling it." She shot Sissy a pointed look.

"A mess? At the tomato farm? The one next door to my house?" Poor Emma looked horrified, and Sissy felt a pang of remorse for bringing it up.

She had momentarily forgotten that Emma lived right next door to the Summerses.

Lizzie reached a hand toward Emma. "It's okay, sweetie."

Emma stepped closer and took Lizzie's hand.

"I can't believe you didn't hear all the sirens and see all the fire trucks and ambulances," Sissy said. Somehow the words came out a little defensive, though she hadn't meant for them to.

"There is a field between the houses," Lizzie pointed out.

Emma nodded. "I heard the commotion but didn't know it was right next door." She turned to Sissy. "Are you sure it was Walt Summers?"

Sissy nodded. "I mean, I didn't know the man, but everyone else agreed that it was Walt."

"It was Walt all right," Bethel said. Her tone carried the weight of the words she didn't say: that Walt was not a well-liked man in their community. Everyone knew it, so there was no reason to belabor the point. Not that Sissy knew the man well at all. But working in one of the few eating establishments Yoder had to offer gave a person front-row seats to the town. Just in the short time that she had been in Kansas, she had heard tales—many tales—of Walt's contentious attitude. Stories ranged from regularly sending back perfectly fine food at the Carriage House Restaurant to forcing a discount at the hardware store for damaged goods that hadn't been damaged before falling into his hands. That didn't mean he deserved to die, but it seemed like his lack of popularity might make it harder on the police to narrow down their suspects.

"Who could have done such a thing?" Mary asked.

"Good luck figuring that one out," Bethel said. She shook her head and then shot a pointed look all around the room. "Supper's ready. And talk at the table will not be about Walt Summers, understood?"

A chorus of *jahs* went up, accompanied by several nods, then everyone piled into the kitchen to fix themselves a plate.

Friday night supper was a casual affair. They held their silent prayer in the kitchen, then everyone grabbed a paper plate and started dishing out food. Everyone but Lizzie, who was still stuck on the couch growing babies.

There wasn't any room at the table for anyone to sit and eat; there was too much food covering the long wooden surface. So everyone made their plate and found a seat somewhere else.

Sissy helped Daniel make a plate for Lizzie, who had already called from the living room with demands of an extra serving of the casserole that Emma had brought and a separate bowl for her watermelon.

"Why don't you ever bring Gavin with you?" Lizzie asked, once Sissy had settled down on the floor next to the couch where her cousin lay. Lizzie was sneaking Duke bites of chicken while Sissy pretended not to notice. Really, the dog was beyond spoiled.

"We're just friends," Sissy said. The words were almost a knee-jerk reaction. She liked hanging out with Gavin, and they had several mutual interests, writing for one, but they also had vast differences.

And then there was the whole matter of him finding out that she was really Aunt Bess. Of anyone she knew, Gavin would most likely take the news itself with relative aplomb, but she didn't think he would like that she had deceived him for so long, even though, in truth, she had been keeping this little tidbit from everyone, even her own mother!

"Lottie comes, and she's just a friend," Lizzie said. She fed another bite to Duke.

"Lottie's different." What else could she say? Plus, she wouldn't want Gavin to get the wrong idea. If there was one thing Sissy wasn't in the market for, it was a boyfriend. Colt had burned her pretty bad, and she wasn't willing to put her heart back out on the line. Not yet, anyway. And certainly not for geeky Gavin Wainwright.

Okay, so sometimes, in a certain light, he was almost cute. Take away his heavy-framed glasses and comb that cowlick off his forehead, then maybe, but no. She wasn't in the market for anything like that.

"Just saying." Lizzie shrugged.

"No thank you," Sissy shot back. "Just saying."

Thankfully, it was the last time Lizzie brought up Gavin at supper. And afterward, once again, the topic of conversation turned to Walt Summers and the events at the tomato farm that afternoon.

"I just can't believe something like that would happen in our little town," Suzanne Yoder said with a shake of her head. Suzanne was another in the never-ending line of cousins, but she and her boyfriend, David Lambright, had come a little late this evening. They had arrived after prayer, when everyone was fixing a plate.

"I can't believe it happened right next door to you, Emma," Mary said.

Emma ducked her head over her plate and merely nodded.

"I suppose something like this was bound to happen sooner or later," Lizzie said.

"Lizzie!" Sissy exclaimed. "I'm surprised at you."

Lizzie merely shrugged. "He's not a well-liked man. Just saying."

"Still," Sissy playfully admonished. "Talking bad about your fellow Yoderidians."

Lizzie chuckled and rubbed a hand over her belly. "Talking bad? I didn't say anything about the time he stiffed us on the catering for his wife's birthday party."

"We cater?" Sissy asked.

"Not anymore," Lizzie quipped. "And I didn't mention a word about the time he demanded a full refund from the meat-packing plant for a piece of string he supposedly found in his ground bison."

"Define demanded," Sissy said.

"Took out a full-page ad in the *Sunflower Express*."

Sissy grimaced. It seemed the tally was definitely not in Walt's favor.

"And they took the tomato plants too?" Suzanne asked getting them back to their previous topic. "I wish we hadn't been late tonight. I feel like we missed all the excitement."

Sissy shook her head. "You didn't miss much. And yes, they took the tomato plants too."

The girls sat quietly for a moment, mulling over the crime that had been committed and the man who had been killed and the little information that they knew about it.

"I just hope Deputy Berry is smart enough to handle this," Lizzie said.

Oh, he's smart enough, Sissy thought. It was more a matter of him keeping his personal opinions out of the investigation.

Saturdays were perhaps the busiest of days at the Sunflower Café. Maybe because they were closed on Sunday, and if you wanted to eat Bethel's biscuits and gravy, you had to come on Saturday or wait until Monday. Or maybe it was because it was the weekend and people didn't want cook after a long, hard week at work. Whatever the case, the place was packed when Earl Berry sauntered in.

Sissy nodded in his direction as she filled the coffee cups for the mayor and everyone seated at his table. Then she made her way over to the waitress station, set the coffeepot on the burner, and turned back to the deputy.

"You want your usual today?"

Earl Berry ate the same breakfast every morning. Three eggs over hard, with half a side of bacon, half a side of sausage, one large slice of tomato, and a piece of toast with a dab of gravy because he was "watching his cholesterol."

The deputy shook his head. "Not today."

Okay then. Sissy pulled her order pad from the pocket of her apron and got a pen poised and ready.

"Three biscuits with sausage gravy—extra gravy— a bowl of grits, a helping of cantaloupe, and two eggs dead fried. Oh, and a side of sausage links, extra crispy."

Would the wonders of the world never cease? Sissy tore off the order and stuck it in the window for her aunt. "That's quite an order there," she said as she dropped her order pad back into her pocket.

"I'm celebrating," he said with a grin.

"Yeah?" Sissy asked.

"That's right." He set up a little straighter on stool number three. "We caught Walt Summers's killer."

"Wow! That was quick." She moved to pour him a cup of coffee.

He shrugged in a humble manner, then admitted, "The killer came in today and confessed."

By now, he had gained the attention of everyone in the immediate vicinity, including the two men on either side of him and Lottie Foster, who worked the cash register at the café.

Lottie propped her hands on her ample hips and waited for him to continue. "Are you gonna tell us who it is?"

Berry seemed to be savoring the moment. He smacked his lips and enjoyed making them wait. Then finally he said, "Emma Yoder."

CHAPTER FOUR

Don't tell fish lies where the people know you;
but more importantly, don't tell them where they
know the fish.
—Aunt Bess

Sissy wasn't sure whose squeal was louder, her own or Lottie's.

"What do you mean Emma Yoder?" Lottie demanded. She leaned in closer to the deputy, who leaned back and held his hands up in a somewhat defensive pose.

"Now just hold on a minute," he said.

"I'll hold on a second," Lottie said. "Then you tell me what that means."

Sissy thought she might have seen a flash of fear in Earl Berry's eyes. Not that she could blame him; Lottie was not a small woman. She was the nicest person you would ever want to meet, but when she was riled up . . .

And right now she was riled up.

Bethel came out the swinging aluminum doors, wiping her hands on a dish towel and looking around at the diners. "What's going on out here? I can hear all y'all clear back into the kitchen."

Sissy and Lottie turned to Bethel immediately, and both started talking at the same time.

Her aunt shook her head. "One at a time, please."

Sissy nodded toward Lottie. "You tell her."

Lottie shot Earl Berry a look that could've melted iron. "Seems our deputy here arrested sweet Emma Yoder for Walt Summers's murder."

"Can you say that again?" Bethel said. Her eyes narrowed, and her face got a little red. Sissy figured she had heard what Lottie had said, and she had heard it right the first time, but she was going to hold herself in check until she heard it once more. Just to be sure.

"Emma Yoder came into the sheriff's office this morning and confessed to killing Walt Summers yesterday."

Bethel's shoulders remained tight, and the high color remained in her cheeks, but she just shook her head. "That's the most ridiculous thing I've ever heard."

"It may be that," Berry said. "But it's exactly what happened."

Lottie rounded on him. "You honestly believe that sweet little girl would kill Walt Summers?"

"Given Walt's standing in the community, I wouldn't put his murder past my own mother."

Lottie pressed her lips together and wagged her head back and forth. "Okay, so I'll give you that. But not Emma."

"It's always the quiet ones," Earl Berry said.

Sissy looked to her aunt. "Bethel, we can't leave her there."

"You'll have to wait until bail is set. If they even give her one." Berry shrugged as if that was the end word of it all.

"You got this?" Bethel looked to Lottie.

"You know it," Lottie replied.

Bethel shook her head. "I hate to leave like this."

"You go on," Lottie said in return.

Bethel turned to Sissy. "Get your purse."

The Reno County Correctional Facility was located in Hutchinson, Kansas.

Sissy supposed they should chalk this up as a red-letter week, seeing as how her aunt had gotten into her car and ridden around in it twice in so many days.

But she didn't say anything to Bethel as they drove. It was safe to note that, on a normal day, her aunt was irritated. Her eyes were usually squinted a bit, and her mouth turned down at the corners. And she always seemed to be looking at something. That, combined with her expression, made it seem like she disapproved of most everything around her. But that look was nothing compared to the one on her face now. Sissy was a writer, and she wasn't sure she could describe it. It was somewhere beyond anger, just south of all-out disgusted, and it was all tied together in a bow of concern.

Never had the just-under-twenty-minute drive taken so long. Bethel didn't say a word as Sissy parked the car; then together they walked into the jail.

Correctional facility. It seemed there was a euphemism for everything today.

They told the officer at the front desk who they were looking for, and they were instructed to wait in hard plastic chairs for their turn. There weren't many other people there, and Sissy hoped it wouldn't take long. Especially since every minute seemed to last an hour and a half.

Finally, after what seemed like an eternity, they were led back to the visiting space, just like Sissy had seen in the movies: chairs and phones on one side of a sheet of plexiglass, with chairs and phones on the opposite side. It was surreal, to say the least. The officer told them where to go, and Bethel took a seat and picked up the phone just as they brought Emma in.

Sissy almost didn't recognize her, dressed as she was in the orange scrubs sets they used at the correctional facility. Emma's hair was parted in the middle and pulled back at the nape of her neck in a small elastic ponytail holder. Her prayer *kapp* was gone. Her eyes were red-rimmed and teary, her nose as bright as Rudolph's.

When she saw them, those tears spilled over the edges of her lashes and raced down her face. She wiped them on the neck of her shirt before she sat down and picked up the phone receiver on the other side.

"What are you doing in here?" Bethel asked.

Emma was already crying, and Bethel's tone only made it worse.

Sissy turned to her aunt. "Why are you being so mean to her?"

"What is she doing in jail?"

"I did it," Emma said. Her words sounded firm and sure, and Sissy wondered how many times she had had to practice them before they gained such a tone. Of anyone capable of committing that murder, Emma was at the bottom of the list. She just wasn't wired up to complete such an act.

Bethel turned back to Emma. "You did not kill Walt Summers."

"I did." Emma repeated. "I didn't want to do it, but he has just caused our family so many problems."

What kind of problems? Sissy wanted to know but managed not to ask. She would ask someone later.

"You did not kill Walt Summers." Bethel sent the same words straight over to her again.

"He was in his greenhouse watering his tomatoes," Emma continued, "so I went right in there and conked him on the head with a spade."

Bethel frowned at Emma. "Why didn't you just run him through with the pitchfork?"

Emma lifted her chin at a stubborn angle that seemed to be a Yoder family trait. "I might have if there'd been a pitchfork around."

Bethel shook her head. "I don't know what it is you're trying to prove by doing this," she said, "but it's just bringing more heartache on your family."

Still more tears welled in Emma's eyes. "Tell my *dat* I'm sorry." She hung up the phone and stood.

She left so quickly that Bethel didn't even have an opportunity to call her name before she was gone.

"I'm assuming that didn't go as planned," Sissy said.

Bethel hung up the receiver and stood. Sissy followed suit.

"That girl is as stubborn as her *dat.*"

"So what do we do?" Sissy asked as they walked behind the guard through the jail and out into the sweet Kansas sunshine. The day was beautiful, sunny and cheery, and it was at absolute direct odds with what was going on with Emma.

"We can't leave her in jail," Bethel said.

"She's innocent," Sissy said. "Did you hear what she said about a pitchfork?"

"She's just talking tough," Bethel said.

Sissy fished her keys out of her purse and clicked the remote lock on her car. "More than that. There was a pitchfork in the growing shed. I saw it. That just proves that Emma didn't do it. She said she would've run him through with the pitchfork if she'd had one. Well, she had one."

Bethel moved around to the passenger side of the Fiat and waited for Sissy to hit the unlock button a second time. "I think you're wishing for more than is really possible," she said. "Those words aren't enough to get her out of jail."

Sissy tossed her purse into the back seat and climbed into the Fiat. "I suppose you're right. Especially since Earl Berry is in charge. But as far as I'm concerned, it's a start."

* * *

There was absolutely one thing that Bethel and Sissy could agree on, and that was the fact that they couldn't leave Emma in the jail.

True, Earl Berry thought he'd found his man—or woman, as the case might be—and he'd look no further for the killer. Not even if it was truly the real killer.

"We've got to do something," Sissy said as she pulled into Bethel's drive.

Bethel retrieved her bag from the floorboard and got out of Sissy's car. "Come out here tomorrow first thing. We'll figure out something."

Sissy nodded and started to put her car into reverse. She stopped. "Tomorrow is Sunday."

Bethel gave a firm nod. "But it's not a church Sunday. We were going to go visiting, but this is more important. Come on out tomorrow. Let's make a plan."

Sissy smiled. "You got it."

"First thing we need to do is make a list of all the people who really could've killed Walt Summers," Bethel said just after breakfast the following morning.

Sissy had come out with Duke as soon as she had gotten up and brushed her teeth. But by the time she had made it to the house, Bethel and everyone there had already finished breakfast. Thankfully there were some leftovers that Sissy scarfed down while Bethel cleaned the kitchen.

"I think Mamm expected you to be out here earlier," Lizzie had said when Sissy arrived.

"I have to get up at the butt crack of dawn six

days a week. On Sunday eight a.m. is first thing, as far as I'm concerned."

Lizzie had just laughed, until her mother came back in the room and everything turned to the serious business once again.

"You guys are really going to do this?" Daniel asked.

Daniel Schrock, Lizzie's husband, was a handsome and patient man. He had to be patient in order to live with Bethel, Sissy knew that right off the bat. He was also a good man. He provided well, worked at the meat-packing plant, and was looking as forward to the birth of his twins as an Amish man would let himself.

"We can't leave her in jail," Lizzie said. "We have to get her out of there."

"You aren't getting her out of any place," Daniel retorted.

The doctor may have said that Lizzie could come out and spend more time in the common areas of the house instead of lying flat on her back in bed, but she was grounded for sure.

"I meant them." Lizzie waved a hand toward her mother and Sissy.

"We're going to make a list," Bethel said again. "We're going to write down the names of all the people who have crossed with him."

"That's most of Yoder," Daniel said with a frown. He might not be willing to allow his wife to join in, but he was certainly on Team Get Emma Out of Jail.

"So be it," Bethel said.

"You'll have to add your name to the list," Daniel warned.

"Oh, that's right," Lizzie looked back to her mother.

"What happened?"

"He gave me a box of rotten tomatoes and wouldn't refund me," Bethel said.

"That's not worthy of murder," Sissy scoffed, then sobered a bit. "Is it?"

Bethel shot her that look again. "Serious offenses only."

"Like?" Lizzie prodded.

"Like Weaver Justice and the To Die for Tomato," Bethel replied.

That was Bethel. She had the tenacity of a bulldog.

"You really think Weaver did it," Sissy said.

Daniel shook his head. He was supposed to be reading *The Budget*, but, instead, he seemed to be hanging on every word they said. "If Weaver had wanted to kill Summers for that tomato, don't you think he would have done that years ago. How long has it been anyway?"

Sissy grabbed up her phone and put the information into her web search. "Fifteen years," she told them.

"There," Daniel said with a snap of the newspaper. He ducked his head back behind the paper even as he continued. "Why would he wait fifteen years to get revenge?"

"Maybe to throw everybody off his trail," Sissy mused.

"Or maybe it's not him and the real killer is using that to his advantage," Lizzie said.

Bethel looked to her daughter. "Have you been reading those detective novels again?"

Lizzie gave a mock pout. "I've got nothing else to do."

Bed rest had to be excruciating, but bed rest without television was beyond Sissy's comprehension. Poor Lizzie!

Bethel turned her attention back to the list. She wrote a couple more names, then tossed the pen aside with a sigh. "There's just too many."

"Then we focus on the most logical," Sissy said.

"When did murder get logical?" Bethel asked.

"No," Lizzie added. "Sissy's right."

"I agree," Daniel said.

"I thought you didn't want to be a part of this conversation." Bethel glared at her son-in-law.

He returned her stare, nonplussed. "Look to the people who are closest to him."

"That's good advice." Sissy shifted in her seat. "Who's closest to him?"

"His wife," Lizzie put in. Duke barked from his perch atop her belly, and she laughed. "Duke agrees."

"She's not even in town," Bethel grunted. "I'm writing down Weaver Justice."

"As you should," Daniel put in.

"But if you put him on the list, you have to put Amos Yoder on it too." Lizzie frowned as she scratched Duke behind the ear.

"Isn't that Emma's dad?" Sissy asked.

"*Jah*," Daniel confirmed.

Perhaps now was the time to ask the questions she had from the day before. "What did Emma mean yesterday when she told you that he had done so much to her family?"

Bethel shook her head, and Daniel took up the

story. He rose from his chair in the living room and came into the kitchen, where they were sitting. It was actually one big room sectioned off by furniture placement. But Sissy figured his coming closer was a sign of him officially joining in the investigation. Good. They needed all the help they could get if they were really going to get Emma out of jail. And that was the most important thing at the moment.

"It's been over a year now, but Walt filed a petition with the city to have the line between their farms resurveyed."

"So a property dispute," Sissy clarified.

"Right. But Amos has two fields. The one in question was where his cash crop had been planted. That's the crop that he's going to sell," Daniel explained. No doubt he noted the confused look on her face. "The other field is where he had planted a cover crop. It's a crop that isn't harvested or sold. Instead, it's turned into the land to add nutrients back into the soil."

Sissy nodded. "So the dispute was over the cash crop."

"*Jah*," Lizzie called from the living room area.

"Amos lost almost half his income that year," Bethel added.

"Walt took it?" Sissy looked around at all three of them to see if they all agreed. Unfortunately, they did. "But if he planted the crops, wouldn't they belong to him? Even if it was on another man's land."

"Amos's wife was sick and dying," Bethel explained.

"Cancer," Lizzie added with a sad shake of her head.

"He just didn't have it in him to fight Summers," Daniel said.

While he had been talking, Sissy had pulled out her laptop and started searching for more info about the situation online. She found one article in the *Sunflower Express*, but almost immediately her low-battery light started flashing.

"Dang it," she exclaimed.

"What's the matter?" Bethel asked.

Sissy shook her head. "This computer battery. I think my charger's gone bad. I don't have any battery left to search."

Bethel shrugged. "Maybe we can try again later."

"I can do it when I get home." Maybe. Or maybe she should head over to Hutchinson and see if she could get a compatible charger at Walmart. She packed up her laptop and stood. "I probably should be going." She had piles of laundry to do. All of it smelled like onions and grease, the downside of working at a café, she supposed.

"I'll walk you out." Daniel went back to the living room and waited patiently while Lizzie kissed the top of Duke's head and whispered silly good-byes to him. Her husband rolled his eyes good naturedly. "It's a blessed thing she's having two babies or she might have to get a dog as well."

Sissy chuckled.

"See you tomorrow at work," Bethel said.

"Yup." Sissy waved to her cousin and headed out the door, Daniel close on her heels.

"Listen," Daniel said as she stowed everything,

including her dog, back into her car. "Emma didn't do this."

"Then why did she confess?" Sissy asked. She waited with the door open for Daniel to continue.

"I don't know. But if you find the answer to that, you might just find out who killed Walt Summers in the first place."

CHAPTER FIVE

Pick your battles. It's the only way to always win.
—Aunt Bess

Sissy's car donged when she was halfway back to town. She checked the dash to see her gas light on. Since moving to Yoder, her gasoline consumption had dropped considerably. It seemed like forever since she had filled up her tank. It probably had been.

But one thing was completely certain: She would have to fill up before heading to Hutchinson. Or even home, for that matter.

She sighed and turned her car toward the highway. She would swing by the Quiki-Mart and fill up. Then it was on to her little house before heading over to Hutchinson. It wasn't hot out, but she didn't want to leave Duke in the car while she ran in to get a charger. Trips into Walmart were never as short as a person planned for them to be. Never.

As she pulled up to one side of the gas pumps at

Yoder's only gas station, she saw him. Maybe the
hottest guy she had seen in a long, long time. Guy
was wrong. He was a man. Something in the tilt of
his head, or maybe the way he had one hand stuck
in the pocket of his trousers as he waited for the
gas to stop flowing said as much. Or maybe because he was wearing trousers on a Sunday afternoon.

Ex-boyfriend Colt was a guy. Gavin was a guy.
This man was all man.

She cut off her engine and got out of her car,
trying to think of something pithy to say to him.
Anything, really. She hadn't seen him around
town, and considering it was a Sunday, she figured
he was either new to Yoder or had come to visit
family. And considering she was single . . .

"Hi." He smiled at her. Even white teeth, perfect
dimple on one side, grin a little bit crooked.

She raised one hand to wave, but it looked as if
someone had glued her elbow to her waist. Hardly
a wave at all, and certainly there was nothing pithy
about it. "I've . . . just . . . pay." Great. Now she
sounded like she shouldn't be left unsupervised.

From his place in the passenger's seat, Duke
barked. He braced his paws up on the side of the
car where the window was rolled all the way down.

Duke approved, but at the rate she was going,
Mr. Handsome was more likely to think she needed
a constant companion. More than just a dog.

"Can I pet him?" the man asked.

Sissy swallowed hard but could only nod. She
turned and walked stiffly to the door of the Quiki-
Mart.

Get it together. She made her way into the store.

When in the world was Eddie Qureshi, who owned the convenience store/gas station, going to install credit-card readers on the gas pumps? She knew there had to be more to it than mere installation, and that was why he was hesitant. But, in the next breath, she was thanking him for giving her a minute to get herself together. Or try to.

What was wrong with her? She had never gotten this tongue-tied in front of a guy . . . man . . . male before. Not since seventh grade, anyway.

She could feel his gaze on her as she opened the door to the store. The bell over it rang as she entered. She could just hear his voice, softly crooning to Duke.

"Hey, Sissy."

Freddie Howard, the young man who worked part-time at the café, greeted her as she came in.

"Hey, Freddie." At least she had gotten her voice back. She handed him her credit card. "I need to fill her up."

Freddie smiled and gave her a small wink. "I gotcha."

She smiled in return and pushed out of the Quiki-Mart.

Now she had to keep her wits around Mr. Handsome. Seriously . . . what was wrong with her?

She had been alone too long. She had never lived on her own before. Maybe she was losing touch with people her own age. It was a terrible theory. She had plenty of interaction with peers. There were Gavin and Josie and Lizzie, and a host of other cousins who came to the Friday-night suppers at Bethel's house.

Thinking about that had her thinking about

poor Emma being in jail. Perhaps that was what got her thoughts and actions back in sync.

"He's a great pooch," the man said as she approached.

She managed a perfect smile, not too big, but still showing teeth. Two and a half years of braces didn't go to waste today. "He is." She opened her gas tank and grabbed the pump.

"I'm Declan," he said sticking out his hand. "Declan Jones."

"Sissy Yoder."

He tilted his head to one side in a charming way. "I swear eighty percent of this town is named Yoder."

"They call it that for a reason."

He chuckled, the sound rich and pleasing to her ears.

Good Lord. Aunt Bess would tell her that it was time to get ahold of herself.

"I'm not from here, though," she continued. "My parents are, but then they moved."

"To?"

"Oklahoma. Tulsa."

He gave a nod. "I love Tulsa."

Sissy noticed then that he had finished pumping his gas. And with the amount showing on her pump, she was almost finished herself. "It's a great town."

"So, Oklahoma Girl Sissy, what are you doing in Yoder?"

The question she had wanted to ask him.

"I came up to help my aunt in her café."

"The Sunflower Café? I love their chili dogs."

Sissy made an apologetic face. Her gas clicked

off, but she didn't place the nozzle back on the pump. "We're not serving chili dogs any longer." Though she was seriously considering talking to her aunt about that decision if everyone enjoyed them so much.

"What?" He looked aghast, but the truth was Sissy wouldn't have picked him out as a chili dog eater. He looked like more of a medium-rare steak and twice-baked potatoes man. And neither one of those things were served at the Sunflower. "Change is not good."

Sissy laughed.

"Say, since you're kin, maybe you could put in a good word to bring the chili dogs back."

"Maybe." At least, her flirting had improved.

He gave Duke one last pat on the head, winked at Sissy, and opened the door of his car. "I'll see you around, Sissy Yoder."

She stood there by the pumps smiling like a fool. "I'm counting on it," she returned.

But as he drove away, she realized she'd forgotten to ask him if he was merely visiting or in Yoder to stay.

Just as Sissy had predicted, all anyone could talk about on Monday were the problems with Walt and the problems surrounding his murder. Like the fact that most Yoderidians couldn't believe that a wisp of a girl like Emma Yoder could hit a man with a shovel hard enough to kill him with one blow.

And since the coroner had just released the report stating that Walt Summers had indeed been killed with one blow to the head, it was practically all anyone could talk about.

"Three whacks," Charlie Otter said. He worked construction around the area, but always seemed to manage to find his way back to the Sunflower Café in time to talk about whatever was going on in the world. "Maybe four."

Copper Callahan shook his head. Copper was another regular. Sissy had been told that Elmer was his given name, and she supposed that his hair had to have been close to the color of hers for him to score such a moniker. Now however, his hair was gray with streaks of yellow. Just like his untrimmed beard. "Did you see her? She was just an itty-bitty thang. Ain't no way she could have killed him without dropping a ton of bricks on his head."

Sissy refilled the two men's coffee but managed to keep her two cents to herself. She completely agreed, but if she stopped and talked to every customer about how there was no way that her cousin could have killed Walt Summers, she wouldn't get anything done.

She moved to the next table, where the talk was the same. In fact, so many of the diners were discussing the murder and the impossibility of Emma Yoder actually being guilty of the crime that they were starting to cross talk from table to table.

"Maybe now we can find out what's in that dirt he sells," Troy Adams threw in.

"I'm not sure I care at all. This last batch didn't do squat for my corn." Glen Ray Donovan shook his head. "Too late to get my money back on that, I suppose."

A chorus of agreement and laughter went up from the tables closest to him.

Over the din, the bell on the door jangled out that someone was coming in or leaving. Sissy finished refilling the coffee at the last table and checked the door to see which it was.

It was Gavin Wainwright, coming in.

She met him at the counter. He slid onto the fourth stool, and she was smart enough to figure out that he did so to be close to Earl Berry when he arrived. She returned the coffeepot to its warmer at the waitress station and filled a glass with ice water for Gavin. She slid it in front of him.

Gavin smiled. "Am I that predictable?"

She grabbed her order pad and pen and got them at the ready. "I've only seen you drink something other than water one time." She shrugged one shoulder and waited for him to decide what he wanted to eat.

"Just the water for now," he told her.

She nodded toward the third stool. "He won't be in for a little bit." She checked the clock. "Maybe forty-five minutes."

"That's all right." Gavin took out his notebook and set it on the countertop. "I thought I might get a feel for the town and what everyone is saying about Emma and the murder."

"It's pretty much the same all over. No one completely believes that she's strong enough to hit anyone with a shovel and kill them with one blow. It's ludicrous." Sissy eyed the pen he held in his hand and tried not to look too nervous over the whole situation. She had almost blown it Friday by quoting her own copy. Gavin might only be a small-town, weekly newspaper reporter, but he was smart. Astute, really, and if she kept making mistakes like that, her secret would be blown in no time. And it was a secret she desperately wanted to keep.

Okay, so it wasn't deviant or crude, but it was hard enough these days to get a date without adding that your job consisted of posing as a seventy-something grandma and dishing out advice like hard candy. Plus, she wasn't sure how the editors would take it if her cover was blown. Who wanted to take advice from a thirty-year-old single woman who was pretending to be something that she was not?

Unbidden, the image of Declan Jones popped into her head. Date, yes.

"Have you seen my cousin about?" Gavin asked.

Sissy shook her head. "I spent most of the day out with Bethel and Lizzie. So if he came by, I wasn't home until later in the afternoon."

"Yeah, okay," he said. "Just wondering."

"Thanks for warning me, though. I would have been concerned if I had seen a strange man lurking around your aunt's house."

Gavin nodded as Josie called from the kitchen, "Order up!"

Sissy moved to take the order out to the table.

"Everybody knows that Jimmy Joe Bartlett has been complaining about the state of his sunflowers this year," someone said.

The statement might have brought up images of a sweet man with a soft disposition who nurtured a small crop of sunflowers just off his front porch. Yet that couldn't be any further from the truth.

Jimmy Joe was a mountain of a man who grew commercial sunflowers in the fields west of town. Sissy had heard what a sight it was to go out there when the crop was blooming and gaze over the sea of golden petals. There was still a while before the sunflowers would be tall enough to make a presence, but it was on her radar to do once the fall hit and they were.

"Jimmy Joe is strong enough to kill a man with one blow," someone added. She thought it was Copper.

A murmur of agreement went up all around.

"He's not the only one having problems with Walt's Special Blend," Charlie said. He had finished his breakfast and was merely hanging around for the conversation. Sissy liked the concept, but she wasn't sure it was appropriate for everyone to lounge around talking about Murder in the First, yet she wasn't about to tell all these farmers and construction workers that they should be talking about something else.

At least, now they were discussing Walt Summers's soil additives instead of who might have killed him. She couldn't say it was great, but it was better for sure.

"He was in the hardware store not even a week ago, saying how he wanted to get his hands on Walt Summers," Copper said, holding up his own hands and mimicking choking someone.

She spoke too soon.

"I was there," someone else spoke up. "He was very vocal about it."

Thankfully, Earl Berry picked that time to saunter in. His swagger was a little more pronounced today, no doubt attributable to the fact that he'd got his man. Or girl, as the case might be. Though it wasn't, because she had turned herself in. And she was innocent, and there was no way little Emma Yoder could have swung a shovel hard enough to crack a man's skull on the first blow.

"Now, now," Berry said as he hoisted himself up onto the third stool. He nodded at Sissy and flipped his coffee mug over—his way of telling her to fill it.

She gritted her teeth and grabbed the coffeepot. Honestly, sometimes she wished she could pour the scalding-hot contents right over his smug head. Well, his expression, anyway. She supposed his head really wasn't all that smug, but she knew what she meant.

"We are confident in our knowledge that we have the correct suspect in custody." He picked up his coffee as soon as she finished pouring and took a tentative sip. Something in that action made her wish she could clunk him upside the head with the coffeepot. Or maybe it was his attitude. It was more than obvious that he had been prepped on what to say. No doubt, the sheriff himself had written the script. And she was certain that they thought they had the right person. You know, with a confession and all that. But the whole town knew that Emma Yoder was innocent. Why couldn't he . . . they see it?

She returned the coffeepot to the warmer with a little more force than necessary.

"Careful," Bethel said, coming up behind her. "Never let them see you sweat."

Sissy turned. "What?"

Bethel shrugged. "Listen, after work, I'm thinking about stopping by Amos Yoder's. Checking on him, you know."

Sissy nodded. Emma's dad.

"You want to go along?"

It was perhaps the first time that Bethel herself had invited Sissy to join in something. A warm rush of light filled her. She tamped it back down. No use in getting overly sentimental. Most likely, it would be reminiscent of Sissy's visit with Darcy Saunders, Kevin the milkman's widow. Chaotic beyond belief, only with two more children. There were twelve Yoders and ten Saunderses. Well, eleven Yoders, she supposed, since Emma was in jail.

"I'd love to," Sissy said and went to pull Earl Berry's order from the kitchen window. And somehow she managed to deliver it to him without dumping the whole thing into his lap.

She should have known, she mused, as she stood next to Bethel in the immaculate kitchen in the Yoders' house. Emma had been in jail for a couple of days, and Sissy knew that she served as a mother to the children, whose real mother had died shortly after giving birth to triplets. At home. With no anesthesia. But that was something to contemplate another day.

Even at twenty, Emma was mature and nurturing. Sissy had imagined that, without her there to oversee the family, things would sort of fall apart. Clothes wouldn't be cleaned, dishes wouldn't be washed, and, in general, the house would be filled with muddy floors, toys galore, and noise beyond reason.

But this was an Amish household, and that wasn't the case. Sissy couldn't decide if telling Emma that her family had stepped up in her absence and taken care of everything would make her feel better, knowing that they were surviving just fine, or worse, knowing that they were surviving just fine *without her*.

"I'll go get Dat," Sheba told them. Or was it Sarah? The twins were sixteen and fraternal and truly looked nothing alike. Sissy just couldn't remember which name to put with which girl.

The rest of the children's names were easy to remember. Mostly. Until you got down to the triplets. They were about a year old, two girls and a boy. The girls, Annie and Abbie, were identical. I-dent-ti-cal. Sissy was glad she wouldn't be called anytime soon to tell them apart. And, thankfully, Amos was obviously a boy and dressed in boys' clothing, so that was a plus.

"*Danki,*" Bethel said.

"Would you like some coffee?" Sarah asked. Or maybe Sheba.

"That would be nice," Bethel replied. She slid comfortably into one of the chairs around the long table. Sissy followed suit.

The twin poured them all a cup of coffee as they waited for Amos to come in from the barn or wherever it was he was working today. Truth be known, Sissy didn't know much about the workings of a farmer. Did they spend a lot of time in their barn? It was a question she would probably never get answered, as anyone she asked would think her a total idiot. So she quietly waited.

"Sissy, will you help me with this?"

Sissy turned as a young girl, maybe six or seven, came in from another room carrying a large sheet of paper and a box of markers. But she wasn't talking to Sissy. She was talking to the twin.

"They call me Sissy too. Sarah was our mother's name." She blushed a pretty pink and gave a small shrug.

Well, that solved the question of which twin was standing in front of her. Sarah Yoder had darker hair and green eyes, while her twin had blond hair and blue eyes.

The other Sissy took the paper from her sister. "Now, Nancy, if I help you with this, how can you say that you did the work when you give it to your teacher?"

"But everyone else's welcome card looks better than mine. Even Elmer's."

"Just do the best *you* can, and don't worry about how everyone else's looks. This is from you to Dee Dee, and I know she'll love anything you give her if you give it from the heart."

Barely sixteen, and already she could serve as a life coach. It just went to show how differently these girls had been raised from your typical *Englisch* household.

"Okay," Nancy said, but she didn't sound too happy about it. "I guess." She took her paper and her box of markers and trudged out of the room.

"School starts next week, and the youngins are making cards to take to their new teacher."

Sissy nodded. She had forgotten about school

starting back. She had learned somewhere along the way that the Amish kids in Yoder either went to the one Amish school or to the charter school with the *Englisch* kids.

"I thought Emma was the teacher," Sissy said. She wasn't sure where she had learned that nugget of information, but it was there all the same.

"Most Amish have a one-room schoolhouse. There's about eight or ten families in each, but somewhere along the line, we decided to do something different."

Sissy nodded and waited for Sarah to continue. She just couldn't call the girl Sissy. That just seemed too strange: two Sissy Yoders.

"The Amish school here in Yoder is a little bigger than most. There are two buildings. The older kids are in one building and the younger ones in the other. Emma teaches the older kids, and Dee Dee Yoder teaches the younger ones. Both have two assistants to help them with the lessons."

That sounded a lot busier than the idea that had been in Sissy's head.

"I hope Sissy hasn't yakked your ears off." Amos Yoder wiped his boots on the mat outside, then stepped into the kitchen. He hung his hat on the wall just inside but didn't try to fluff his hair free from the invisible band around it.

"She was just telling us about Emma's classroom." Bethel stood to greet him. For a moment, Sissy thought she might give the man a hug, but Bethel just wasn't the huggy kind.

Amos Yoder nodded toward Sissy and took the seat opposite her at the long table. He looked like most all the other Amish men she had encountered in Yoder. Blue shirt, black suspenders, broad fall pants, long, untrimmed beard, and a bad case of hat hair. He was a little dusty and a little sweaty from working outside, but he accepted the coffee that Sarah poured him. Sarah grabbed her own cup, but instead of sitting around the table with them, she headed into the room from which Nancy had emerged. "I think I'll go help the kids with their cards. It was good to see you, Bethel." She squeezed her aunt's shoulder and with a small tilt of her head in Sissy's general direction, she made her way out of the kitchen.

Amos watched her go, then shook his head. "Lord, save me from my own mistakes."

"We all make mistakes," Bethel said.

Sissy felt a little like she had walked into the middle of a conversation, so she kept quiet and allowed the two of them to visit.

"*Jah,* but they aren't all as big as mine."

"Amos, you know as well as I do that the fences were put up wrong long ago. How Walt Summers got ahold of those old survey records, we'll never know."

Nope. Especially now that he was dead, but Sissy kept that comment to herself.

"You couldn't help that mistake. It was someone else's to begin with."

"I could have fought harder."

For a moment, Sissy thought she saw the sheen of tears in his eyes, but it must have been just a trick of the lighting.

"You did what you could in the circumstances that surrounded you. The rest was up to God."

Then Sissy remembered. Walt Summers had

contested Amos's ownership of a large parcel of land. A very large parcel. Unfortunately, the field in question was where Amos had planted his cash crop for the year. When he lost the field, he lost the crop as well, since he hadn't bought mineral rights from the true owner. But at the time, Sarah—his wife Sarah—had just given birth to the triplets. She was ill, and there were three new babies in the house all at once. Sissy was certain that the man couldn't have had the energy or the time to fight against a powerful force like Walt Summers. Nor did it seem that he had the heart. In the end, he had given over his crop and the land and concentrated on healing his wife, who eventually died.

It was surely enough to warrant killing someone—speculatively speaking. Most people would be in the state of mind to seriously hurt the person who had taken advantage of them in a weak moment, but sitting with Amos Yoder didn't give Sissy the feeling that he was capable of murdering anyone. Not even Walt Summers. The whole Amish pacifist thing aside, he just wasn't the kind to take up arms when things didn't go his way. He was more of a "find a different solution" problem solver.

And all that went double for Emma.

"It wasn't enough." His voice was thick with emotions, most likely regret and remorse. "I don't know why she's telling everybody . . . the police that she killed Walt Summers. She didn't. I know she didn't."

Bethel reached across the table and patted his hand. "Of course she didn't."

Sissy wanted to share the story of Emma and the

pitchfork with Amos, but she wasn't sure how the anecdote would be taken, so she kept quiet.

"I know she didn't because she was at the school at the time when he was killed," Amos continued. "And there are at least four, maybe even five witnesses who can attest to the fact."

The other teacher and their assistants, Sissy assumed. But she was certain Earl Berry would consider all that "circumstantial" when held up against a signed confession.

"I went out to see her yesterday," Amos said.

Sissy got the feeling he needed to talk to someone.

"She's still holding firm to her story."

"Emma's nothing if not stubborn," Bethel put in.

"So what do we do?" Amos asked.

Bethel gave a small, stiff shrug. "Do our best to talk her down and wait it out."

From the look on Amos's face, that was not what he wanted to hear.

CHAPTER SIX

*A farmer has to be an optimist or he wouldn't still
be a farmer.*
—Aunt Bess

"**D**anki for bringing me out here," Bethel said
the following afternoon.

She said the words, but she didn't appear thankful. To Sissy, her aunt looked like she had swallowed a whole lemon, one itty-bitty piece at a time. She had one hand braced on the doorframe in the opened window, and the other clutched her prayer *kapp* as if her life depended on it.

"You're welcome." Sissy chanced a second glance at her aunt. She was as stiff as the dead, sitting there, all locked in, as if expecting a crash at any moment. "Have you always had such a problem riding in cars?"

Bethel didn't take her eyes from the road. "No," she replied. "Just this one. Is it made from recycled soup cans or something?"

Sissy managed to resist the urge to roll her eyes. It wouldn't do any good. "No. This is a perfectly safe, finely engineered Italian motor car."

"*Jah.* Uh-huh."

"Do you want me to roll the top up?" Maybe that would make her aunt feel a little safer. She reached for the button, but her aunt used one sharp elbow to knock Sissy's hand away from the controls. "Don't. I already feel like I'm riding in a baby shoe with wheels. Don't close me in."

Sissy dropped her hand back to the steering wheel and hid her smile. It wasn't that she was happy that her aunt was suffering; it was just that her aunt had her own list of things that bothered her—just like everyone else. And she didn't mean bother her like the way the size of Sissy's dog bothered her.

But to get to Jimmy Joe Bartlett's house, it was either take Sissy's car or Bethel's tractor, and Sissy wasn't sure she herself could take another tractor ride after the one they had taken yesterday out to Amos's house.

The only good part about standing on a piece of tractor that she wasn't sure she should be standing on while they had slowly chugged through the farmland was that it had given her time to look around at the scenery and get a better feel for the countryside. For the most part, the road where Weaver Justice, Amos Yoder, and Walt Summers had lived had all the houses on one side, while there was nothing but fields of crops on the other. The field that had been in question between Walt and Amos sat between their two houses. Sissy didn't know what it had been planted with last year, but this year there was corn. Tall enough that it blocked the view from Amos's to Walt's. And for some reason, she wanted to get another look at Walt's property, his growing shed, and the hunks of dirt where the missing tomatoes had been planted. Maybe they had missed something the first time. But Bethel had a different plan.

She had overheard the talk in the café about Jimmy Joe Bartlett and his sunflowers. How they weren't growing right, and even Walt Summers's special soil mix, his Special Blend, which cost an arm and a leg, wasn't helping. Bethel didn't come right out and say it, but Sissy got the feeling that her aunt thought perhaps Jimmy Joe had just about as much motive as Emma. And he was definitely strong enough to swing a shovel and kill with one blow.

When the pavement ran out, Sissy had to roll up the windows to keep too much dust from getting in the car. But Bethel made her leave the top at least halfway open. What they called the "sunshine mode," which left just the very top of the car open. Bethel had insisted, so Sissy had complied.

Thankfully, the distance between where the road turned to dirt and where Jimmy Joe's farm sat was negligible, and they were there in no time.

Bethel sighed when Sissy pulled the car to a stop in Jimmy Joe's driveway and turned off the engine. Sissy hadn't even unhooked her seat belt before her aunt was out of the car. She couldn't help but feel a little bad that riding around in her car stressed her aunt so badly, but she hadn't known any of this was going to happen when she bought it. That she would be here, driving her poor Amish aunt around, and trying to figure out who really killed Walt Summers. Of course, with as much as she loved her little Italian import, even if she had known, it wouldn't have made a difference. She had come to care about her aunt in the weeks that she had been in Yoder, but it was a Fiat! A convertible. It was her one concession for spending her secretive days handing out advice as a seventy-year-old busybody who overshared in the newspaper.

"Bethel Yoder, is that you?" A man came out of the open garage attached to a small brick house. He was wiping his hands on a faded red grease rag as he approached.

Jimmy Joe Bartlett was exactly what he appeared to be—a farmer. He wore a dingy white wife-beater under Liberty brand overalls and dusty, mud-caked muck boots. It was just that his crop seemed a little unusual to Sissy, but again . . . what did she know about farming? And farming sunflowers seemed a lot more pleasing that farming soybeans. Nothing against soybeans, but sunflowers were a lot more beautiful. And Kansas was the Sunflower State.

"At the café yesterday, I heard you say something about Walt Summer's Special Blend of fertilizer."

"Yeah." He nodded toward Sissy, and she supposed it was in both agreement and greeting.

"It's not the same this year, or what?" Bethel asked.

Jimmy Joe tilted his head to one side and thought about it for a moment. "Why you want to know?"

"Daniel had me come out. He's thinking about growing some strawberries next year and—"

"He can grow strawberries, but he won't be getting any of Walt's Special Blend."

Because he's dead, Sissy thought.

Yet that wasn't a stopping place for her aunt. "I guess he won't be needing it if it ain't any good."

Jimmy Joe stuck the rag into his back pocket. "See for yourself." He gestured toward the field on the left side of his house. Then he turned and headed off in that direction. Sissy and Bethel followed behind.

"Even without Walt's Special Blend, these should be in full bloom, but they're not. Usually, with a good batch of fertilizer, I get blooms half the summer. These buds are all closed up tight. They won't be opening for a while. And I'm already a hundred days in." He shook his head. "Sunflowers can be profitable even in bad years. But this . . ." He shook his head sadly. "This is worse than bad."

"And you think his fertilizer did this? I mean, your plants are growing."

"But not like they used to. I'll still manage to get some crop out of it, but if they don't hurry up and bloom, then the frost will hit, and it'll all be over."

"How's Ashely doing?" Bethel asked.

Sissy didn't know who Ashely was, but if she had to guess, it was either Jimmy Joe's wife or his daughter.

"We've still got a few more weeks left. That's another thing. I was hoping to get everything harvested before the baby comes."

Wife, Sissy thought.

"But now . . ." He shook his head and made his way back over to the house. Sissy wasn't sure, but it seemed like Jimmy Joe was turning his back on the crops like he couldn't bear to look at them. Maybe he couldn't.

Was that enough to commit murder? A pregnant wife, a failing cash crop?

"I went over there last week and told him I wanted my money back, but he refused. Said I had already used it, and once it left his farm, he had no control over how it was used. He had no guarantee that I had done it correctly. Like I haven't been getting that Special Blend from him all these years." Jimmy Joe shook his head. "This new stuff doesn't even smell the same. Here." He went over to the side of the house and brought back one of the blue not-pickle buckets stacked there.

Both Bethel and Sissy took a step back.

"We'll take your word for it." Bethel held up both hands.

"I'll say this," Jimmy Joe started, "I don't wish anybody dead, but I'm not at all sad to see him go. That just makes me one of many."

"What do you mean?" Sissy asked.

Jimmy Joe shrugged. "I challenge you to find one person in this town who is grieving that sumabitch."

"His wife," Sissy offered.

Jimmy Joe shrugged again in a way that clearly displayed his doubt about that. "Maybe you should go ask her."

Sissy stewed on that as Bethel thanked Jimmy Joe for his time and his input.

"Good luck with them strawberries," he said.

"What?" Bethel squinted at the man.

"The strawberries. The ones Daniel is gonna grow," he explained.

"*Jah.* Strawberries. Right. Thanks."

They climbed into the car and waved goodbye to the young farmer.

"Do you think it's strange that no one has seen Mary Ann Summers since Walt died?" Sissy asked as she started the car.

"She's in Wichita."

"And?" Sissy prompted.

"She could have come home and gone back without anyone knowing. It's only forty miles or so. Easy in a car."

"Right," Sissy said. "But her husband just died. She has a funeral to plan."

"Maybe. Maybe not." Bethel shrugged, then braced herself in the car and clapped one hand over her prayer covering. "I've heard all kinds of things about *Englischers* planning out their own funerals. I've even heard some people will pay for it in advance all so the grieving widow or whoever doesn't have to worry about a thing."

"Does Walt Summers strike you as the kind of man who worries about what his wife is going to do for his funeral after he dies?"

"*Nee.*"

They hit the blacktop again, and Sissy stopped on the side of the road to let the top all the way down. She loved riding with the wind in her hair, and it seemed her aunt needed the openness the sliding roof gave her.

"So you're saying that she could have come back into town and possibly put all of Walt's plans into motion." Sissy glanced at her aunt for verification.

"Only if he had plans."

"Which we don't think is the case."

"Right," Bethel said.

"Truth is, the only person besides Mary Ann who would know if she was coming back to Yoder to plan his funeral would be—"

"Dustin Moore," Bethel supplied. "Funeral director and part-time coroner."

Sissy checked the clock on the dash. "I've got about another hour before Duke will start trying to escape his kennel. Is that enough time?" she asked. She didn't include the destination. She didn't have to.

"I guess it will if it's all we got."

Sissy turned the car around and headed back to town. To the Moore Funeral Home on Westwood Avenue.

They drove back to town in silence. Sissy figured her aunt was thinking about the conversation they'd just had with Jimmy Joe. Thinking about it, just like she was. But was her aunt thinking the same thing?

"How well do you know Jimmy Joe?" she finally asked. They were almost to the funeral home, so if she was going to bring up her doubts, now was the time, while they were still fresh in her mind.

"What are you getting at?" Bethel asked. Ah, her sweet-talking aunt.

"I don't think he's the one who killed Walt Summers."

"Because?"

Sissy shrugged. "He's big enough. And he's definitely strong enough, but he seems like a big ol' teddy bear."

"That big ol' teddy bear was the number-one defensive lineman for the Hutchinson High Salthawks back in the day."

"The Salthawks?"

Bethel shot her a look.

Okay, ignore the bizarre school mascot. Focus on what is important. "Just because he's a good football player doesn't mean he's a killer."

"Tell that to Randy Coleman."

"He killed Randy Coleman?" And he was still out walking around?

"Broke his neck."

"On the football field?" It happened, unfortunately. The gridiron was no place for sissies. No pun intended. "How do you know all this?" It didn't seem like something that would be talked about in the close-knit Amish community.

"People talk," she said. And when Sissy started to ask, she supplied, "*Englisch* people."

"So you heard it at the café that he broke Randy Coleman's neck."

"In a bar fight, right after he came home from college."

"What was the fight about?"

"It was over a girl. Ashely, who is now his wife. But it cost him. He had to serve a little time for assault and battery. Ashely started dating someone else. Ended up pregnant. That guy died shortly after Jimmy Joe got out of jail."

"This all sounds like a soap opera."

Bethel shrugged, then grabbed the window

frame again as Sissy swung wide to enter the narrow drive at the Moore Funeral Home.

"So he didn't kill the guy, I'm assuming."

"No one was able to prove anything, but the fight and the jail time set him up as a man with a temper. Not many people are willing to forget that. So he turned to farming."

"What was he doing before?"

"Selling insurance or something."

"Making steady money." She turned off the engine and twisted around to better see her aunt. "If farming is the only job he can get and Walt Summers messed up his crop—or even if Jimmy Joe thinks that he did . . ."

"Then Jimmy Joe, the big ol' teddy bear, turns into Jimmy Joe, crushing lineman."

It was something to consider.

"All right, then," Sissy said. "Let's go."

They walked shoulder to shoulder to the entrance of the Moore Funeral Home. The whole setup looked like a washed-out colonial. Instead of crisp red brick, the building stones had been painted a milquetoast beige. The what-should-have-been-white columns were painted dark ecru and the black shutters a soft fawn. All in all, it was an off-white nightmare. But, as far as Sissy knew, it was the only funeral home in Yoder. So it would stand to reason that this was where Walt would be buried. Or, at least, that's what they were counting on.

Bethel opened the large, pale tan door and motioned for her to enter. "Go right ahead."

Sissy felt more than a little conspicuous as she

stepped into the cool beige interior. Whoever picked the colors for the outside had most likely done the same for the inside, though Sissy briefly wondered if they'd just bought too much paint and used it up on the foyer. The beige upon beige upon beige was only broken up by a cherrywood podium and a potted palm with leaves so perfect she wanted to feel one to see if it was fake.

"May I help you?" A man stepped around the corner to what appeared to be a hallway. He, at least, was wearing a somber gray suit. Sissy didn't know what she would have done if he'd come out dressed in beige to match everything else. His hair was close, though. It was a thick, hay-colored blond shot with white. "Bethel." His steps stuttered in surprise. "I trust everything is okay?"

Sissy knew that the Amish community wouldn't use the services of a funeral home such as this. The Amish had a coffin maker for the community, the bishop conducted the service, and the viewing would be held at the deceased person's house. She figured the man knew Bethel like everyone else did—from the Sunflower Café.

"Everything's fine, Dustin. Have you met my niece Sissy?"

Dustin took a step forward and shook her hand. "Nice to meet you, Sissy."

He spoke in such a soft and kind way that Sissy wondered what sort of training funeral parlor directors received. Every one that she had met had displayed the same gentle demeanor. They all had an almost ethereal aura and spoke in soft tones (if they had a color, Sissy was sure that it would be beige). All had gentle voices as if the person they were speaking to might shatter like a fine crystal wineglass.

"Likewise," she whispered. Otherwise, she would have felt like she was shouting.

"I've come to ask you a question," Bethel abruptly stated.

Dustin's forehead wrinkled as he frowned. Sissy wasn't sure if it was because of the question or if it was her aunt's normally brusque manner that had him concerned. "What's that?"

An interrogative statement used to gain information, Sissy thought. Honestly, one day, her movie references were going to get her into trouble. Now was not the time to be quoting *Airplane!* Plus she was certain neither of her companions had seen the movie and wouldn't appreciate the humor in it. Well, her aunt hadn't seen the movie. Dustin Moore, she was certain, had had his sense of humor surgically removed as he had gone into funeral parlor director training at the Beige Academy. Where was Gavin when she needed him?

"Have you seen Mary Ann Summers?"

Dustin drew back. He had been leaning forward as if to encourage Bethel to speak softly since he was so close. "Not lately. Why?" He shook his head sadly. "What a shame about her husband."

Yeah. Poor old Walt.

Sissy might not have had the chance to meet him before he died, but it was obvious there weren't any people in Yoder who mourned his passing.

"*Jah,*" Bethel said. "But no one has seen Mary Ann. At least, no one that I've spoken to. And I figured . . ."

Dustin smiled. "You figured that if anyone had seen her, it would be me." He seemed pleased that he was included in her thoughts. "Walt had his funeral all planned out. All Mary Ann had to do was call me and tell me to put his plan in motion."

"And she did that?" Sissy asked.

The funeral director nodded. "I've talked to her on the phone, but I haven't seen her in person. She called me from Wichita just yesterday. Though she promised the next time she's in town, she'll stop by and sign all the papers."

"*Danki,*" Bethel said. "I've just been concerned about her."

"That's mighty kind of you, Bethel."

Her aunt nodded, but otherwise didn't acknowledge the compliment.

They said their goodbyes and headed back out into the bright Kansas sunshine.

"So Walt didn't trust his wife to make his funeral plans," Sissy surmised as they made their way across the almost empty parking lot to where she had left her Fiat.

"Or he loved her so much that he didn't want to put her through having to make all those decisions."

"What are the odds of that?" Sissy asked. She fished out her keys and unlocked the doors.

"I believe the correct term is slim to none." Bethel opened the passenger side door and worked herself into the small seat.

"That favorable, huh?"

Bethel chuckled as Sissy got in. She started the car and sat there for a moment, just taking it in.

"I thought you only had an hour before you would need to check on that rat of a dog."

Sissy didn't take offense. She knew her aunt secretly liked Duke. She had seen Bethel petting the beast when she thought no one was looking. "Yeah. But isn't it a bit strange that she didn't come right home to see for herself or identify his body or some such?"

Bethel shrugged. "Knowing what you do, if you were married to Walt Summers, would you rush right home?"

CHAPTER SEVEN

*When you have ruled out the impossible, whatever's
left has got to be the truth.*
—Aunt Bess

"Word around town is that no one has been
in to visit with Emma Yoder," Lottie said
the next day at breakfast. She poured Earl Berry a
refill on his coffee as she waited for him to respond.

She wasn't the only one listening in.

Wednesday at the Sunflower Café was pretty
much Tuesday Part Two. Gavin had come in early
and parked his behind on stool number four, waiting for Earl Berry to come in and park his behind
on stool number three, so everyone in the immediate vicinity could get the news on what was happening next firsthand. Or, at least, as firsthand as
they possibly could. As Lottie had just mentioned,
no one had been to see Emma Yoder. Or that's
what everyone was saying.

Berry did not disappoint. He picked up his coffee cup, smacked his lips once before taking a small sip of the mostly fresh brew. "That's right." He straightened up importantly.

"You mean her dad hasn't even been in?" This from Gavin. Sissy could tell he was taking furious mental notes but didn't want to tip his hand to Earl Berry by actually writing everything down in a notebook.

"Nope." The deputy shifted on his stool. "But don't be thinking hard on Amos," he continued. "That man's got eleven youngins to look after and a farm that's about to come in. The way I see it, this couldn't happen at a worse time for him."

Sissy couldn't think of what a better time would be for your daughter to confess to murder, but who was she to judge?

"What about Samuel?" Lottie asked.

In all the commotion, Sissy had sort of forgotten about Samuel Glick, Emma's fiancé.

Earl Berry shook his head. "She's refusing to see anybody."

Bethel came out of the kitchen at that point, wiping her hands on a dish towel and frowning. Sissy wasn't quite sure if it was a deeper frown than her normal walk-around-town frown, but it seemed to be. "Lottie, I think the mayor needs a refill."

Lottie nodded. "Right." She moved away toward the table where George Preston set up counsel most mornings until his secretary came and made him get on into the office. Preston wasn't really the mayor, though most people considered him the voice of the town. He was, after all, the postmaster and a very respected person in these parts.

But his office wasn't in City Hall—there wasn't a city hall in Yoder. It was in the back of the small post office smack dab on Main Street.

Bethel pulled Sissy to one side. "How about you and me go check on Emma this afternoon after we close. You got anything else to do?"

Of course, she needed to take Duke for a walk, and there were two loads of laundry she had to do, but laundry fell way behind a visit to the Reno County Correctional Facility to see Emma. And Duke's walk could be cut a little short on the promise of a longer one before supper.

But she must've hesitated too long, for Bethel continued, "Anything that can't wait?"

Sissy shook her head. "Just let me take the poochie out for a quick stroll and we'll go."

Bethel dipped her chin in a motion of thanks. "Right after work."

And that's how Sissy found herself on the highway headed to Hutchinson, with Bethel in the passenger seat once again, holding onto her prayer covering for dear life with one hand and the doorframe with the other.

"What do we do if we get there and she refuses to see us?" Sissy asked.

Bethel turned and shot her a look.

"Right." Sissy was fairly certain Bethel had never taken no for an answer in her life. It wasn't that she was contentious, though some could say that about her aunt; it was more that she was stubborn, persistent, and somehow had a way of making people do what she needed them to do. Most people Sissy had known like that had a sunny disposition and were always smiling; she could only suppose

that Bethel's skill behind the cookstove contrib-
uted to the jump-and-fetch attitude she seemed to
inspire. But Sissy was just guessing.

Sissy opened her mouth but closed it again.
She'd been about to say something to the effect of
they didn't have to bring Emma out to see them if
she refused, but she had a feeling she would only
receive another of those looks from her aunt. She
thought it best to kept quiet.

"She will not refuse to see me," Bethel said.

Okay, well, that made a little more sense. She
wasn't counting on the guards and other law
enforcement doing what she wanted rather her
niece . . . cousin? Kin. She would go with kin.
Bethel was counting on Emma to not deny her.
And Sissy was fairly certain she was right.

And she was. They were led into the same room
they had been in before, with the little booths and
telephones and plexiglass with chairs and telephones on the opposite side. Emma came shuf-
fling out in orange jailhouse scrubs and rubber
slide shoes. Her hair was lank and listless and
hung in a ponytail over one shoulder, but, at least,
she gotten her prayer *kapp* back. Sissy supposed
that was an improvement for the young girl, but
she still looked as miserable as any one person
could look.

Bethel picked up the phone and waited for
Emma to do so on the other side. "Are you ready
to come home yet?" Bethel asked as soon as the
young girl picked up the receiver.

Bethel leaned closer so Sissy could hear.

"They're not gonna let me out of here. I committed murder," Emma said, but her voice didn't

have quite the same confident ring to it that it had had on day one in jail. It'd been less than a week, but life in captivity was starting to take its toll on the girl.

Sissy couldn't say that *Englisch* kids would have an easier time of it than one who was Amish, but, at least, most of them had sort of an idea about what they were getting into if they got sent to jail. There were shows on TV with jail scenes, reality shows and movies and all sorts of whatnot that depicted, at least, some sort of jail or prison life. But an Amish girl would be solely unprepared in that way.

"You didn't commit murder," Bethel said. Each word was succinct and clear, almost as if her speech had bullet points.

"I told you I did."

"And I know your mother didn't raise a liar," Bethel shot back.

At the mention of her mother, tears rose in Emma's eyes. At least, that's what Sissy thought must've caused them. Bethel's tone didn't change. Her words were just as forthright and uncoated as they always were. But the tears were there all the same.

"Mamm is gone."

Sissy could tell that Emma was doing her best to strengthen her tone. She straightened her backbone, she gritted her teeth, but somehow the words still remained near whisper level.

"Your *dat* may be too, if you keep stressing him out like this."

The tears that threatened made themselves known, racing down her cheeks and dripping off the edge of her jaw. Sissy may have only been in Yoder for a few weeks, but it was still strange to her to see this young girl sitting there, her hair incorrect, her prayer *kapp* tied in place, orange outfit instead of an Amish dress and apron.

"If you tell them the truth, they will let you go home."

Emma closed her eyes and shook her head. "It's too late for that."

"Emma," Bethel said. But the girl wiped away her tears with an angry gesture and stood. "Don't come back here." She hung up the phone and turned toward the guard.

"Emma," Bethel said once more, but the girl was already gone, her phone hung up, and the words lost somewhere between the two receivers.

Bethel hung up the phone and dropped her head. Her chin touched her chest, and she took two big breaths as if to try to get the world back into the correct order.

Sissy sat there and just felt helpless. There was nothing she could say or do to make Emma tell the truth, as they all knew she was lying. And there was nothing she could say to make Bethel feel like she had done the best she could to try to talk Emma out of whatever crazy idea had entered her head. And she surely couldn't convince Bethel to feel better about the whole situation. She had only been in Yoder a short time, but she had come to like Emma. She liked most of this extended family she had never met. And she wouldn't want any of them to go to jail for any reason, especially not when they were innocent. But what could they do?

Bethel stood abruptly. "Let's go."

Neither said anything as they made their way out of the jailhouse and across the parking lot to Sissy's car. She unlocked it, and they got inside before Bethel turned to her. "I'm sorry I made you drive me all the way out here for that."

"You don't have to apologize to me," Sissy said. "I wanted to come see Emma too."

Bethel snorted. "A lot of good it did us."

"She's weakening," Sissy said and started the car. "It won't be long before she breaks."

"And then what?" Bethel said. "They have a confession that she signed. How are they going to all of a sudden believe that she's telling the truth when she tells them that she didn't kill Walt Summers?"

Sissy backed the car out and sighed. "Good point." And it just went to prove that they were going to have to find the real killer before they could get Emma out of jail or, at least, to admit the truth.

"She's doing this for her *dat*," Bethel said.

"Amos?"

"That's the only *dat* she's got."

Sissy decided to let that one slide. "Why is she doing it for him?" That just didn't make sense.

"I thought about this last night," Bethel said. "I was lying in bed, and I thought to myself, why would Emma say she was guilty, and the only thing I could come up with is that she's trying to protect somebody. And the only person that she could be trying to protect would be her *dat*. Because she believes that he killed Walt Summers."

Sissy slammed on the brakes, sending them both jerking against their seat belts. There was a screech of tires, and the car behind them honked loudly.

"Sorry." Sissy waved her apology to the other driver. He sent her back a rude gesture and drove off. Not that Sissy could blame him. She'd stopped in the middle of the road. But she had not been expecting those words to come out of Bethel's mouth. "I hadn't thought of that."

"Well, I have." Bethel shook her head. "That family lost a lot of money because of Walt Summers."

Bethel didn't need to say it; Sissy understood. It was a lot of money they didn't have to lose and at a time when they needed it the most. And with Amos being right next door . . . "Do you think he did it?"

Bethel sighed. "I don't know what I believe about Amos. I haven't gotten through all that yet. But I do believe that Emma is trying to protect him."

At the sacrifice of her own life. A life that was really just beginning. Emma had been planning her wedding. Talking about the fabric she was going to get for the attendants to wear, what her own dress was going to look like, where she and Samuel would live, and a host of other things that came with joining one life with another. But now none of that would happen.

"Maybe Samuel can help." Sissy shrugged one shoulder. It was certainly worth thinking about. Bethel and Sissy couldn't get through to Emma, and it was obvious that her father couldn't. Perhaps her fiancé would be the key.

"She's refused to see him too."

"I don't know. We got in. Maybe if we grease a few palms, we can make it happen," Sissy said.

"Greased palms?" Bethel asked.

"You know, in the way we do best. Like a couple of pies to the jail employees might override anything that Emma has dictated about visitation."

Bethel slowly started to nod as if warming up to the idea. "Then we prep Samuel on things to say to her. Maybe he can get through to her where we can't."

"Exactly." Sissy said.

Bethel checked the clock on the dash. "How much longer till you need to let that rat out again?"

"My purebred Yorkshire Terrier can last another hour if you want to head out to Samuel's house and see what we can do."

"Then head that way," Bethel said with a flick of her wrist and a point toward Yoder.

The Glick house was pretty much a reflection of most of the Amish houses in Yoder. White clapboard, no shutters, two stories, no power lines connected, and a tractor parked outside.

"Good. He's home," Bethel said as Sissy pulled her Fiat into the drive. The house itself seemed sort of nostalgic to Sissy, probably because it resembled her aunt's house so much. And she did remember a few of the times at Mammi Yoder's before she'd stopped coming to visit. She remembered nights sleeping on the porch with Lizzie, the two of them huddled in their sleeping bags side by side. Back then, Lizzie had worn pajamas that looked just like Sissy's, complete with the latest cartoon character plastered on the front. And with their hair braided the same, the differences between them were whittled down to nothing more than eye and hair color. Sometimes, she wished she could go back to that. Other times, she just wished she could remember it more clearly and could somehow savor those sweet and special days when the only thing that seemed to matter was what kind of pie Mammi was making that night.

As they got out of the car, a young woman pushed out the front door. The screen door slammed behind her. "Hey, Bethel," the young girl said. Sissy didn't recognize her, but figured she was somehow kin to Samuel.

"Hey, Katie."

The girl stopped briefly. "Mamm's inside," she told them. "I've got to go to work."

"I'm looking for Samuel," Bethel told her.

If it was surprising to Katie, she managed to hide it well.

"He's inside too," she told them. "Sorry." She started for the tractor just a few steps away. "Gotta run."

"Be safe," Bethel said.

Katie nodded and climbed on the tractor and started it up. Sissy supposed she would eventually get used to the sight of young Amish girls in their bright pretty dresses and their pristine prayer *kapps* driving around on dirty old tractors like it was their preferred mode of transportation.

Then again, it was faster than a horse and buggy for sure. And part of her hoped she didn't get used to seeing that sight so much that she couldn't enjoy it. It did bring a smile to her face. It was just so quintessentially Yoder.

They waved to Katie and started up the porch steps. Bethel opened the screen door and poked her head inside. "Martha?" she called.

"In here," the voice came in return.

"I love when people say that," Bethel said. "Where exactly is here?" She wagged her head and started for what Sissy was soon to find out was the kitchen.

"What brings you out today?" Martha asked. She had her hands in a huge mixing bowl, stirring up what had to be bread. She was practically up to her elbows in flour and every so often would rub her nose against her shoulder. Sissy knew her pain. Why was it that the minute your hands were dirty or clean or otherwise previously occupied was the exact minute your nose started itching?

"Sissy and I want to talk to Samuel."

Martha nodded, her gaze shifting to Sissy. "He's in the barn. Just had a new litter of pups born a couple of days ago. He's gone out to check on them."

"Thanks, Martha." Bethel moved toward the back door. It was obvious that she had been here many times before. Sissy started to follow behind.

The woman continued to knead the bread dough and spoke to Sissy. "You're Mary's daughter, *jah*?"

"That's right." Sissy stopped. "You knew my mother. *Know* my mother?"

"Haven't seen her since she last visited, but *jah*. I know her."

Just one of the beautiful and ugly things about

Yoder. It was really easy to get to know everybody in town. "I'll tell her you asked after her."

"*Danki*," Martha said.

Bethel gestured for Sissy to pick up her pace so they could get out to the barn.

But first they passed through the large screened-in porch, complete with cushioned lawn chairs and occasional tables. It was neat and orderly, but still looked to be the perfect place to relax on not-so-hot summer evenings.

Sissy could imagine Emma and Samuel out here on the porch, talking about their future and making their plans, praying that their plans and God's plans for them would line up. So far, it seemed that was a prayer hadn't been answered. At least, not in the way that they had desired.

Sissy pushed the image to the side as they continued down the porch steps and across the yard toward the large red barn. She hoped there would come a day real soon when that prayer would be answered in a way that would benefit the young couple.

"Samuel?" Bethel called as they neared the barn.

"In here," he hollered in return.

Bethel rolled her eyes but headed for the open side of the barn's double Dutch doors.

Sissy stepped into the building behind her and blinked to allow her vision time to adjust from the bright sunlight to the dim interior of the barn. It only took a couple of seconds, but in that time a large animal came sauntering out from one of the stalls and headed straight for Sissy. She took a step back, unable to determine with her cloudy vision if the dog was friendly or not. For that matter, she wasn't entirely sure it was a dog. She thought it was, but it took a couple more seconds for her vision to return to normal so she could definitely see that the beast was friendly. And it was a dog. A very cute Airedale terrier. He was adorable, but just so big! Or maybe Sissy was simply more accustomed to the smaller breeds.

"Rusty," Samuel called from his place at the stall. He whistled, and the dog immediately sat on his haunches and raised a hand to shake with Sissy.

Sissy laughed and accepted the proffered paw. "That's very good training," she said. "I can barely get Duke to sit on command when a treat is involved."

"It's consistency," Samuel said.

"I suppose so," she replied, though she knew he was right. Sissy was a pushover where her pup was concerned.

"Your *mamm* said you had some new puppies," Bethel said.

As Samuel nodded, Sissy took note of his appearance. He was dressed the same as most all the men in Yoder when they were working. Blue shirt, black pants, straw hat, muck boots. He wasn't married yet, so he was clean-shaven. He looked the same as she had always seen him at the Friday-night suppers, except there was a sea of sadness surrounding him, threatening to drown him. But, for the moment, he had come to the surface for air. He was treading as fast as he could, but she could tell that he was about to go down. Any hint of joy or happiness on his face was a show for those who loved him.

"Rusty here is the new *dat* of a litter of eleven."
He gestured to the stall where he had been standing. "Just born two days ago."

Sissy and Bethel moved closer. Rusty eased
along with them as if he was proud of his off-
spring.

"This is Ellie," he said, gesturing toward the stall
where the mama dog and her puppies rested.
"This is her first litter, so she's a little nervous right
now."

Sissy peered over the top of the stall door at the
squirming mass of black and tan puppies. Their
eyes were still closed, and they were about the
most precious things she had ever seen. Though
they were mere newborns, they were about as big
as her full-grown Dukester.

Bethel must have noticed the correlation as
well, for she turned to Sissy. "See? This is the size a
dog should be."

"I beg to differ. And if you're such an expert on
dogs, why don't you have one of your own?"

"*Jah*, Bethel. And I'll have bright and shiny fresh
ones ready to go in about eight weeks."

"I didn't come here to talk about dogs," Bethel
harrumphed.

"Now you're trying to change the subject," Sissy
teased.

"I sure am." Bethel turned to Samuel. "We've
got to do something about Emma."

Immediately, his demeanor fell. "Emma." Her
name on his lips was like a prayer whispered into
the wind. Just a puff, and it was gone. But it said so
much. It told of his sadness, his hopelessness, his

helplessness. And despair. All-around despair, but in it, as well, she heard the first stirring strains of acceptance.

"You can't give up," Sissy told him. She wanted to step forward. Put her hand on his arm, get him to look at her so he could see the support in her eyes, but she stayed in place. It wasn't a move she should make with an Amish man she didn't know extremely well. And she only knew Samuel from the nights he had come out to Bethel's for Friday-night family supper. Not well at all.

But she did know that he cared for Emma. Loved her and wanted to build his life around her. Now both of their dreams were on hold, perhaps even dashed to pieces. And all because of Walt Summers.

He shook his head. "Did you know we were supposed to get married last year?" he asked.

"*Jah,*" Bethel said.

While Sissy said, "No" at the same time.

"We were supposed to get married in October, but when her mother got ill, we postponed everything. Then when we saw that she might not make it, it was too late to get a wedding together."

"But it's not now," Sissy said.

"Not if you can convince Emma to tell the truth about her and Walt Summers," Bethel added.

To Sissy, it sounded like Emma and Walt had had some sort of clandestine affair, but Samuel seemed to know what Bethel meant.

"Convince her? She won't even let me in to see her." His voice rose.

Rusty whined, then walked over and pushed his nose into Samuel's palm. He knew his master was upset about something, even if he didn't know what it was.

"She doesn't want you there because she knows you'll be hard to resist. But get over there and see your girl," Bethel said.

Samuel sighed. "These days . . ." He shook his head. "These days I wonder."

"Don't wonder," Bethel said sternly. "Act. You can't leave her in jail for killing a man we know she didn't kill. Not even if she lied and claimed she did in her confession."

"But what if?" he quietly asked. His words were hesitant, as if he had never said them aloud before and was worried about the consequences if he did. "What if she isn't lying? What if she really did kill Walt Summers?"

CHAPTER EIGHT

If you want something done right, do it yourself.
—Aunt Bess

"It's going to be up to us," Bethel grumbled on the way home.

Sissy made a noise that Bethel must have taken for acceptance.

"Has to be. Everyone else has given up on her."

"She did confess," Sissy reminded her.

"Not you too." She turned back in her seat so she could look out the front window. They were in Sissy's car, headed back to Bethel's house. They'd had enough of playing detective for one day. Sissy was tired, she still smelled like the grill at the café, and she needed to take her pup—however small he might be—on a walk.

"I'm just saying that sometimes when things look impossible to solve, it's because the answer is too simple."

"Simple? Are you out of your mind? That girl didn't kill Walt Summers."

Sissy kept her eyes to the front and continued to drive. She didn't have anything helpful to add, so she thought it best to do what her mother had always told her to do—when you don't have something productive to say, don't say anything at all.

"She didn't," Bethel said again.

"I hate to say it, but she had motives of her own," Sissy quietly admitted. "That man ruined her wedding with all the trouble over the crops and the land." And that grief had been compounded by the loss of her mother.

"Her *dat* says she was in the school with the other teachers getting ready for the school year to start."

Sissy had heard through the grapevine that another young woman had stepped up into Emma's vacant position. She had said that she would be there until Emma came home, but Sissy didn't think that she really meant it. Sarah Hostetler wanted that coveted position of teacher. Of course, she would have gotten it eventually when Emma married Samuel, but this route was definitely quicker for her. Emma was in jail, and the kids had started back at the end of last week.

"Maybe if we can get one of the other teachers to come forward and prove that she's lying—"

Sissy shook her head. "All that stuff is for the trial. All anyone cares about right now is the fact that she confessed."

"This is highly frustrating."

"Tell me about it."

"I just did." Bethel shot her an annoyed look. "But maybe we should talk to them anyway," Bethel said. "I don't suppose any of them would still be at the schoolhouse . . ."

"Even if they were," Sissy started, "I need to get home to my dog." And rest for a while. Sleuthing could really take it out of a person. Or was it all the murder suspicions and worry over a loved one locked away? Most likely a little of both.

"Sorry," Bethel said. "I guess I got a little caught up in this whole thing."

"It's okay," Sissy said. "We can regroup tomorrow. Maybe come up with a few more ideas about how to help."

"I hate her being in jail. She doesn't belong there."

Guilty or not, Sissy agreed with her. Jail was no place for someone as sweet as Emma Yoder.

Thursday brought with it some much needed rain. But even the gray skies couldn't keep the good folks of Yoder from coming into the Sunflower Café and speculating on Emma Yoder's innocence or guilt.

In her time at the tables, Sissy had heard all sorts of theories about why Emma had killed Walt Summers. Everything from something he might have done to her when she was a child to a basket of rotten tomatoes he'd sold her at canning time last year. All in all, the reasons were not as believable as the one that Bethel had come up with— that Emma was trying to protect her *dat*.

"I say we go back out and talk to Amos tomorrow." Bethel pinned Sissy in the storage room between the bursts of customers, each of which coincided with a slack in the rain.

"Why not today? Tomorrow we have the family supper," Sissy reminded her.

"And Walt's funeral." Her aunt's normal frown deepened.

Sissy stopped stacking the boxes of straws that had just arrived in this week's order and turned to give Bethel her full attention. "You're not thinking about going . . ." The words fell somewhere between a statement and a question.

"I have to." Bethel shrugged.

Sissy scoffed. "You don't have to."

"In Yoder, you do. If I don't show up, everyone around town will start spreading rumors about me."

Sissy squinted. "Seriously? Even with Emma in jail?"

"*Jah.* By closing time, I'll be her accomplice. Or I'll be letting her take the rap for my crime."

Take the rap? Where did her aunt get this stuff? "So we're going to the funeral?"

"I'm going," she said insistently. "You don't need to, I suppose."

"If you're going, I am too." As much as she hated the thought of attending another funeral, she shook her head when her aunt started to speak. "There might be something that we've missed. The killer almost always turns up at the funeral. I need to be there to see if I can ferret him out."

"Or her," Bethel corrected. "And where did you get that information about the killer?"

Sissy shrugged unapologetically. "TV."

"Good enough for me." Bethel nodded. "Good enough for me."

"You really don't have to bring me home every day," Bethel said as she held on for dear life in the tiny confines of Sissy's pride and joy.

"I drive you in the mornings," Sissy reminded her. "How else are you going to get home?"

"That's another thing," Bethel started. "You don't have to bring me every morning either. Problem solved."

"Hardly." Sissy pointed to the side yard at the Yoder-Schrock house. Three strange tractors sat in the grass. The tractors themselves weren't strange. They were just regular ol' tractors. One green, one blue, and one a very oxidized silver and red. They were strange because Sissy didn't remember ever seeing them before—not that she was keeping up with everyone's tractor make, model, and color. And she didn't know why they were there. Though, no doubt, they had been left there by occupants who were inside visiting.

"Probably just some of Lizzie's friends stopping by to check on her." It was a logical answer, but Bethel's voice didn't sound all that certain.

Sissy put the car in park and sat with the engine idling.

"Are you coming in?" Bethel asked.

She wasn't sure what she wanted to do. She just kept looking at the house, hoping for some inkling about what she should do.

"Fine," she finally sighed. "I'm coming in." She

shut off the motor and walked with her aunt into the house.

Lizzie had set up to receive her guests on the couch, which seemed to be her custom these days. Three young women sat around her. All had glasses of something to drink, and Sissy prepared herself for what Bethel would say if Lizzie admitted to fixing her company a drink.

"Bethel." One of the young women stood as the two of them came into sight. "I got us a drink." No doubt coached to say that by Lizzie herself.

The *mamm*-to-be just smiled innocently at her own mother.

"Girls." Bethel nodded at the three young women.

The Getter of the Drinks returned nervously to her seat. Though Sissy hadn't remembered seeing these three particular women around town, she had a feeling Bethel knew each and every one of them.

"Right on time," Lizzie said with a deepening grin. "Hi, Mamm. The girls here wanted to come by and talk to you about something. They got here a few minutes ago, and I assured them you'd be along directly."

"You want to talk to me?"

The woman in the middle, the tallest of the three, nodded her head. Her *kapp* strings danced about her shoulders. Just another indication of her age. Most of the older, married women in Yoder tied their *kapp* strings. It was only the young people who went around with them hanging loose.

"*Jah*," the other two said, as the first woman nodded.

"About?" Bethel asked them the question, but then turned her gaze onto Lizzie, as if she wondered what all they had said to Lizzie in order for her to let them come in.

"Emma Yoder."

And that would do it.

Bethel dropped her purse by her chair and came around to sit in it. "What's this about?"

The Getter of the Drinks elbowed the woman to her left. "Dee Dee, show her what you found."

Dee Dee. Sissy knew that name. She was the teacher who taught the younger kids opposite Emma, who taught the older grades. That would mean that the other two women with her were the assistants at the larger-than-normal Amish school.

Dee Dee looked at the other women, then reached into her bag and pulled out a small silver camera. She switched it on, then handed it to Bethel. "If you push the circle on the left, it'll take you through the pictures."

Sissy moved behind Bethel's chair so she could look over her aunt's shoulder at what Dee Dee had captured.

"Those are the pictures that we took when we were setting up the schoolhouse."

"These pictures—" Bethel started.

Getter of the Drinks shook her head. "We know that we aren't supposed to take pictures, and we're definitely not supposed to pose in them, but look at them."

Bethel peered a little closer at the tiny digital

screen. Sissy did the same but couldn't tell any difference between them after she squinted, so she squinted some more. There were pictures of all three women pinning up colors, the names of books, trains with cars showing how to write each letter of the alphabet. Pencils and apples with the names of the students and their families written on each. But there weren't just pictures of the three of them. There were pictures of Emma too.

"Look at the date stamp," Dee Dee said.

The same day that Walt Summers was killed. And the time was anywhere from eight o'clock in the morning till just after noon. Just about the time that Sissy and Bethel had found his body.

Bethel handed the camera back to Dee Dee. "What am I supposed to do with it?"

"It proves that Emma was with the three of us when Walt was . . . killed." The third woman in the bunch finally spoke up. It was obvious to Sissy that she was reluctant to say the ugly "M word."

"I can see that," Bethel countered. "It still doesn't tell me what I'm to do with it."

"We thought that perhaps you could take it to the deputy and show him. Maybe he'll believe you."

"You should take it," Sissy gently interjected. "If you three are the witnesses, I'm sure that the sheriff will want to talk with you personally."

Dee Dee shook her head as she turned off the camera and dropped it into her bag. "He didn't. He didn't care one thing about it. Said that it was evidence that could have easily been—" She stopped and turned to the Getter of the Drinks. "What did he call it, Nell?"

"Tampered with, or something like that," Nell replied.

"We tried to tell him that we didn't even know what that meant exactly. At least, not when it came to what we were showing him, but he said we could have changed the date on the camera to make it show an incorrect date so it would look like Emma had been at the schoolhouse when she really hadn't been."

"Susan is right, but none of us know how to do that," Nell said.

"The guy at the store where I bought the camera," Dee Dee added, "he set all the particulars for me. I didn't even do it the first time."

"But don't tell the bishop," Nell said. "We don't want Dee Dee to get in trouble. We just thought it would be fun to take some pictures of the rooms so we could look at them next year."

"And since this was going to be Emma's last year to teach . . ." Susan's eyes welled with tears. Obviously, she was the most sensitive of the bunch. Or perhaps Emma's arrest had just affected her differently.

"I won't tell the bishop," Bethel said. "But why are you telling me?"

"We thought that if you took it to the sheriff that he would listen to you?" Nell's voice turned the sentence into a question.

"I don't have any sway with Kennedy South," her aunt said.

Dee Dee shook her head. "Actually we took it to Earl Berry."

"And that was your first mistake." Sissy pressed

her lips together to keep from saying more. If only . . .

"How so?" Dee Dee asked.

"Because Emma confessed to Berry," Bethel explained. "If you had taken it to South maybe . . ."

"But it's probably too late now," Sissy added. "You take it in to the sheriff now, he'll call his deputy in, and his deputy will say that all these little Amish ladies are a bit hysterical, since one of their own is involved, and that will be that."

"Hysterical?" Bethel asked, shooting Sissy a look.

Sissy shrugged. "His words, not mine."

Bethel shook her head. "I wish there was more that we could do."

"Us too," Dee Dee said.

The three teachers stood.

"You should keep those photos for evidence," Sissy said. "Once this goes to trial—if it even goes to trial—the DA's office might want to see them."

"So they might still be able to help Emma."

"Yeah." Sissy nodded reluctantly, praying against all odds that she hadn't gotten their hopes up. Yes, those pictures might still be able to help Emma, but only because miracles sometimes happened.

"I guess I should be going," Sissy said a half an hour after Dee Dee, Nell, and Susan left. She had stayed to have a quick glass of water with Lizzie and, of course, to talk over Emma's situation a bit, but only because it seemed like their efforts were going nowhere fast. How were they supposed to find out the truth with a roadblock at every turn? And the part that bothered Sissy the most? If they did figure out who really killed Walt Summers, would Earl Berry even listen?

"Give Duke extra kisses from me," Lizzie said.

Daniel, who had just arrived home from his shift at the meat-packing plant, rolled his eyes. "These babies can't come soon enough," he joked. "Otherwise, I might end up with a Duke of my own."

Sissy smiled at her cousin once removed. "All in good time," she said. "There are worse things than dog ownership."

Daniel shot a loving look at his wife, her large, protruding belly high in the air as she "bed rested" on the couch. "*Jah*," he said. "I suppose there are."

Sissy hugged her cousin goodbye and started for the door.

"Here," Bethel said, "I'll follow you out."

"Where are you going?" Lizzie, Sissy, and Daniel asked, all at the same time.

"Out to check on Amos." Her aunt snatched the tractor keys from the hook by the door.

"If you wanted to check on Amos, why didn't you just ask?" Sissy stopped at the edge of the living room and gave her aunt an inquisitive once-over. "Are you planning something?"

"That's what I want to know," Lizzie put in.

"No. I thought you had a puppy to take care of."

"It doesn't take him that long to potty," Sissy said. "And once he takes care of his business, we can take him with us to see Amos and the rest of the family."

Bethel shrugged. "Suit yourself." She hung the keys back up.

While her back was turned, Daniel gave Sissy a thumbs-up. Seemed her almost cousin didn't completely trust his mother-in-law. Not that Bethel wasn't the kind to go check on someone, but to go without food seemed a little suspicious. Only just a little.

"I'll have her home in time for supper."

Lizzie checked the beautiful ceramic clock that rested on the mantle. Sissy had heard stories from both Lizzie and her mother about the ornate timepiece. It had once belonged to John and Bethel's great-*grossmammi* and had been handed down for all those generations. When Lizzie had gotten married, it had passed to her. Sissy supposed she had just as much claim to it, but only if she got married. And even then . . . well, when was that going to happen? At the rate she was going, probably never. "It's almost time for supper now," Lizzie pointed out.

"Then we'll get something on the way," Bethel said, steering Sissy out the front door.

"What's the hurry?" Sissy asked as Bethel hustled her over to the Fiat. "I've never seen you this eager to ride in my car."

"I'm not," she said and waited for Sissy to unlock the door.

"Sorry." She clicked the button, and her aunt immediately climbed into the car.

Sissy shook her head. Curiouser and curiouser. She got in and started the engine. "Are you going to tell me what this is about?"

"I want to talk to Amos," she said.

"And you need to do that right now?" Sissy asked.

Bethel nodded, then slapped a hand on the top of her prayer covering as Sissy started down the road. "Before tomorrow."

"Why so soon?"

"Because Walt Summers's funeral is tomorrow, and if I know my nephew, he's got plans to go."

"I'm sure most of Yoder will turn out for it," Sissy replied. *Even if to make sure the despised man is really dead.*

"But you said the real killer always shows up at the victim's funeral," Bethel said.

"I said almost always," Sissy corrected, but Bethel wasn't listening.

"With everybody going 'round showing evidence that Emma can't truly be the killer, then if Amos shows up . . ."

"You think he might look guilty?" Sissy frowned and turned her eyes from the road to stare at her aunt.

"Pay attention to your driving," Bethel admonished.

"You know that sounds crazy," Sissy said, but she turned back to face the front. "Just because he shows up at the funeral doesn't mean he *is* guilty. Just as him not showing up doesn't mean he isn't guilty."

Bethel shook her head, and Sissy couldn't blame her. She had said the words, and she was having a hard time keeping up with them herself. "Just take me there," Bethel said. "If Amos is guilty, then Walt Summers's funeral is the last place he needs to be."

CHAPTER NINE

*It is better to hold out a helping hand than point
an accusing finger.*
—Aunt Bess

They stopped by the Chicken Coop first, let
Duke take care of his business, then Sissy bundled the happy dog into her car, and the trio set
off to Amos Yoder's.

"Do you really believe that Amos could be
guilty?" Sissy asked as they turned down the road
that led to Amos's farm.

Sissy just couldn't imagine. Amos was . . . so
Amish. It was the only way to describe him that
combined all of his traits into one. He was peaceable and peaceful. He was kind and quiet and
seemed so godly. You could practically see the
faith coming off him like heat waves off the pavement in July. It was that faith that gave her doubts.
The Amish believed in God's will. They were
taught it from the time they were born until the

time that they died. Everything that life threw your way was God's will—wife dying, tractor broke, crop didn't come in. Basically, every bad country song was, to the Amish, part of God's will. So why would a man with faith like that take matters into his own hands? It just didn't make sense to Sissy. Just like Emma's confession didn't make sense.

"Amos has been wracked with grief this last year. He's held on for as long as he could."

"And you're afraid he just snapped."

"*Jah*. I suppose that's a good a way as any to put it."

Sissy supposed that could happen to anyone, whether they believed in God's will or not. What if Amos had been struggling with accepting this as God's will, then snapped, like she said. He would be regretting his actions. He would be wringing his hands over his daughter in jail. He just might do something stupid. Yes, she supposed it was a good idea to try and keep him from the funeral.

"I've been thinking about it," Bethel said. "I love my nephew, and he's a godly man, but he is only human."

Sissy nodded but waited for her to continue.

"We had just come down the road when Walt was killed."

"Yep," Sissy said, hoping the word would serve as encouragement.

"We didn't pass a car that day. So whoever killed Walt had to be close."

"Or they drove out the other way."

"That would mean that they don't live in Yoder," Bethel surmised. "The only thing out that way is cornfields and the highway to Buhler."

"So you think that because we didn't pass a car as we were coming in that the killer may have been still around when we found Walt's body?" The thought was chilling.

"I think the killer may have lived close. And the only two houses on this road other than Walt's are Weaver's and Amos's."

"So what about Weaver?" Sissy asked. "They have quite a history."

Bethel shook her head. "They do, but the two men have lived side by side for over thirty years. If Weaver had wanted to kill Walt over the tomato hybrid, as you said yourself, he would have done it long before now."

"So that just leaves Amos."

"Now you're catching on."

Maybe her aunt was onto something here.

Sissy slowed her car just as she turned down the road next to Weaver's house. Normally, she would have sped back up to head past Walt's and down to Amos Yoder's, but there was so much going on at the Justices' place that she continued to inch along the road.

"What in the world?" she asked, but of no one really.

"Looks like he's putting in a new septic tank," Bethel said. "Pull over."

That was another thing about small-town living: Everyone just had to know what everyone else was doing. It was a wonder any crime went unsolved.

"Oi!" Bethel called, slipping out of the car before Sissy had even gotten it stopped all the way. "What's going on, Weaver Justice?"

Weaver waved but apparently couldn't hear her question over the sound of the machinery.

But Sally Justice saw and came to the edge of the yard, where Bethel had stopped.

"What's going on?" Bethel asked. Sissy had just managed to arrive next to her, Duke securely hooked to his leash. He was barking like mad at all the equipment, engines roaring as they dug up a large chunk of Weaver Justice's yard.

Sally shouted to be heard over the din of engine noise and crazy barking from Duke. "Weaver decided that we needed a new septic tank." She turned and looked back over her shoulder at the mess in her backyard. All the overturned earth. "I don't know why. This last one's only been here a couple of years. But who knows what goes on in the mind of a man?"

Sally shook her head. Sissy chuckled, as was expected.

She supposed that they would have to dig up the old septic tank first, take it away, and then set the new one in its place. It was a good thing that they had already found Walt Summers's body. If not, then this would be the perfect opportunity—

She shivered, despite the heat of the day.

"This new one is made of some special material. I don't know. You'd have to ask Weaver about it if you want to know more. I'm just out here to make sure no one runs over my azaleas."

"And your tomatoes." Bethel nodded toward a small garden on the other side of the yard. Sissy could see the tall tomato plants heavy with fruit staked up in even rows.

Despite the noise, Sissy heard Sally's sigh. "Those are Weaver's."

Bethel nodded as if she expected as much. "Looks like they're growing good this year."

The man running the mini excavator shut it off in the middle of her words, leaving her shouting into the now peaceful day.

"Thank heavens," Sally said. "Weaver decided on something different this year. Didn't go with Walt's Special Blend."

Tomatoes. Right.

"You don't say." Bethel half-turned to Sissy but didn't say anything else.

Sissy knew what she was thinking: There was an awful lot of talk about Walt's Special Blend this year.

"Sally, have you met my niece Sissy?"

"I don't believe I have," Sally said.

The normal pleasantries were exchanged, then Bethel turned her attention to Sally. "That's something about Walt, *jah*?"

Sally nodded. "It's kind of scary. Just right next door. But I heard you two found him."

Bethel nodded.

Sally closed her eyes briefly. "That must have been awful. Just knowing it happened next door is giving me nightmares."

Sissy nodded sympathetically. She had had a few herself. Even if she didn't know Walt and even if she was most likely the only person in Yoder he hadn't crossed, she didn't wish anything on the man.

"I mean, we've had past troubles, but tell me any long-term neighbors who haven't."

The way Sissy saw it, stealing all the credit for a revolutionary tomato hybrid was a little more "trouble" than parking on someone's grass or playing music too loud after dark.

This was the perfect time to bring up the past forgiveness and see if perhaps old bygones weren't so bygone any longer. But Bethel beat her to it.

"Did you hear that the tomato plants were all gone from his growing shed?"

"All of them?" Sally asked, eyes wide. "That's a lot of plants."

Sissy couldn't tell if she was genuinely surprised or if she was putting on a covering act.

"*Jah,*" Bethel agreed. "Someone just ripped them out of the ground and carted them away. Left all the tomato baskets in the shanty."

Across the yard, the digging looked as if it had come to a stop for a while. The men, Weaver included, were standing around, looking into the hole that had been dug. They were talking among themselves, though at this distance, Sissy couldn't tell what was being said.

"That tomato." Sally shook her head once again. "It was more trouble than it was worth. Don't get me wrong, it was . . . it *is* a good tomato, but not worth the heartache."

To die for.

"I told Weaver back then, it's time to let it go."

"You did?" Bethel asked.

"I did." Sally seemed quite pleased with that decision. "I told him it was going to be the ruin of our marriage and our lives if he kept trying to fight Walt for it. It was just too hard to prove what work he had done after Walt claimed all the glory.

I told him it was better to just let it be and have a happy life rather than battle him in court after court with the possibility of still losing it all."

"Smart," Sissy said. And she truly believed it. Sometimes a person just had to learn when to let go.

"And he handled that all right, it seems," Bethel added.

Sally looked back to where her husband and the other men were still debating whatever had stopped the digging for the time being. "At first, I think it was almost too bitter a pill to swallow, but I started making him go to church, and I'm sure the good Lord has seen fit to help him. Weaver's just a man, you know. He does what he can. I suppose, like us all, he's a work in progress."

"*Aemen,*" Bethel murmured. "How are you holding up?"

"At the time, I struggled, but Mary Ann was a big help," Sally said.

Sissy pointed to the eerily quiet house next door. "That Mary Ann?"

"One and the same."

"You've been friends a long time?" Sissy asked.

Sally shrugged. "I suppose it depends on your definition of friend."

"I suppose," Sissy murmured.

"Have you seen her since . . ." Bethel trailed off with a jerk of her head toward the Summerses' place.

Sally's sunny disposition clouded a bit. "Not since, no. But I talked to her last night. She's driving back tonight for the funeral."

Big of her.

Sissy squelched that hateful thought. It wasn't

her place to tell anyone how to grieve, but it sure seemed strange that the widow hadn't made it back to town yet.

The driver of the digging machine climbed back into his seat, and the big diesel engine rumbled to life.

Sally shook her head. "I guess I should go," she said. "I have some canning on the stove."

Sissy and Bethel watched her disappear into her house as the men on the other side of the property continued to dig.

"Are you thinking what I'm thinking?" Bethel asked.

"If you're thinking that Walt's dead and Mary Ann is in Wichita, so there's no one going to notice if we take another look at the crime scene, then yeah."

Her aunt smiled. "Exactly."

They waved to Weaver and the other workers, climbed into Sissy's car, and drove away with a purpose. And a plan. To drive around to Amos's property, leave Sissy's not so inconspicuous car in her cousin's driveway, and sneak back over when no one was looking.

Sissy supposed that quick and non-trespassing was the attitude to have, so they made their way as quickly and as nonchalantly as they could across the cornfield that separated Walt's house from Amos's. The corn was growing taller, but Sissy knew that it had been tall enough to hide a man who was most likely crouched down as he moved between the rows of green stalks.

But she drew up a little short when they got to the door of the growing shed. The yellow CAUTION tape was still across the entrance, and it made Sissy shiver, despite the late August heat. Part of her wanted to stop and turn around, leave it be. But another, she supposed bigger, part was curious about how accurately she remembered the details from that day.

"You going in or you going to stand out here all evening?" Bethel prodded her in the ribs.

"I'm going," Sissy said. "Just give me a minute."

Bethel harrumphed and nudged her out of the way. She took ahold of one end of the tape and pulled it free. Then she swung open the door and stood to one side to allow Sissy to enter. "After you."

The last thing she wanted to do was walk into the growing shed where she had found a dead body less than a week ago, but what choice did she have? It had been half her idea to come in here, but now that she was here . . .

Duke growled as Sissy finally found the courage to enter the mesh-enclosed building. "It's okay, puppers," she told him and hoped that she believed it herself.

"What do you see?" Bethel asked from behind her. Her aunt's subtle way of reminding her to move.

Sissy inched forward and to the side so Bethel could enter.

"About the same," Bethel said.

And it did. With the exception of no dead body and the addition of the charcoal-colored fingerprint-detecting dust left behind by the detectives.

The shovel was gone. The pitchfork remained, and the piles of earth still marked the spots where the plants had been.

Duke squirmed to be released, but Sissy held on tighter. "You have to stay with me, baby." The last thing she needed was him running amok in a crime scene.

He whined in protest but settled down a bit into the crook of her arm.

"What are we looking for?" Sissy asked.

"Anything that we might have missed before." Bethel strode over in the direction of the potting table. She stopped short a bit from where Walt had been lying. "Walt was here, right?"

Sissy nodded, suddenly realizing that they could have missed more than they realized. That day had been shocking, and they had been reluctant to stay in the growing shed while Walt's body was in there. Once the police arrived, they weren't allowed back in. It only stood to reason that they had missed something.

"Right." She took a more confident step forward. "The water hose was under him; water was all leaking out from under him."

"The shovel was over there." Bethel pointed to one side, where the shovel had been carelessly resting. As far as Sissy knew, the police, along with the help of the medical examiner's office, had determined that the shovel had indeed been the murder weapon. "Feet down here." She mapped it out with her finger. "One hand was under him, I suppose holding the water hose, and the other one—"

"Was extended," Sissy said in awe. She had forgotten that part. It was extended but not empty. "He was holding a piece of paper."

Bethel nodded grimly. "I didn't get a good look at it. Didn't know it would be important, but I think it was some kind of invoice. It was pink, like a customer copy. I thought I saw P-I-P written across the top, but it could have just as easily been B-L-B or P-L-P or even B-I-B."

Sissy nodded. "I get it." But it was a start. "Maybe we can get Earl Berry to spill the beans about who the invoice was from or what it was for."

"Maybe," Bethel said. She grew quiet as she continued to survey the area around the growing shed.

"They took his plants, but not the Special Blend."

Sissy scoffed. "With the way everyone is fussing about the Special Blend, I'm not surprised. It seems to be crap this year." She smiled a little at her own pun.

"Or not enough crap," Bethel quipped.

Sissy spun around so fast Duke yelped. She stroked his head. "Was that a joke?"

Bethel shrugged. "Just saying. A manure blend has one main ingredient. No matter how 'special' it is."

Sissy smiled and continued down the long row of tomato plants. Why would they take the plants and not the tomatoes out front? To keep customers and passersby from knowing there was a problem until it was too late and they came upon his corpse?

And what did they do with the plants after they pulled them out of the ground? Could they be transplanted? Or were they already wilted and rotting in some dumpster as she mulled it over in her head?

"What's in those containers?" Bethel asked.

"Walt's Special Blend," Sissy said without even looking up from her search. Honestly, she didn't know what she was searching for, so looking around when it wasn't necessary could cause her to miss something vital. Especially when they already knew the answer to the question her aunt was asking.

"Not the blue containers," Bethel said. "These white ones over here."

Sissy came around the back side of the row and looked to where her aunt was pointing. To one side of the potting table, there were several white pickle buckets, but Sissy supposed that, like their blue counterparts, they didn't contain pickles. "Are there any labels on them?"

Bethel peered from one side to the other, careful not to touch the buckets themselves. "There are some letters, but they don't make sense. PHOS and HMNR and CMNR."

She didn't have any idea what those letters could mean either. She supposed it was too naïve to wish that the buckets had been labeled *Evidence to clear Emma's name.*

"I guess we could open one of them," Sissy said.

But Bethel shook her head. "I don't think we should go that far. Fingerprints and all that."

"I suppose you're right." Sissy started around the side of the row and back up to where her aunt waited. She wasn't sure what they'd hoped to find by coming in here today. They should have been checking to see if Amos and the family needed anything instead of wasting their time here—

Sissy paused. "Look," she told her aunt. "Come here and look at this." She motioned her over, and Bethel was at her side in a heartbeat. "Is that what I think it is?' Sissy asked.

"It looks like a shoe print," Bethel replied.

"Maybe that's why the deputy wanted us to give shoe impressions."

"*Jah*," Bethel nodded, catching the direction her thoughts were going. "He was trying to see if one of us left that print."

"But I don't think I ever came back this far," Sissy said.

"Me either. And this isn't a regular shoe print," her aunt continued.

"It's not?"

"This is a boot print."

"So it's probably Walt's," Sissy said. "He was wearing boots that day." One fact that she didn't think she would ever forget.

But Bethel was shaking her head. "Walt was wearing *work* boots. This is a muck boot print."

"How do you know?" Sissy asked.

Bethel shrugged. "Everyone in these parts has a pair of muck boots."

"I don't."

"I rest my case," Bethel deadpanned.

"So whoever killed Walt was wearing muck boots." Despite the fact that Bethel said everyone in Yoder owned a pair, the thought gave Sissy a small rise in hope. At least, they knew something about the killer that they hadn't known before.

"Size eleven, from the looks of it."

Sissy frowned and squinted a bit, staring at the partial, faded print there in the earth. "How can you tell that?" Sissy asked. "There's not even an entire print there."

Bethel pointed to a small oval to one side of the impression. "The size is stamped on the bottom. See? Size eleven."

How convenient.

But when she said as much, Bethel shook her head. "Not hardly," she said. "Of all the muck boots in Yoder, Kansas, most of them are size eleven."

CHAPTER TEN

Mistakes are just proof that you're trying.
—Aunt Bess

And, just like that, Sissy's hope bubble burst. But there for a moment . . .

"I guess we should be going," Bethel said, though she sounded reluctant to leave. She obviously felt just as disappointed in their lack of a new lead as Sissy herself did.

"I guess." She allowed her gaze to wander over the rows of bright yellow marigolds still growing and blooming between the rows of earth piles. It really was a shame. Not only that the plants were gone, but the fruit as well.

"Did you happen to notice if there are any tomatoes out in the fruit shanty?" she asked Bethel. They had come in the side way and hadn't gone to that side of the growing shed.

"I didn't. Though I suppose whatever was left Earl Berry and his bunch took with them."

"Probably." But something was still nagging at her. Something about the tomatoes? Or was it merely lingering disappointment over not discovering anything new. Well, aside from a muck boot print in the reportedly most popular size in Yoder, Kansas.

"What do you suppose the killer did with the tomatoes?" Sissy asked Bethel.

"What?"

Together, they turned and made their way carefully toward the door. Both wanted to stay longer, and neither wanted to leave traces of their visit. It was just so frustrating. Sissy felt like the answer to it all was so close, like they could be stepping on it right that moment and not even realize it.

"The tomatoes. The ones on the plants when he took them. We did agree that the killer took the tomato plants."

"*Jah.*"

"Well, there was fruit on them. What happened to that?"

"How am I supposed to know?" Bethel said.

"Just asking," Sissy grumbled. It seemed a shame that the fruit would go to waste. Not when so many people, women mainly, in the area canned tomatoes on a regular basis—

"Wait a minute," she said, turning to Bethel. "Sally Justice was canning something. Didn't she say so?"

"*Jah,* but that doesn't mean it's tomatoes."

"But it could be."

"And that would mean she was a thief, but not a murderer. Why would she go and steal tomatoes from her neighbor? You saw Weaver's tomatoes.

They look better than practically everybody in the county's."

"Right." So that wasn't it.

Duke whined a bit as she stopped, not following Bethel out the door. Sissy turned and looked back into growing shed. What was it? She took a quick inventory one more time: mounds of dirt, yellow marigolds, potting table, buckets of Special Blend. And no more clues.

Wait.

"Bethel, why would Walt Summers be holding an invoice in his hand while he's watering his plants?"

Her aunt stopped just outside the growing shed. "Your guess is as good as mine."

She mulled over the problem all the way back to her aunt's house. What in the world could the invoice be for? Did it mean that he'd had a service truck at his house just moments before his death? Could the driver of the service truck be their real killer? She supposed it was as logical as anything else they had come up with. Walt Summers had managed to tick off just about everyone in Yoder, so the idea that he'd had a run-in with the service-man was viable.

She turned into her aunt's drive and put the car into park.

"Are you coming in?" Bethel asked as she straightened her *kapp* and grabbed her purse from the floorboard.

Sissy shook her head. "I need to get home." Not really. The one thing that would dictate her time was lounging in the back of the car in his special doggie seat. But she felt a little overwhelmed with all the things they had done and seen that afternoon. They had been busy, and she needed a minute to process it all.

"Lizzie's going to be upset if you don't."

"I know." Sissy smiled. "Tell her I'll stay late at supper tomorrow to make up for it."

Bethel nodded and got out of the car.

Sissy put the little Fiat into reverse as Duke began to whine. "It's not that far to the house," she told the pup. "Not far enough to warrant moving your seat, buddy. Just stay put for now."

He barked out his displeasure.

"Shush," she said. "You're okay."

He quieted down by the time they got to the main road, most likely having realized that he wasn't going to get his way this time. She supposed that's what she got for spoiling her dog, but, to date, he was the one man other than her father that she could always depend on.

Once Duke settled down, her thoughts returned to the piece of paper that Walt had been holding when they'd found him.

There were just endless possibilities as to why he was holding it at that particular moment. Maybe it was a note from his wife that had been written on the back on the invoice. Maybe it wasn't even his at all. Maybe it had blown into his growing shed and he'd merely picked up as he was watering.

Actually, that made the most sense of all. If a truck had come to his house, then she and Bethel most likely would have passed it during their trip out to the farm. She didn't remember encountering any truck that would be the kind to perform a service that would require handing out invoices. But she hadn't exactly been looking either. She had been talking about tomatoes and enjoying the beautiful day.

She just wished that she had paid more attention to the paper when she had seen it. But in her defense, she had just found a dead body. That had a tendency to shake a person a bit. But if it wasn't random trash, why was he holding it? Was there a trash can near the potting table where he could have possibly pitched it out instead of carting it around? Surely. But, once again, she hadn't noticed. Or perhaps he hadn't wanted to throw it away. Maybe it was important to him somehow.

What the invoice meant might be a bigger mystery than who killed Walt. Or maybe it had the potential to solve the whole thing. Who knew?

Sissy sighed as she pulled into the drive at the Chicken Coop. Her thoughts were centered on one thing and still managed to be all over the place.

She rolled up the top of her car and turned off the motor before catching Duke's sweet brown gaze in the rearview mirror. "Come on, puppy," she said to him. "We're home."

Duke waited—albeit a little impatiently—for her to come around and rescue him from his seat in the car. He licked her face as if he'd just been sprung from a maximum-security dog pound.

"Cut it out," she told him, laughing all the while, "and I'll take you for a walk."

He was immediately on his best behavior while Sissy dropped her purse and her other things just inside the little house. Then she relocked the door, let him down on the end of his leash, and the two of them started through the neighborhood. Yes, it had been a while since Duke had been allowed a potty break, but his excitement at the mention of a walk came from his desire to prance through the neighborhood like he owned it. She supposed he did, if ownership had anything to do with how many bushes he peed on. And he peed on plenty of them. In fact, their walks were a series of pee stops up and back down the road where they lived.

Sissy didn't mind. It was good to get out for a bit, stretch her legs somewhere besides the Sunflower Café, the funeral home, and the crime scene. And it was always interesting to linger a little in front of Gavin's aunt's house and to peer and see what unusual items she had in her flower beds this week. This day, really. You never knew when she would change out the eclectic mix of trash, treasures, and silk flowers she had assembled there. In fact, the arrangement was altered daily, and sometimes even more often.

Sissy had yet to meet dear Aunt Edith, but she was hoping to. She wanted to see if the real deal was in any way similar to the vision she had of the woman in her head. As far as Sissy's overactive writer's imagination was concerned, Edith Jones wore flowy, Indonesian-print caftans, large hoop earrings, and a scarf wound tightly over her hair. Incidentally, the hair underneath the scarf was dyed Lucille Ball copper-pink-red and hung to the middle of her back. Of course, she wore it up—makeshift turban and all that. But, to Sissy, that's what she looked like.

She moved farther onto the side of the road when she heard a car pull into the lane behind her.

"Well, hey."

She turned at the sound of the vaguely familiar voice behind her. And there he was: Declan Jones. The oh-so-handsome man from the Quiki-Mart. Driving his sleek black Mercedes and looking all the more like he didn't belong in Yoder but somehow managing to fit in.

Super. After the day she'd had, she probably looked like she'd been caught in a tornado. She stopped and resisted the urge to pat her hair back in place or pull up her sagging jeans. Extra super. She was still wearing what she'd had on for work: a Sunflower Café T-shirt and jeans that had seen better days, but not in a fashionable way. And she smelled like hamburgers. Double extra super.

Of course, he looked as cool and as put together as he did when she'd met him earlier. Like he'd just breezed in from the pages of *GQ* magazine.

"Hey." At least, she managed to sound confident and competent. And after their first meeting, that was something.

"Out for a walk?" he asked.

Duke barked, his tail wagging enthusiastically at the sound of the man's voice.

"Every evening," she said. "He likes to patrol the neighborhood."

"That's right." He snapped his fingers. "I heard you were staying in the Chicken Coop."

"Where'd you—" She stopped. "Never mind."

He laughed. "Do something in Yoder and the whole town knows by sundown."

That was true, with the exception of murder. Of course, the deputy thought he had "solved" the case when Emma had "confessed." And since Sissy knew for a fact that Emma wasn't guilty, then that point was moot.

"I guess I'll let you go," he said. "I was driving by and saw you. Thought I would say hi."

"Hi."

He grinned. "Hi." His car rolled a little bit forward. "I'll be seeing you, Sissy Yoder."

She waved and watched as he turned around in Aunt Edith's driveaway. Then he drove to the end of the lane, the brake lights on the back of his Mercedes shining at the stop sign there.

She might look like death warmed over, but it really didn't matter. He wasn't the kind of person who would go for a person like her.

He was way out of her league. But it was fun to dream about a handsome man sweeping her off her feet in the back of a Mercedes S-Class.

But just like her getting back with Colt, that was not happening.

CHAPTER ELEVEN

*Some people are such treasures you just want to
bury them.*
—Aunt Bess

On Friday morning before the funeral, it was
business as usual at the Sunflower Café. Talk
was of the weather and the chance for rain, but
not in relation to how it would affect the funeral.
It was of the crops that the local farmers had growing that everyone was concerned about. Occasion-
ally, someone would mention Walt Summers and
the fact that his burial was later that afternoon, but
it wasn't at all like when Kevin Saunders was killed.
Was it because Kevin had died there at the café?
Or because Walt was really that hated among the
typically nice residents of Yoder, Kansas?

Perhaps the everyday vibe that continued in the
café had sparked her to look at the feet of almost
every customer who waltzed in the door. She was
looking for size-eleven muck boots. The problem

was she didn't know how to tell the size of a boot just by looking at it. Could anyone? And almost every man who sauntered in wasn't wearing muck boots, despite Bethel's claim that nearly everyone in town owned at least one pair.

They closed at two, and Sissy rushed home to change into her one and only black dress, the peasant-style frock that she had bought for Kevin's funeral. She supposed it wasn't a bad thing to have a "funeral dress," but she would have to put a sweater on over it if anyone else died before the end of the year. And—God willing—that wouldn't happen. Two funerals in one year was enough for her.

After taking Duke out for a short walk—which had nothing at all to do with Declan Jones and the off chance that she might see him again since he seemed to be familiar with her neighborhood—she promised him a longer one later. Then with two treats to wipe the sad look from his cute little face as she locked him in the kennel—Duke, not Declan—Sissy headed over to the funeral home to meet the rest of the Sunflower staff.

It was standing room only at the service. But there were many more people in the room than flowers.

"I wonder how many of these yahoos are here just to see if he's really dead," Lottie Foster said, leaning in close so that no one else could hear. Well, almost no one else. Bethel, who was seated on the other side of Sissy, frowned, and someone behind them shushed her.

Lottie threw a frown over her right shoulder, then turned back around. "Say what you want, but it's true," Sissy heard her mumble under her breath.

True, but maybe not in good form to mention. Or, at least, that's what Aunt Bess would say about the matter. Which worried her. She was starting to think like Aunt Bess even when she wasn't writing. Which meant she was having trouble separating her alter ego from her real one, and sooner or later, she would slip up, and her secret would be revealed. Not a secret she wanted to get out, mind you. It was hard enough to find a date these days. Even harder in a town the size of Yoder. All she needed was the right guy to feel she was too old-fashioned or a little bit kooky since her secret day job had her pretending to be a seventy-something grandma.

She pushed those thoughts away and concentrated on the real reason she had come to the funeral. It certainly wasn't to pay her respects to the man. Even though she and Bethel had been the ones to discover his prone body, she didn't know him. Had never met him. She was here for the widow.

Mary Ann Summers didn't look at all like Sissy had imagined a tomato farmer's wife would look. Her slimming black dress hugged a curvy body that Sissy would have expected to see on a much younger woman. Sissy supposed she probably worked out regularly, something she herself had promised she would start doing . . . soon . . .

The woman's makeup looked professionally done; her hair was obviously dyed blond, and the upswept coif had the signature of an exclusive salon. Sissy wasn't sure what about it was so striking, but she could tell that Mary Ann Summers spent a lot of money on her appearance—makeup, hair, even a tanning-bed tan. Did they even have a tanning salon in Yoder? Doubtful. Which meant she went out of town to maintain it. Wichita or Hutchinson, Sissy supposed.

And like everyone else in the room, Mary Ann's eyes were dry. Sissy had the disturbing feeling that it wasn't an effort to save her perfectly applied mascara. Mary Ann Summers was not a typical grieving widow. In fact, she looked like she would rather be someplace—anyplace—else. Sissy was certain the aura of discontent that surrounded her had nothing to do with attending her husband's funeral. She merely looked like she had somewhere more important to be, and she wished the preacher would hurry this thing up, thank you very much.

But a lack of love for her husband didn't necessarily mean that Mary Ann Summers had killed him. She seemed to be living well off the money he had provided for her. And she had been out of town at the time of the murder. Reportedly anyway. She had been only about forty minutes away by car and could have easily come back to town, killed him, then headed back to Wichita. That theory could go two ways: Why would she come home and leave and go through all that when she could have just killed him while she was home? Then there was the fact that it made a pretty solid alibi.

Sissy allowed her gaze to travel around the room. She supposed that just about everyone there had a reason or two to want Walt Summers dead. That was

the problem with trying to solve the murder of a
hated man, but she had to try. For Emma.

That made two people that she knew weren't in
attendance: Emma and her father. Amos had told
Bethel that he wanted to come and pay his respects, but given the circumstances, he would wait
until the crowd cleared. He didn't want to start
anything.

And still she had to wonder if the real killer was
standing there among them. Not to be dramatic or
anything, but she had seen a show on television
about serial killers and how they usually showed
up at funerals and wakes to see the destruction
they had caused. This was not a serial killer murder, but that didn't mean whoever had killed Walt
wasn't there to see firsthand how satisfied the town
was that the most hated man was gone.

"Ding dong, the witch is dead," Sissy muttered.

"What was that, dear?" Lottie whispered in return.

The man one row behind shushed them once
again.

Sissy shook her head as if to say it wasn't important and turned her attention back to the service.
Maybe when they got out to the gravesite, the
crowd would thin a bit, and the true killer might
be more easily identified.

Maybe.

But the gravesite was just as crowded. It seemed
as if everyone who had been to the viewing and
service had made the trip out to the cemetery to

see the man laid to rest. Most likely to see for themselves that he was buried in the ground. Like a despised treasure chest.

Once again, Sissy looked around at the people gathered there. The service at the cemetery was short, and she didn't have time to scan the crowd like she wanted before it was over and the people all started milling around.

Mary Ann Summers stood at the gaping hole where her husband had been placed in his sleek black coffin. She looked elegant and dramatic as she stood there in head-to-toe black, including her large sunglasses. It seemed as if she was playing the part of a grieving widow. She tossed in a handful of dirt, then looked at the dust on her hand and turned to the woman beside her.

Sally Justice opened her tiny purse and pulled out a package of handwipes and gave one to Mary Ann.

The new widow cleaned her hands on the disposable cloth, then looked around. Sissy supposed she was trying to figure out what to do with the soiled wipe. Mary Ann glanced over at Sally, then shrugged and tossed the wipe into the open grave.

But the strangest part of all was no one blinked an eye. Not even the preacher, who somehow had missed the disrespectful exchange.

Sissy knew, though. Just because Mary Ann had tossed her trash into the man's final resting place didn't mean that she had killed him. She might be glad, thankful even, that he was gone, but that didn't prove anything other than a bad marriage had existed between them.

And how many bad marriages were milling around in the crowd of "mourners"? Most likely, more than anyone even knew.

Sissy moved around a group of men who were holding a conversation about Walt's Special Blend—a conversation they could have had anywhere but apparently decided to have there in the cemetery—and over toward the swarm of women that had gathered around Mary Ann Summers.

"But murdered," one of the women was saying. Sissy had never seen her before, but she seemed to be on close terms with Mary Ann. She was holding the other woman's hands, pumping them up and down with each syllable. "It's unbelievable."

"It is." The murmur went up from the collective group. All the women nodded their heads sympathetically.

"It's hard to believe he's gone," Mary Ann said.

Sissy couldn't judge the sincerity of her words. Her eyes were dry, and her chin didn't wobble as if she was fighting back tears. All in all, she looked like she was attending the funeral of a distant cousin she had never met rather than her husband of thirty-plus years. Sissy supposed her words could be interpreted in a number of ways.

And then the thought struck her. What if Mary Ann was also a target for the murderer? No one really knew if she was safe. And with a murderer on the loose in Yoder, were any of them really safe?

That was up for debate.

"Honey," another woman started, drawing out the word to ensure she got Mary Ann's full attention. "Surely you aren't staying at home tonight. You don't need to be by yourself at a time like this."

"I am." Mary Ann lifted her chin as if in defiance of the woman's words, practically daring her to counter her response.

"I'm staying there with her." Sally Justice wrapped a protective, almost possessive arm around Mary Ann's shoulders. "There, there," she said, patting Mary Ann soothingly on the arm. The motion was all for show, for the benefit of the other women. Mary Ann didn't look like she was in need of comfort of any sort.

But, Sissy told herself once again, lack of grief didn't make her a murderer.

"Are you coming out to supper now?" Bethel asked as Sissy climbed into her car.

Sissy plucked at the ruffled fabric on the bodice of her dress. "I want to change out of this first," she said. "And I've got to get Duke. If I show up without him, I may have a riot on my hands."

Bethel nodded in an understanding way. "I think you might be right about that. Well, come out as soon as you can. Lizzie needs all the company she can get."

Sissy gave her aunt a saucy military salute and started her car. Bethel rolled her eyes and slid into the passenger's seat of Lottie's sedan.

It didn't take long to change out of her funeral clothes, grab the bowl of potato salad she'd made last night, bundle up her sweet pup, and get back on the road to Bethel's house. She needed this, this family dinner. It was simply amazing to her how much these get-togethers meant to her after such a short period of time. But they did. Even Duke looked forward to visiting with so many of his adoring fans.

She just wished Emma could be there tonight. Of course, she would in spirit because she was all anyone would be able to talk about. Especially after just burying the man she'd confessed to killing.

Blame it on the writer in her, but she just wanted to know *why*. Why had Emma confessed? What if in that *why* lay the identity of the true killer?

But that would mean that, if Bethel's prediction were true and Emma was trying to protect Amos, then he was the killer.

Sissy glanced over to where Duke stood, braced up in his car seat and gazing out the open window, pink tongue hanging out, silky fur ruffling in the wind. She wished she could be so carefree. If only for a little bit.

But lately, it had seemed to be one thing after another. First, Colt cheating on her, then having to move out of her apartment, because really . . . could any woman happily live with the sister of the cheating man she had once loved? So Yoder had been her salvation. She could come and reinvent herself for six months while she helped out at the café and waited on the birth of Lizzie's twins. But since she had been in Yoder, there had been two murders and a bunch of drama.

Then she made herself a promise. Just as soon

as everything settled down, she was going to work on that whole relationship and reinvention thing.

Now why did Declan Jones's face pop into her thoughts at that exact moment? She didn't want to examine that too closely, so she gently nudged it away and turned onto the packed gravel road that led to her aunt's house.

CHAPTER TWELVE

*What you don't know can't hurt you . . . until you
find out about it.*
—Aunt Bess

When she walked into her aunt's house, Daniel was reading to Lizzie from *The Budget* newspaper. Sissy had finally gotten used to the fact that everyone—well, the Amish really—just walked in without a knock or a previous warning. They came in, shouting out a greeting, and that was that.

"Sissy!" Lizzie called as if it had been eons since they had last seen each other and not just a couple of days. "I'm so glad to see you."

"Me too," Daniel quipped. "You can take over now." He handed Sissy the newspaper as Duke climbed over Lizzie's belly to flop down and snuggle into the crook of her neck.

Sissy shook her head. "He's going to be heartbroken when the babies come and he can't be the center of your world."

Lizzie gave a mock pout. "Well, maybe you should give him more attention then."

"Uh-huh," Sissy said. "That's exactly what he needs."

"I'm going . . ." Daniel pointed toward the kitchen and disappeared through the doorway that led into the large room.

Lizzie rolled her eyes. "He's been reading to me in the evenings," she said. "But I don't think he likes it."

"Why not?"

"I don't know." Lizzie stroked Duke's silky head, and he let out a blissful puppy sigh. "He says it's because he's already read them all and that I get argumentative about the articles. But I just want to discuss them. With a person. You know, a living, breathing person, something I haven't seen in hours and hours."

Sissy gave her an understanding smile. "Bored, are you?"

"Beyond belief," Lizzie admitted. "And then scared. I want the babies to come so badly, so I can get up and move around, but when they come, am I going to be ready?"

"Of course you are." Sissy patted her hand, and Duke let out a small growl. He was possessive of Lizzie. Maybe he could sense her fear and doubts. Whatever it was, she decided to let his impertinence slide. "What are y'all reading about?"

"He just finished the one about the Swartzentruber community in Pennsylvania that moved out of state because they don't want to add safety triangles to the back of their buggies. I guess Pennsylvania requires that."

Sissy found the article and scanned it while Lizzie rubbed one of Duke's silky ears between her thumb and forefinger. "I don't get it," Sissy said. "What do the triangles have to do with following the word of God?"

One thing she had truly learned while living in Yoder was that Amish was a religion, first and foremost. She felt like people on the "outside" lost a sense of that when they started talking about buggies, one-room schools, and no electricity. When they contemplated whether or not they could "become" Amish, whether or not they believed the same doctrine as the community was never brought up. Most times, such conversations centered on what they would have to give up in terms of convenience—curling irons, cars, and computers. But being Amish was a religion. And following their interpreted word of God would always lead the way.

"I don't think it said in so many words," Lizzie replied. "But I feel like it has to do with trusting in God."

Sissy nodded. "Trusting in God is good. It's the fellow man you have to watch out for."

Lizzie chuckled. "Read the next one."

Sissy started to read aloud the next article on the page. It was about a certified organic farm in Ohio that had started using human waste as fertilizer. "Ew." She looked up from the paper and made a face.

"Agreed," Lizzie said with a shudder. Then she stopped. "They are talking about poop, right?"

Sissy scanned a little farther down on the page, just to be certain. "Yup."

"Where do they get it?" she asked, then called out before Sissy could answer, "Daniel, come here."

Her husband appeared immediately in the doorway between the two rooms. The look on his face was slightly panicked, a little excited, and a whole lot expectant. "What is it?" he asked. "The babies?"

She shook her head. "Did you read this article about the farm in Ohio using"—she paused as if looking for the best way to phrase it—"outhouse materials to fertilize the fields?"

He exhaled, the relaxation visible. Then he tossed the dish towel he held onto one shoulder and nodded. "I did."

"And what do you think of that?" his wife asked.

He glanced to Sissy, who waved for him to continue. Daniel was nothing if not an Amish gentleman. "It's been up for debate for some time now. There are farmers who consider it a basic, natural resource that is being wasted. Others feel that it's not sanitary. Mostly, the talk in that piece is about the definition of organic and organic matter."

Sissy nodded, even though that last bit went right over her head.

"But where do they get it?" Lizzie asked. "Surely not from the outhouse."

Sissy had a vision of a large poop truck similar to the grease truck that came to the restaurant. It had a big hose that sucked all the grease out of the grease trap. Except this one was designed for poop.

Double ew.

Daniel shrugged and shifted a bit in place, obviously a little uncomfortable with the subject matter. Truth be known, Sissy was a little weirded out by it herself. "Septic tanks and the like, I suppose. Now I gotta—" He ducked back into the kitchen without finishing his sentence.

Sissy turned back to her cousin.

"What do you think?" Lizzie asked.

Sissy grimaced. "I think it's a little gross. I mean, we can talk all we want about it being a natural part of life, but to put it on growing food doesn't seem sanitary."

"Putting cow patties on the same food is okay?"

And this must be what she meant when she said Daniel thought she was argumentative about the subjects in the paper. Still, Sissy wasn't going to be dissuaded. "We expect farmers to use some sort of fertilizer, and I would rather them use manure than chemicals." She had never really thought about it much before, but that part was true. "Out of the accepted possibilities, human . . . manure seems the least appetizing."

There. That was the real problem.

"But if you don't know that the farmer used human manure?" Lizzie raised her eyebrows, awaiting a response.

"I suppose that's part of the issue," Sissy said. *What you don't know can't hurt you . . . until you find out about it.* But she decided that was one Aunt Bess quote she would keep to herself. "No one wants to be deceived. Or even to feel like they've been deceived."

Lizzie relaxed back onto her pillows and thoughtfully scratched Duke behind one ear. "I don't think I would like it if I didn't know."

"And if you did know?" Sissy asked. "Would it

still be a problem? Or would you go ahead and eat the vegetables grown with . . . you know?"

"I'm not sure," Lizzie said. "I'll have to get back to you on that."

"Supper." Daniel's entrance interrupted their conversation—thankfully. In one hand he held a heaping plate of all the good things that Bethel and Daniel had put together, along with the potato salad that Sissy had brought. She had been surprised that no one else had shown up for the supper, but Bethel shrugged it off when Sissy said something about it. "Some weeks are just like that," she said.

Sissy had no reason to doubt her aunt's words, and yet she did. The Yoder clan had a lot going on at the time. They were gearing up for babies to arrive. They had just attended a funeral that very same afternoon, and they were all worried about one of their own having confessed to murder. Sissy supposed that was enough to keep most people in bed, and not traveling around and visiting. But still she felt like the lack of people had more to do with Bethel's explanation rather than lack of interest.

Shame, really. Sissy would have liked a few others to bounce some of her theories off of—like if Amos could really be guilty of murder and if Emma was indeed covering for him. But, instead, she and Lizzie had talked about poop.

And she couldn't feel but just a little bit guilty that she hadn't been conversing about something more important to them all.

* * *

"Lottie." Sissy pulled the café worker to one side as the traffic in the eatery had slowed down enough that they could, at least, catch their breath. It was as if, now that Walt was well and truly gone, the whole town had turned out for breakfast at the Sunflower. It was barely ten-thirty, and Sissy's feet ached all the way up to her knees. "Why aren't the men wearing muck boots?"

"Pardon?" Lottie asked. She stopped straightening the supplies in the waitress station and gave Sissy her full attention.

"Bethel told me that most everybody in Yoder has a pair of muck boots. So why aren't they wearing them when they come in here?"

She had been watching all morning, even with all the hungry customers they had had, perhaps even especially with all the customers they had had. But only a couple out of all the men had been wearing muck boots, and those two had taken their orders to go.

"Does this have anything to do with Walt Summers?" Lottie asked.

"Can you just answer my question without another question?" Sissy countered. She didn't have time to explain it all to Lottie, though Sissy was fairly certain that Lottie already knew all the main points from Bethel. The two had been friends for longer than Sissy had been alive.

"I'll take that as a yes." Lottie nodded, satisfied by her own detective work. "And to answer your question without another question, most farmers leave their muck boots in the barn."

"So they don't wear them around town?"

"Would you want to tramp all over town in those things?"

Well, when she put it like that . . .

"So if we were going to find a certain pair of muck boots, say size eleven—"

Lottie laughed, that big-hearted chuckle that Sissy remembered so well. "Sweetie, you'd be better off trying to find a diamond in Miss America's crown."

Sissy frowned. That wasn't what she wanted to hear. The thoughts had been plaguing her all night and into her workday.

"Not what you wanted to hear?" Lottie asked gently.

Sissy shook her head, her thoughts racing.

"What's the matter?" Bethel picked that time to come out of the back and stare at them like some Amish overlord.

"It's just . . ." Sissy started, hesitant to let her thoughts go free. She wasn't sure she could contain them if she did. "It's just that whoever killed Walt Summers was wearing muck boots. That's a solid fact. But if the men—or to be fair, the women—in this town don't go jaunting around in their muck boots, then surely that means one of two things. Either the person is comfortable in their boots and wears them out all the time, or they were in their own fields and got the sudden urge to clonk Walt Summers on the head with a shovel. In which case, they walked over wearing their muck boots. In which case, that means whoever it was lived close. In which case, that makes both Amos Yoder and Weaver Justice prime suspects. And truly that would make Emma a prime suspect as well. After all, she could have slipped on her father's muck boots to help disguise her footprints in the mud."

Bethel tucked the dish towel she held under the tied strings of her cook's apron, then propped her hands on her hips. "Girl, you need a hobby."

Lottie smiled. "I think she has one."

"So now I'm the only one who cares about getting Emma out of jail?"

"No one said that, but your theories just made her a top suspect." Bethel paused to see if she was going to say anything back.

But it was Lottie who spoke next. "I thought we had all agreed that Emma wasn't strong enough to kill Summers with one blow?"

It was true. They had. But even that evidence was small when compared to a signed confession.

"So that leaves Amos and Weaver," Bethel said.

Lottie shook her head. "It wasn't Weaver," she said emphatically. "That man has been through so much at the hands of Walt Summers that if he had wanted to kill him, he would have done so long before now."

Bethel nodded in agreement, even as she frowned. Or maybe that was her thoughtful look. "Maybe something changed in their friendship."

"I wouldn't call what those two men had a friendship," Lottie countered.

"Then what would you call it?" Bethel asked. "A bromance?"

Sissy turned to her aunt. "Where did you hear that word?"

Bethel shrugged. "I know things."

"It's no bromance," Lottie said. "More of a love-hate sort of weird neighborhood thing going on."

"Can I get some more coffee?" A man in overalls and work boots—not muck boots; Sissy had checked when he came into the café—stood at the counter, coffee cup in hand.

"Gracious," Lottie said and moved to pour the man another cup.

Bethel turned and made her way back into the kitchen.

Sissy went to bus a recently vacated table, her theories no clearer now than when she had voiced them. If she ever hoped to be an investigative journalist, she needed to step up her game. Maybe solving this murder would help. But it seemed like Lottie had more insight than Sissy had first realized. At the rate they were going, finding the killer might just prove to be as difficult as finding a diamond in Miss America's crown.

It couldn't be that popular, Sissy decided sometime after the lunch rush died down. She had looked at everyone's feet—even the women—during their busiest time, and aside from only seeing one pair of muck boots in the whole lot, she discovered that the people of Yoder had very different-sized feet. From each other, that was. And to say that a size eleven was the most popular was merely her aunt's own opinion and observation. And just to prove it—

"I'm going to take a smoke break," she told Lottie.

There was only one person at the counter and

one table that held a young couple who looked to be from out of town. All the rest had been bussed and wiped down. If she was going to be able to go, now was her time.

"You don't smoke," Lottie reminded her.

"I know, but Josie takes so many, I feel I should get one too."

Lottie gave a one-shoulder shrug. "I suppose that's fair."

Sissy had been counting on it. "I'll be back in fifteen."

Lottie nodded and went back to filling the salt-shakers and wiping them down.

Outside was sunny and bright, the perfect Kansas day, if you hadn't been locked up for murder. Truth was, Emma's face haunted her at night. The poor girl had no call to be in jail, and yet there she sat. Sissy wasn't sure if this little "smoke break" of hers was going to yield any more knowledge than she already had, but the thought had occurred to her during lunch, and she wanted to act on it as soon as possible.

"Where you off to?"

Sissy turned to see Gavin striding toward her.

She smiled at him. "The hardware store." She faltered as he changed his direction and fell into step beside her. "They sell muck boots, right?"

"Yeah." Gavin chuckled. "You thinking about taking up gardening?"

She shook her head. "Anyplace else sell them?"

"I'm sure you can get them in Hutchinson, but in Yoder, yeah. That's probably it."

She nodded and continued on. She couldn't check all the stores in Hutchinson to see if they had recently sold any size eleven muck boots. Or if they remembered any of their customers who wore a size eleven. Truthfully, it was a dead-end prospect, but she had to see for herself.

"Why muck boots?" Gavin asked.

"There was a footprint at the crime scene."

"Crime scene? Oh, you mean Walt Summers."

"Yes. There was a footprint that we believe was made by a size eleven muck boot. My aunt seems to think that it's the most popular size and therefore not a good clue at all, but—"

"You want it to be."

Sissy nodded.

The wind gusted and ruffled Gavin's hair. He reached up and fingered it back into place in that gesture she was starting to associate exclusively with him.

"Where are you going?" she asked.

"Well, I was coming to see you and chat for a minute."

"Anything important?"

"Nah." He shook his head and stopped at the entrance to the hardware store. "After you."

She stepped inside and stopped, allowing her gaze to meander around for a brief moment.

Every time Sissy had been to the iconic Yoder Hardware Store, the front doors of the buttery-yellow building had been propped open. She supposed that was typical for an Amish business here, to allow the breeze to come in. And despite the fact that there was no electricity in the building, it was cool inside, a little dimmer, and smelled of rubber and leather.

"Hi." Jeremiah Glick greeted them. Like the hardware store itself, Jeremiah was something of a fixture in the town. Sissy had asked a few people how long he had worked at the store, and most couldn't remember a time when he hadn't manned the counter. "Help you find something?"

Gavin pointed to Sissy. She took a step forward. "Muck boots," she said simply.

"Right over there." Jeremiah pointed to the far wall, where the boots were stacked up, one on top of the other, with a random sample pulled out to show the style.

"I'm not really here to buy," Sissy tried to explain. "I just need to know a fact or two."

Jeremiah didn't blink. Sissy began to wonder if it was merely his demeanor or if people came in often asking for trivia on the boots. "*Jah?*"

"Is size eleven really your most popular size?" she asked.

He gave a small rise and drop of his shoulders. "I suppose it's on up there. Maybe with a size ten, but definitely popular."

"So you sell a lot of size elevens."

"I suppose."

Sissy felt like she was dragging out each word from the man. Not because he was reluctant; he just wasn't chatty. She needed someone chatty who would spill tons of information about the boots, and then she would somehow find a nugget of evidence/proof/anything to help clear Emma's name. Or at the very least make Earl Berry realize that the girl was lying and take her home to her family instead of keeping her locked up.

"Do they last a long time? I mean, do you sell a lot of them to the same people?" That question definitely hadn't come out quite like she wanted it to, but she decided to let it rest and see what Jeremiah might reveal. She could always work on a rephrase next.

"They'll last for years if you want 'em to. Long as your feet aren't growing."

"So it's safe to say that people may only buy one or two pairs after they reach adulthood."

"*Jah.* I suppose you could say that if you wanted to." His tone clearly stated that he didn't know why any rational person would need to say such a thing.

Even so, the information was a help. Or really not a help at all. But it did answer her question.

"All right then, thanks."

"*Jah.*" Jeremiah waved, and Sissy turned for the door.

"That wasn't in the paper," Gavin told her as she stepped back into the bright afternoon sun. "About the boot print. The police didn't release that to the papers."

"I know," Sissy said. "But I found the body, remember?"

"Right." He fell in beside her, shoulder to shoulder, as she started back toward the café.

"It was a long shot," she told him. Her aunt and even Lottie had warned her that it was a long shot, but she'd had to see for herself.

"Still trying to get Emma out of jail?" he asked.

"That girl is innocent. She has her whole life in front of her."

"She confessed," he reminded her.

"She lied," Sissy shot back. "Ugh." She looked down to see that she had stepped in a puddle of water just outside the café.

She had been concentrating on the information that she had received at the hardware store and her conversation with Gavin, and she hadn't seen the standing water. Apparently, neither had Gavin.

"What the—" Gavin raised one foot, water dripping from the sole. "You could have warned a guy."

Sissy shook her head. "This wasn't here when I left." She opened the door to the café to find Lottie with a squeegee pushing the water out of the dining area and toward the front door. Bethel was on the phone, pacing back and forth in her wet, no-nonsense shoes. Josie was nowhere to be seen.

"What happened?" Sissy asked.

"Drain," Lottie said, huffing with the effort of pushing the water.

Great. While she'd been out chasing needles and diamonds and size-eleven muck boots, minor disaster had struck the café. The hits just kept coming.

"Well, that should about do it." Vern McDaniel of Yoder Pumps and Pipes tore the top invoice off the pad he held in his work-stained hands and offered it to Sissy. She pointed to Bethel, who glared at her, then accepted it from him.

"You'll bill me, *jah*?" her aunt asked the man.

"Yeah." Vern switched the wad of tobacco from

one side of his mouth to the other and grinned. "You need to have those drains checked regularly or it's going to happen again," he told them.

"*Jah*." Bethel nodded, but she wasn't looking at Vern. She was studying the invoice, looking for discrepancies, no doubt.

"All right, then." Vern adjusted his hat, then started to turn away. "Oh," he said, spinning back around. "I almost forgot. We got these new invoices last month. This is your copy too." He flipped through the pads, tore out the pink paper, and offered it to Sissy.

This time she did take it, and she stared at it as if she had been handed a winning lottery ticket. Maybe it was even more valuable.

"I guess it's time to get to mopping." Lottie moved to go into the kitchen and start cleaning up the mess that the backup had caused.

According to Lottie, just before closing time on that Saturday, the kitchen drain started to gurgle, and all of a sudden, water seemed to be everywhere. Water and gunk, what appeared to be water-logged leaves, pieces of lettuce, and who knew what else. Even a few of those plastic straw wrappers.

At the time, Sissy had made a mental note to talk to her aunt about doing away with straws altogether—in hopes of them leaving a better planet behind—or, at least, the ones with plastic wrappers, but for now, all she could do was stare at the invoice she held in her hand.

"Bethel," she whispered.

Her aunt grunted, and without even looking at her, Sissy knew that she hadn't bothered to look up from the copy of the invoice she held, but Sissy needed a little more from her than that.

"Auntie."

That got her attention. "What is it?" Bethel grumped.

"This is it," Sissy said in awe, holding out the pink slip of paper that Vern McDaniel had bestowed on her. "This is what Walt Summers was holding when he died."

CHAPTER THIRTEEN

You don't have to be perfect to be amazing.
—Aunt Bess

"How did you talk me into this again?" Sissy asked the next morning.

It was Sunday, and she and Gavin were going out for a bicycle ride. Last night, she had wanted to question Vern about whether or not he had been the one to go to the Summerses' farm on the day Walt died, but it seemed a little accusatory. And though Vern McDaniel didn't appear to be a violent man, he still wasn't the type to be accused of murder and take it lightly. So she had let it rest. Though now anything she wanted to do would have to wait until tomorrow. It was a church Sunday for the Amish in Yoder.

"Are you going to say that every time we ride?" he asked.

Sissy shrugged. "Maybe." Because every time he managed to talk her into donning his spandex cast-offs and helmet and climbing on the extra bike he had insisted she keep at her house, "just in case you want to ride without me," she wondered how he had managed to get her on the bike in the first place.

"Well, quit. I've got you everything you need, including a basket for your baby."

As if he knew they were talking about him, Duke sounded off from his place in said basket.

"Are you sure he's going to be okay in there?" Sissy eyed the small compartment warily.

"Stop," Gavin said. "He's going to love it. He's harnessed in and completely safe."

"Until I crash," she muttered.

Gavin shrugged one shoulder and donned his helmet. "So don't crash."

Sissy sighed and straddled the bike. How did she let herself get talked into these things?

But Gavin was right: Duke loved riding along, his pink tongue lolling in the wind as they rode.

Okay, truth be known, after that first ride that had her walking like Yosemite Sam, she sort of enjoyed going out riding with Gavin. Just as long as she kept herself in check and didn't blurt out any Aunt Bess-isms that had yet to be printed in the paper. After her last slipup, she was sort of worried about saying anything at all. If she quoted her alter ego again now, Gavin might put two and two together. And he seemed pretty good at math.

But it was fun seeing Yoder at a slower pace, and the countryside just to the west of town was a lovely sight: green fields of soybeans and corn in neat rows and pastures dotted with Dutch Belted cattle. Wildflowers grew along the side of the roads, adding sprinklings of color everywhere she looked. And the sunflowers. Yes, she had known when she had arrived in Kansas that it was the Sunflower State—it was on the welcome sign at the side of the highway when you crossed the line and all—but she hadn't expected fields of them. Okay, so she had seen fields in pictures on the internet, and she knew that they existed, she just never dreamed she'd be riding by on a midsummer's day with an impossible blue sky overhead. And, of course, she never imagined that she would be wearing brightly colored spandex and weird shoes that looked like she was about to coast down to the finish line at the Tour de France.

She motioned to Gavin that she wanted to stop for a minute.

He nodded, and they pulled to the side of the road.

"What is it?" he asked as he took off his helmet. He tucked it under one arm and waited for her answer.

She shook her head. "It's so beautiful out here I didn't want to just ride right by."

He looked around, the wind lifting the strands of his blond hair. Hair that had been stuck into place by the weight of his helmet and the sweat it and the exercise produced. "It is beautiful," he said. "These are Jimmy Joe Bartlett's fields."

"Jimmy Joe, as in the one who wanted to kill Walt Summers Jimmy Joe?"

"One and the same."

That changed a few things. She turned back to the field and looked a little more closely at the flowers. "But this isn't the road his house is on," she protested. Which meant these weren't the fields that she and her aunt had seen a week or so ago. Those flowers weren't only closed buds still struggling in their reach toward the sun. These were in full bloom. Beautiful flowers as large as dinner plates.

"Well, word around town is Jimmy Joe found a few barrels of Walt's Special Blend that he'd bought a year or so ago. He fertilized these flowers with the old Special Blend, while the ones nearer his house are treated with the new blend he'd purchased this year." He gestured toward the north, and Sissy could only assume that was the direction of the field and the house where she and Bethel had talked to the mountain of a farmer.

She was no expert on farming or on flowers, but she could see the difference in the crops. Anyone could.

"What exactly do you do with a field full of sunflowers?"

"Sunflower seeds are a pretty hot commodity. I mean, I like them, and the birds like them."

"So mostly food stuffs. Packages for consumption and bird feed."

"And seed packets. And they are pressed for their oil," he added.

"So it's a good living," she said, the words a half question.

"I don't know for sure. Good enough, I suppose. Jimmy Joe's not rolling in dough, but he seems to be doing all right. When the crops are good."

Jimmy Joe, Sissy thought, as she stared out over the field of swaying sunflowers. He went to the top and back down to the bottom of her suspect list with alarming regularity. Yes, he could kill a man with one blow. Yes, he was suffering at the hands of Walt Summers. Yes, he went around in muck boots most of the time and would be one of the few people who would drive across town in them even if he was aiming to kill someone. But after meeting the man, he didn't seem to be the type to murder someone. Not even in the heat of anger. And every time he fell to the bottom of the list, her uncle Amos Yoder rose back to the top. It all made perfect sense, even adding in Emma's confession to protect him. There was no concrete evidence, and Sissy was almost afraid to dig further in case she found it. And it definitely wasn't the answer she wanted.

Gavin pulled his phone out from some magic pocket in his spandex and started thumbing in something.

"What are you doing?" she asked.

"Internet search on sunflower usages." He lifted his phone to the sky and moved it around in an arc as he continued to stare at the screen. "I don't have much signal out here."

Sissy reached for her phone, which she had placed in the basket before they left. Duke gave her a sweet lick on the hand as she pulled it out. She patted his head with her other hand, then scratched him behind the ear as she tapped the screen with her thumb. "I don't have any signal at all."

Gavin looked back to the east. "We could head back into town. Maybe stop at the Carriage House and get some pie."

Sissy shook her head with a smile. "For someone who's always concerned about eating healthy, you do love your pie."

"What can I say?" He grinned. "I'm a man of simple needs."

One thing Sissy could definitely say about Gavin was that he wasn't embarrassed by his body. Most of the men she had known weren't. But she didn't know many men who could strut around in skintight spandex and not give it a second notice. Of course, they lost weight more easily and gained it more slowly, and Gavin watched every morsel he took in, so he could eat pie whenever he wanted.

Sure, he was toned tight from all his cycling, and that counted for something, but his confidence amazed her. He didn't seem to mind the weird shoes or the helmet head, and she was certain everyone was looking at her every fat roll and sag as the hostess seated them in one of the high-backed booths.

They had stopped by the Chicken Coop on their way to the Carriage House and dropped Duke off in his kennel. He was pouting when Sissy shut the door behind him, no doubt puppy-dreaming about the good times the humans would be having without him.

"Your waitress will be over in a moment," the Amish hostess said, placing their menus on the table in front of them before heading back to the front of the restaurant.

"Are we really just here for the pie?" she asked.

"And the internet connection," he reminded her.

She opened her mouth to ask him if he was going to remove his goggles, then remembered he probably hadn't brought his glasses to replace them. And he needed them, of that she was certain. She had peered through them one time and about fell on her rear. The poor boy was practically blind!

Instead, Sissy picked up her menu as the waitress approached.

"How're y'all doing today?" she asked, placing their rolls of silverware and two water glasses in front of them. Her name tag read Carol.

"Good," Gavin said. He handed her back the menu. "I already know what I want."

"Okay then." Carol got out her pen and had it at the ready.

"I want a piece of chocolate peanut butter pie," he told her.

"That's it?"

He nodded.

She turned to Sissy. "What'll you have?"

She almost said, "The same," but something stopped her. "A piece of pie," she told her. "Just surprise me."

"Oh." Carol blinked a bit as she took the menu. "Okay. I'll surprise you." She nodded at them, then hustled away to get their order.

"Is that today's paper over there?" Gavin asked, pointing to the folded newspaper next to the condiment caddy.

She picked it up and examined the date. "Appears to be," she told him.

He motioned for her to hand it to him. "Let's see . . ." he muttered as he opened it.

Something in his tone sent a bit of a chill running down her spine. A total overreaction, but for some reason she wasn't ready to fess up to being Aunt Bess.

"When's your birthday?" he asked.

"Why?"

"Horoscope."

"I'm a Libra," she told him.

"Umm," he said, no doubt reading it first before delivering the prediction to her. "Says here, new friendships are on the horizon, but be careful to continue to nurture the old friends as well. Secrets can quickly come undone in the heat of passion." He peered over the edge of the paper and waggled his eyebrows at her. The effect was diluted by the frames of his goggles, but the intent was just as strong.

"It doesn't say that." She snatched the paper out of his hands.

"Does too." He laughed as she scanned the horoscope section. Which just happened to be right next to the "Aunt Bess Knows Best" column.

"Okay," she grudgingly said after reading what was under the Libra heading. "So it does."

"Read Aunt Bess Knows Best," he urged.

Sissy's heart sank. "You don't want me to read her."

"I do," he said.

She searched his face for some deception. Was he trying to trip her up? Was he trying to trap her and force her to admit her secret?

"Really? She's so . . ."

"So what?" he asked.

"Trite." It was the only word she could come up with on such short notice. Yes, she was a writer, but there was a lot to be said about the editing stage. That's where all the best words and phrases entered the scene.

"You're crazy. She's not trite." He shook his head. "She's got a great voice. She's fun and sassy, and she tells it like it is."

This was the only time that Sissy was able to truly open up and say what she usually wanted to say about Aunt Bess; she usually didn't have the nerve or the lack of manners to do so. "Whatever. I still don't read her." Truth.

Gavin shook his head. "You don't know what you're missing."

She didn't have time to respond as the waitress came back with their pie.

Chocolate peanut butter for Gavin and . . .

"For you," the waitress said, placing the small plate in front of her, "pecan, fresh from the oven with a scoop of ice cream. A la mode is on the house," she continued. "Since it was warm. Well, that's the best time to eat it with ice cream. Can I get you anything else?"

Gavin shook his head and cast a brief but longing look at her pie.

"Thanks," Sissy said.

The waitress moved away as she picked up her fork. Then she set it down and grabbed the spoon, which was better suited for melting ice cream on warm, gooey pie.

"You are going to share, right?" he cajoled. "Since I'm, you know, your best friend in Yoder."

She took a big bite of the pie and closed her eyes. She had meant to tease Gavin, but it really was that good. She opened them again and swallowed. "What did you say your name was?"

"Please." Gavin batted his lashes at her.

"I'll think about it. In the meantime, your pie is getting . . . room temperature."

He picked up his own fork and took a bite. "Yum," he said around the mouthful, his reaction a bit much for someone who ate that pie at least three times a week. "That is good. You want to trade bites."

"I'll think about it," she said again. She spooned up another bite and allowed her gaze to roam around the restaurant. By sheer habit based on what she'd been doing the last week, her gaze went to everyone's feet. But it was Sunday, after church, and there were only ladies' pumps, men's dress shoes, and a few pairs of athletic shoes that must have been saved for Sunday dress, for they were clean and mostly new-looking. No muck boots would be found, she was certain. She felt a little foolish for even looking.

"Have you thought about it?" he asked.

"What if I don't want to share my pie?"

"I thought Libras were generous."

"We're also self-indulgent," she told him, scooping up another bite. Self-indulgence was perhaps her worst trait. It had her carrying around five extra pounds, dating men like Colt, and hiding her career behind the persona of a seventy-something grandma.

"Please," he said once again.

Sissy sighed, making a big deal out of releasing

the breath. She wasn't really unwilling to share. She just liked to tease Gavin. Other than the whole hiding her career from the world issue, she could be herself around Gavin more than anyone she had ever met. Even her ex-roommate, Stephanie, whom she hadn't talked to since the whole Colt fiasco, which was natural considering that Stephanie was Colt's sister. Joking with Gavin was as easy as . . . well, pie.

She reached across the table and snatched up his spoon. "I suppose." Her tone was grudging as she scooped him a bite and handed it to him.

"Cozy."

The familiar voice sounded close to her elbow, but Sissy hadn't been paying attention to any of her surroundings as she teased with Gavin.

"Hey, Declan." Gavin accepted the bite of pie and shoveled it in, then realizing he hadn't made introductions, he quickly chewed and swallowed.

"Sorry, Declan, this is Sissy. Sissy, my cousin Declan."

"Your cousin?" Sissy managed to keep her voice down to a soft screech. If there even was such a thing.

"We've met." Declan shot her that winning smile.

"Really?" All of a sudden, his expression closed, and he looked from one of them to the other.

"Yeah. At the gas station, then in the neighborhood."

"I see." Gavin centered his gaze on her, and Sissy immediately felt like she had done something wrong. Which was ridiculous. She hadn't done a thing. But the feeling was still there, mixed with the embarrassment of how she looked. Aunt Bess always said never go anywhere underdressed because you never knew who you might run into, and yet here she sat, having failed to follow her own advice. She resisted the urge to run her fingers though her hair to fluff up the helmet hair she was certain she had. But she had pulled her shoulder-length tresses back into an elastic band before they left for their ride. She would have to redo her ponytail in order to straighten out the mess, and she couldn't very well do that seated at a center booth in the Carriage House, now could she? Like it mattered. Even if she could repair the damage done to the efforts of her volumizing conditioner and root spray, she was still wearing . . . wince . . . spandex. Gavin's spandex. Ugh.

"What are the two of you out doing?" Declan asked. He had one hand in the pocket of his slacks, his smile as warm and sexy as ever. Why was she forever to be pitifully dressed every time she ran into the man?

"Just out for a cycle," Gavin said. "You?" His expression was still closed. Still guarded.

"Just got out of church," he said. "And Mom wanted me to pick up a pie for later."

"Auntie is here?" Gavin looked around as if expecting his aunt to be somewhere nearby.

"In the car," Declan said.

"Mr. Jones." The hostess held up a to-go sack just the right size for a pie box.

"I'll let y'all get back to it," Declan said. "See ya."

"See ya," Gavin said, but he didn't take his eyes off Sissy as his cousin disappeared from view.

"What?" she asked as he continued to stare at her. "The pie is gone."

"Why didn't you tell me you met my cousin?"

Why didn't you tell me your cousin is the Kansas version of George Clooney? "I didn't know he was your cousin."

"I told you he'd be in the neighborhood."

"You did, but you didn't tell me his name."

"Jones," Gavin said. "Wasn't that enough?"

"No," she said, curious as to why he was so upset about the matter. If she had known that Declan was Gavin's cousin, she could have had him put in a good word for her, but with the look on Gavin's face, she was pretty sure he would have told her to go jump in a lake. Cousin rivalry. Had to be. Sissy had never had to deal with that since her family had moved away and her cousins had lived in another state her whole life. But she'd had enough to deal with in sibling rivalry, thank you very much.

Gavin stood and tossed a couple of dollars onto the table. "You ready?"

Did it matter? Seemed not. She stood as well. "You got the tip. I'll get the pie this time."

He grunted, and she took the sound to be affirmative. It was her turn to buy, after all.

They made their way to the front of the restaurant, where the cashier's stand stood between the charming gift shop and the entrance.

Sissy fished her debit card out of one of those magic pockets of the spandex shorts, but she couldn't say she did it with as much finesse as Gavin.

The door behind them opened, and a man stepped inside. Vern McDaniel, employee of Yoder Pumps and Pipes, walked into the Carriage House.

Automatically, Sissy's gaze dropped to his feet, where she saw muck boots. Perhaps even muck boots in a size eleven. Just like their killer had worn.

CHAPTER FOURTEEN

When tempted to fight fire with fire, keep in mind
that the fire department uses water.
—Aunt Bess

"Gavin," Sissy whispered, "that man's the killer."

"What?" He swung around to see who she was talking about. "Vern?" he asked, and not very quietly.

"Hey there, Wainwright."

"Working hard on a Sunday?" Gavin asked the man as Sissy reined in her suspicions, but only just.

"Not too much. We ran into a problem with the septic tank over at the Justice place. I got voted to come and pick up food for everyone."

"Lucky you," Gavin replied with a laugh.

Sissy stuffed the debit card back into the secret pocket in her borrowed shorts. The invoice, the boots, the opportunity. It was all there. But it wasn't like she could do anything about it herself.

"Check you later." Gavin lifted one hand in a small wave and made his way out of the restaurant. Sissy had no choice but to follow after him.

"Gavin," she said as he started to unchain their cycles.

Yoder was a small town with small-town values, but that didn't mean it didn't have its share of petty crimes. And leaving a bicycle unattended and unchained was just asking for it to be taken. If only for a joyride.

"Yep?"

"Did you hear what I said? I think—" She stopped as Vern McDaniel came out of the Carriage House.

"Later, Wainwright."

Gavin waved in return and went back to unlocking her bike chain.

Sissy caught Vern's gaze and did her best not to let him see her suspicions. She wasn't equipped to tell the man that she knew he had killed Walt Summers. But she was equipped to tell Earl Berry the very next time she saw him, which would be in the morning for his usual breakfast and his stint on Stool Number Three. And in the meantime . . .

"We need to follow him," she whispered to Gavin, even though McDaniel had already gone around the back of the building where most of the parking was, especially for trucks and the tractors that the Amish drove.

"Over to the Justice place?" Gavin had his helmet at the ready, but he paused before actually placing it on his head. "What's wrong with you?"

"I told you. Vern McDaniel killed Walt Summers."

Then Gavin did the most unlikely thing. A thing she would have never imagined he would do. Gavin burst out laughing, and he laughed so hard he bent over at the waist.

"What's so funny?"

Gavin couldn't answer. He was still laughing too hard.

"The evidence is all there," Sissy explained. She figured Gavin's crazy guffawing was kind of like when you got the giggles in church. You knew you shouldn't be laughing, and that made you want to laugh all the more, even though nothing around you was really that funny. It had to be that. Even though they weren't in church and he could laugh all he wanted. "The invoice, the boots, the opportunity. It's him."

The helmet hit the ground as Gavin tried to recover himself, bracing his hands on his knees. His chuckles were interspersed with sighs of "Whoa, boy."

"You better now?" She crossed her arms and hid her annoyance. Okay, so she didn't hide it. She had come up with the real murderer, and this was the last way she expected anyone to react to the news.

"Vern McDaniel did not kill Walt Summers."

"How can you be so sure. The evidence—"

"The evidence is wrong," Gavin said. "Vern McDaniel is the most gentle and kind-hearted person in Yoder. Maybe even in Reno County."

"Anyone can snap," she protested, still not convinced. Gavin's claims were one man's opinion. Take that and stack it against the evidence, and the evidence definitely won out. She started to launch in again about the facts she had in the case, but stopped as Gavin shook his head

He wiped the tears of mirth from his eyes. "Vern McDaniel wouldn't hurt a fly."

"Vern McDaniel? Are you out of your mind?" Lottie looked from Sissy to Bethel and back again.

Bethel shrugged.

"What's wrong with Vern McDaniel?"

"That man wouldn't hurt a fly," Lottie proclaimed.

"So I've been told," Sissy muttered.

The three of them had gathered in the kitchen on Monday morning, and Sissy had seen the opportunity to test her theory again. It was sound enough. Vern McDaniel wore muck boots that looked to be a size eleven. With muck boots it was hard to tell. He wore them everywhere for his job, she assumed, and his job was working for the same company listed on the invoice that had been in Walt Summers's hand when he was killed.

"Anyone can be pushed beyond their limits and snap," Sissy protested. "Maybe he just snapped."

"Over what?" Josie pipped in. "A sink trap?"

Bethel frowned at her, and Josie went back to the eggs she currently had sizzling on the grill.

"It's a valid point," Bethel said. "Without motive, the rest is just circumstantial evidence."

Sissy sharply turned to stare at her aunt. "Where'd you learn something like that?"

Bethel shrugged. "Maybe I've seen an episode or two of that cop show on TV. The one with all the letters."

"*NCIS?*" Sissy asked.

"That's the one." Bethel gave a quick nod.

"And she's right," Lottie said. "Plus Vern wouldn't hurt a fly."

"So you've said." She had so hoped that she had been onto something. And maybe she still was. Anyone could snap, right? Even those who wouldn't hurt a fly.

"Why, once I saw him scoop up a spider and put it outside rather than squash it."

And even those who scoop up spiders and set them free.

"Okay," she said. "Okay. It was just a theory."

"I know, dear, but on this one you're barking up the wrong tree."

Sissy nodded, though she wasn't completely convinced. And she and Lottie pushed back out into the dining area. Sissy immediately grabbed the coffeepot and started refilling cups, while Lottie took up the water pitcher.

Maybe there was motive. And no one would question what Vern was doing out at the farm. Plus, hadn't that been one of the original theories about who could have killed Walt? A deliveryman or repairman? It all seemed to fit. Now she would have to do a little digging in order to find that motive.

Since she was at work and basically confined to the café, Sissy decided some professional-grade eavesdropping was in order.

When all this had started and Emma had confessed, Sissy had started a list of people who had something against Walt Summers. Perhaps today she could pick up some insight into Vern McDaniel. Perhaps someone might let something slip or tell a story about the time that *fill in the blank with a negative story concerning Vern and Walt*. But, try as she might, no one had anything to say about Vern, and she wasn't able to come up with a good way to question people without them knowing that she was questioning them.

Her investigative journalist skills had taken a hit while she'd been pretending to be a seventy-five-year-old woman and handing out advice. She didn't have to dig for the answer then. People sent her the questions they wanted answered instead of the other way around. But she was grateful that she had a career at all. Right?

Gavin slipped into the booth, and she slapped her notebook down on the tabletop.

"What's that?" he asked.

"That's a list of everyone who complained today about something Walt Summers did."

He turned the pad where he could read it, lifted the page, and whistled under his breath. "That many?"

"I know, right?"

"And this long after he's been gone."

Sissy shrugged. "It's only been a couple of days. It'll take a while for people to forget."

He looked at the names again. "You think the killer might be among them?"

She wished. She wanted the killer to be Vern McDaniel. But more than one person thought that theory was impossible. The problem was, if it wasn't Vern, then it was most likely Amos.

Could she put her uncle in jail in order to free her cousin?

It was unimaginable.

"What?" Gavin asked.

She shook her head. "I'll get you some water. You eating today?"

He nodded. "Hamburger—"

"Without the bun and a side salad instead of fries," she finished for him.

"Predictable, eh?"

"Consistent," she corrected with a small smile. "Be right back." She left to put in his order and get him a glass of water, the problem of her cousin being in jail and innocent, even though she had confessed, weighing on her. She hoped that Emma was doing okay.

"What's wrong now?" Bethel asked, as she stopped at the waitress station.

"Emma," Sissy replied simply. "I'm worried about her."

"Want to go check on her after work?" Bethel asked. "We could go together."

Sissy nodded. "Let's do it. We can make sure she's okay and put some money on her commissary. She might need cigarettes or something."

"Cigarettes?" Bethel drew back a bit. "What for? She doesn't smoke."

"Cigarettes are like money in jail. Or is it in prison? I can't remember."

"Is there a difference?" Bethel asked.

"I think so." Sissy wrote out Gavin's order and handed it to her aunt. "Here," she said. "For table five."

Her aunt studied the order. "We should call this the Wainwright Special."

Sissy laughed. "Have you met his cousin? Declan?" She hadn't realized it was still on her mind until that moment. So much had been happening.

Lottie picked that moment to come up. "I have. Handsome man."

"*Jah,*" Bethel agreed.

"I thought the Amish didn't care about such things," Sissy said.

"We don't, but I ain't blind."

Sissy and Lottie laughed.

"Why do you ask?" Lottie pinned Sissy with a speculative look.

She could only shrug and play it off like it was no big deal. "I've met him a couple of times. Then, yesterday afternoon, we were in the Carriage House—"

"Who's we?" Bethel interrupted.

"Me and Gavin," Sissy replied. "And Declan came by. I didn't know he was Gavin's cousin. And Gavin got sort of weird."

"Weird?" Bethel asked. "How so?"

"I dunno," Sissy replied. "Kinda quiet and reserved. He seems okay today. But yesterday . . ."

"That's because that boy likes you," Lottie said.

Sissy scoffed. "As a friend, yeah."

Lottie shook her head. "Much more than that."

There was entirely too much to think about. Declan. Gavin. Cigarettes and invoices. But Sissy was ready to go see Emma again. She liked the girl.

And she worried about how such a young Amish
person would handle the confines of jail. It was a
different world, made up of seedy *Englisch* people
the likes of whom Emma had probably never seen
in her life. Probably didn't even know that they
existed. Now she was rubbing elbows with them.

"Do you think they are making fun of her in
there?" Sissy asked Bethel as they drove the highway to the Reno County Correctional Facility.

"Emma?" Bethel asked.

Sissy sighed. "Of course, Emma. Who else would
I be talking about?"

Bethel thought about it a moment. "No one, I
suppose."

"So . . . are they making fun of her? The other
inmates?"

"Probably." Bethel shook her head. "I don't
know. People are mean. And the meanest people
are in jail, *jah?*"

"Most likely." Though she knew a few had to
have escaped justice.

"They are making fun of her prayer *kapp*, but
that's all that would physically set her apart from
the others. I saw how she was dressed last time."

It was a good point, but Sissy hated the thought
of Emma being made fun of to any degree. But she
supposed that was life. Thug life. Amish thug life.

She shook her head at her wayward thoughts
and turned into the parking lot.

Just as on their previous visits, they were asked
to wait before being escorted back into a long
room with a plexiglass divider and phones for
communication.

Emma was led out to them by a female officer

who would have made two of Sissy. She couldn't imagine how helpless Emma felt. And it aggravated her that the sweet girl continued to maintain her guilt. When you went to jail, weren't you supposed to deny anything and everything, whether you did it or not?

She sat down across from them and picked up the phone. "I told you I didn't want you to come back." Those were the first words out of her mouth. But Sissy couldn't concentrate on that. She was too busy examining the horrifying myriad of colors in her cousin's black eye.

"What happened?" Bethel asked.

Emma shook her head. "Pudding."

"Pudding doesn't cause bruises like that," Bethel countered.

"It does when someone bigger and meaner than you wants it and you refuse."

"Oh, Emma." Sissy had been right all along. Emma was ill-equipped to handle the jail situation. Most people would be, but Emma even more than most.

"You need to quit this nonsense and tell them that you didn't do this." Bethel glared at her kin with what Sissy would have called the "stink eye," but Emma wasn't looking. She had closed her own eyes against the flood of emotion Sissy could read on her face.

Slowly, Emma's lashes parted. Tears trailed down each cheek. "I can't," she finally said. "Me being here is the best thing."

"You being here is what's keeping the police from finding the real killer." Sissy did her best to make the words gentle, yet firm. She didn't want to cause Emma anymore undue stress, but dang it! She didn't belong behind bars.

"That's right," Emma said quietly.

Bethel glanced over at Sissy just as she looked over to her aunt. It was as close to a reverse confession as they had managed to get from her, but it was a start.

"Emma," Bethel quietly started, "is there something you would like to tell us about this situation?"

Emma shook her head. Two more tears found their way from the corners of her eyes down to the edge of her jaw.

"Let me," Sissy said. She leaned forward in her seat and looked Emma dead in the eyes. "Emma, do you know who killed Walt Summers?"

The young girl nodded, and the tears really began to flow.

"Who?" Sissy quietly asked.

Emma swallowed hard. Sissy could almost see her gathering her courage and the bravery she needed to answer the question. It was a hard question, But one that they needed the answer for. It was imperative, and all three of them knew it.

The young girl sucked in a breath, glanced over her shoulder as if to see if anyone was listening in, then very quietly said, "Dat."

CHAPTER FIFTEEN

Life is too important to take seriously.
—Aunt Bess

Sissy's heart began to thump hard in her chest. Her mouth went dry so fast her lips stuck together.

"And you know this for a fact?" Bethel asked.

"*Jah*," she whispered.

"You saw him do it?" Sissy asked. The idea itself was sickening, gruesome, and depressing. The mere thought of this poor girl seeing her father kill another man because that man had practically ruined his life, his family . . .

"I didn't see him," Emma said. "But I know he did it. I know."

Bethel exhaled, and she seemed to shrink two inches. She had been so keyed up that it looked as though the tension just seeped out of her. "How do you know?" she said gently.

"Because of what that man did."

"If you say you know he did it, why did you confess?" Bethel asked.

Emma hiccupped lightly, then let out a shuddering sigh. "I can't take care of eleven children. They need Dat more than they need me."

"Oh, Emma." It was a tragic tale, and one that would be hard to reverse now that it had been set into motion.

"What about Samuel?" Bethel demanded. "He would have been there for you."

"I couldn't ask that of him." Emma sniffed. She was bringing her emotions under control now. Her expression was clearing up, her shoulders leveling off, rising. She was getting back to the Emma they saw during their first visit to the jail. "That's why you have to stop looking for the real killer."

"Emma." Sissy hoped the one word would be enough to talk some sense into the girl. Mainly because it was all she had. Emma had sacrificed herself for her siblings. To help her family. In her mind, it was the only choice she had.

But if it hadn't been her father who killed Walt Summers . . .

"No. You must. Otherwise, you'll leave me to care for them, and I can't do it. It's better this way."

"How do you know that we're trying to find the real killer?" Bethel crossed her arms and waited for Emma's answer.

"I'm in jail, not on the moon. Word gets around in here faster than it does in our community. People talk, you know."

"I know," Bethel grumbled.

Emma turned as one of the guards behind her said something. "I've got to go," she said facing them once again. "Stop, okay? Just stop." Then she hung up the phone and was gone.

Bethel looked to Sissy. And all she could do was look back.

They had discovered what they needed to know. But did that mean they had finally landed on the truth?

"What now?"

Sissy hit the unlock button on her key fob. "I have no idea."

Sure, they could go to Earl Berry or really anyone in the Reno County Sheriff's Office, and they would most probably be told the same thing. They had a signed confession, and they were moving forward with the process.

"Even if we could convince someone that she's innocent, that would only leave her father open for further investigation." And a family without a bread winner. A large family. She shook her head. "It's just so unfair."

Bethel grunted her agreement as the two of them climbed into the little Fiat and headed back to Yoder.

"I mean, she was about to get married." Sissy couldn't get her mind off of it. A young woman sacrificing her life for her siblings. It just didn't sit well with her. "There's got to be something we can do," she said. "We just haven't thought of it yet."

"I don't see anything from where I'm standing," Bethel said. She had both hands braced on the dash, but, at least, she had stopped clamping one hand over her prayer *kapp* as they drove along. It wasn't much, but it was a start.

"Let's assume that Amos is innocent," Sissy said.

"Why would we do that?" Bethel asked.

"Because we want him to be. And if we're going to get Emma out of jail and correct this whole mess, then we don't need to put Amos in the pokey."

"Pokey?" Bethel raised her eyebrows.

Sissy couldn't decide if she didn't know the word or if her aunt was just surprised that Sissy herself did. "Yes, pokey. We need for someone else to be guilty. We need to be looking for evidence that will incriminate someone other than Amos Yoder."

"Evidence," Bethel repeated in a tone that almost made the word into a question. "Like that invoice? When you thought Vern McDaniel was the killer?"

"Exactly," Sissy replied. "Sort of, anyway. That invoice seems like a good clue. And maybe it still is." The thought crept up on her so quietly that she almost missed it. "What if Vern McDaniel wasn't the one who came out that day? What if it was someone else? Someone not as kindhearted. Someone who had a beef with Walt Summers. You and I both know that's not a hard person to find in this town."

Bethel nodded.

"And Vern can't be the only person who works at Yoder Pumps and Pipes." Or the only employee they had who liked to wear his muck boots around town. And wore a size eleven.

Okay. So her theory was starting to stretch thin, but she didn't want Amos to be guilty. She wanted to get her cousin out of jail, keep her uncle out of prison, and find the real killer.

Really. She wasn't asking for much.

"I guess you'd need to know if someone had a call out there that morning."

"At the tomato farm?" Sissy asked.

"*Jah.*"

"If we had the invoice, it would be on there. The time, date, person attending. All of it." And it might even tell them who the killer was. And if they knew that . . .

But how were the supposed to get the invoice? No doubt, it was in the evidence box shoved under someone's desk at the sheriff's office, deemed unimportant in light of a confession.

"If someone had been out there that morning— and it seems that they had been, since Walt was holding an invoice—then the main office would have a record of it."

"Yes!" Sissy exclaimed. She was so excited by the thought she almost missed her turn. "We don't need the invoice. We just need to know their schedule." But her excitement quickly went flat as the realization hit her. "How are we going to get someone to tell us if there was a call out to the Summerses' place that day?" Maybe she could talk Gavin into calling and pretending to—

"Where's your phone?" Bethel demanded.

Sissy pointed to the resting place where she kept her phone while she was driving. "Why?"

"We've got a call to make."

"We do?" Sissy asked. "Who are we going to call?"

Bethel smiled. "Amanda Yoder."

"Another cousin?"

"*Jah*, but she's *Englisch*."

"And she works at Pumps and Pipes?" Sissy asked.

"*Jah*. And she has for years."

Twenty minutes later, the hope that had bloomed in Sissy's heart had deflated like an old balloon.

"Okay. *Jah*," Bethel said, nodding as if the woman on the other end of the line could see her. Sissy didn't need to hear the other side of the conversation to know what was going on.

"What'd she say?" Lizzie and Sissy asked at the same time.

"She said that no one went out to the Summerses' farm that day. She even checked the day before, just to be certain."

"Maybe—" Sissy started but stopped as Bethel shook her head.

"She checked for two weeks. No one from Pumps and Pipes went out to the tomato farm for any reason."

"So where'd the invoice come from then?" Lizzie asked no one in particular. Sissy suspected she didn't even expect an answer. She was merely voicing the thoughts that all of them had. The invoice could possibly point them in the direction of the killer, but not if they couldn't figure out who wrote it out and what it was for.

"I'm beginning to feel like this is hopeless."

Sissy flopped down on the chair next to the couch. She didn't want to give up. She hated giving up, but facing dead end after dead end was disheartening at best.

"It's only hopeless if we say it is," Bethel said.

"*Jah*." Lizzie playfully punched at Sissy's arm. "So quit saying that."

"I will. I will." But—and this was a very important *but*—she couldn't help but wonder if there was something huge they were missing.

"What if it wasn't from Pumps and Pipes?" Lizzie mused.

"It was," Sissy said. "That I'm certain of. Absolutely positive."

"One hundred percent?" Lizzie asked.

"A hundred and ten," Sissy countered.

Bethel frowned. "You can't have more than one hundred percent."

Sissy smiled a little and shook her head. There was no sense in trying to make her aunt see the exaggeration for what it was. Bethel Yoder saw everything literally. To her, the world was black and white.

"So if we know for certain that the invoice was from Pumps and Pipes, and we know for certain that it wasn't for a call to Walt Summers's place, then we need to figure out who it does belong to."

"That could be anyone in the county," Bethel protested. "Maybe even more than the tri-county area."

And that was a lot of people.

A light dawned in Lizzie's eyes. She pushed herself up onto the pillows a bit higher and motioned for Bethel to call again. "Get Amanda back on the phone," she said. "We're looking at this all wrong. We don't need to know if they were at the Summerses' place. We need to know what calls went out that morning. If anyone in the county could be guilty, let's go out and find them."

CHAPTER SIXTEEN

*Don't ask the good Lord to guide your footsteps if you
aren't willing to move your feet.*
—Aunt Bess

New plan, Sissy thought on the way to work the following morning. Right.

The second call to the plumbing company yielded nothing but static and headaches, as Amanda kept getting interrupted by customers who were actually paying the company to do work. She looked and continued to look while Bethel held on and held on and the battery in Sissy's phone got lower and lower. Finally, it died altogether with no answer to their biggest problem.

But today Sissy had come up with a new new plan. If she couldn't get the invoice and she couldn't get the record of the calls to match up, the last thing she could do would be trick Earl Berry into revealing what was on the invoice. Who had been at the farm that morning? It had to be someone from that morning. After all, who went around watering their tomatoes holding an invoice from a week ago.

Nope, she had practically meditated on the issue, and she could visualize a man handing the invoice to Summers while he was watering his tomatoes. An argument breaks out and then a physical confrontation, a shoving match. Walt turns away, thinking the matter is done. The faceless, unknown man picks up the shovel, and wham! Walt Summers is dead.

More and more, as she thought about it, this became the truth. No matter the evidence they had against Amos. It didn't stand up to that one little detail. That one little piece of paper and who had handed it to Walt.

And as soon as Earl Berry came and plopped his keister onto stool number three to eat his morning eggs, she was going to put her plan into motion.

She didn't have to wait long.

Fortunately, the café was having a slow morning. Just one of those days, like Tuesdays tended to be. The Monday rush was over, and the push for the weekend hadn't yet begun.

Sissy grabbed the coffeepot from the warmer and made her way behind the counter where Berry was sitting.

"The thing I can't understand," she started as she refreshed the man's brew, "is why there was a plumber out at Walt Summers's place the day he died."

Subtle, Yoder. Real subtle.

Super. Already her plan was not going as planned.

He looked up at her with squinted eyes. "How'd you know there was a plumber out there?"

She shrugged, trying to recover her nonchalance. Well, not that she ever really had any. She had been trying for it, but her mouth got ahead of her on this one. "I figured there was since Walt was holding an invoice when we found him. An invoice from Yoder Pumps and Pipes."

"Yeah," he said, easing back onto his stool. Until that moment, she hadn't realized that he had risen a little in place, not quite standing but not entirely sitting either. He went back down, but he looked poised and ready to pounce.

"Just makes a body wonder if the person who killed Walt works as a plumber." She hated to throw someone else under the bus, but she had to get Emma out of jail. If the girl wasn't going to retract her confession, then it would be up to Sissy to prove someone else had killed the man.

"The person who killed Walt Summers is in jail." This time he did relax. He was confident and positive that he had gotten his man—or, in this case, his woman. A young woman who shouldn't be in jail at all.

"What about the footprint at the scene?" Sissy asked.

She couldn't wait for Berry's answer. Across the dining room, a man waved her over, and she had to see what he needed. "Be right back," she told Berry, and took the coffeepot with her, just in case he wanted a top-off while she was there.

In minutes, she was back behind the counter and facing down Earl Berry. "Well?" she asked, "what about the footprint?" Size eleven muck boot.

The deputy just shook his head. "Signed confession," he said with a smack of his thin lips.

"Have you ever thought that she might be lying?" Sissy asked. She returned the coffeepot to the burner and propped her hands on her hips.

"Why would she do something like that?" Berry asked.

She could give him several reasons, but she needed him to discover them for himself. "Why indeed."

But Berry wasn't biting. And Sissy couldn't tell him the real reason without possibly implicating Amos. So she waited for Berry to come to his own conclusion. But the only thing he concluded was the conversation and his breakfast.

Another dead end.

"Sissy, phone's for you." Lottie handed her the cordless phone that belonged to the café.

"For me?" She took it with a bit of hesitancy. After all, who would be calling her on the café's line? No one she could think of.

It was after two, and she was mopping the front of the café in preparation to going home. It would be the perfect end to the workday.

"Hello?" A small flicker of hope had her imagining that it was Earl Berry and he had seen the light, but another male voice greeted her.

"Declan?" she exclaimed. "What a surprise."

"I didn't have your number, and I knew you worked at the café. So I thought I'd try you there."

"Well, you found me." Awkward. Was she forever to be a hopeless dork around this gorgeous hunk of a man?

He chuckled the sound rich and warm. "So I was wondering if you're busy tonight."

Sissy's breath caught. Perhaps she hadn't been as dorky as she felt. He wondered if she was busy? Heck no, she wasn't busy. And if she had been, she would clear her calendar for the likes of Declan Jones.

But was she ready for this? After Colt and his betrayal, was she ready to date again?

She didn't know, but she had a feeling that Declan wouldn't wait around forever. If she was going to have a chance at anything more than a casual acquaintance with him, she had to get back on that horse.

"No," she heard herself say. "Nothing going on tonight." After all, it was a Tuesday in small-town Yoder. But she kept that last part to herself. See? She was starting to cure her dorkiness already.

He sighed across the phone line. "I know it's short notice and all."

"Yes?" Her heart thumped in excitement. A date! A date with a gorgeous man. The first date since she and Colt had split up. Her first Yoder date. It was exciting.

"Well, my regular babysitter has some sort of stomach virus. It's Mom's birthday, and we have plans for supper. Would you be able to watch Hayley for me while we go out?"

"Hayley?" Did he have a dog or something? He hadn't mentioned.

"My daughter."

She should have realized he had said babysitter, not puppy sitter. But she hadn't known that Declan had a child. Why hadn't she known this? Why hadn't she been told before she made a fool of herself, even if only to herself. But still.

"She's four," he was saying. "And no trouble at all. I thought of you because of Duke. She would love to come play with him. I'll buy pizza," he said, obviously trying to sweeten the deal. "And maybe Gavin could come over too. Y'all are friends, right? And that way there will be someone there who Hayley already knows. Like an icebreaker."

Sissy closed her eyes. She was eight kinds of fool, but what else could she do? She'd already said she was available. "Yeah," she said, doing her best to hide her disappointment. Okay, so the truth was she wasn't really ready to date again, but when she had imagined that a man like Declan Jones had an interest in her . . . Well, what woman wouldn't want that? "Bring her over."

"Great," he said. "We'll see you at about seven."

"What's on your mind, girl?" Bethel asked as they pulled up in front of Amos Yoder's house.

"Nothing," she lied. There was too much on her mind to tell her aunt even half of it. Emma, Gavin, Declan, and Hayley. Then Lizzie and her babies, who, blessedly, were still content to live inside their mother for a while longer at least. And the tribe of Yoders who lived inside the two-story white clapboard house in front of them.

Her aunt made a noise that Sissy was certain she

used instead of calling her out on her fib and got out of the car.

They had decided today would be a good day to check on Amos and the younger Yoder siblings. It seemed like Emma had been in jail for an eternity, but since she had sisters who weren't that much younger than she was, Sissy figured the house would be much like they had seen it the first time— clean, neat, and organized. Everything caught up and in order.

The Amish tended to take care of each other. Even with three teenage daughters around, the church would have come to help. So neat and orderly was what they expected when they came to the house.

"Knock, knock," Bethel said as she pushed her way inside.

But instead of neat and orderly, they found the main room cluttered with toys, books, and shoes, while the kitchen was piled high with dishes.

The triplets—Amos, Abbie, and Annie—had been baby-gated into the living room, which had been stripped of any sort of breakable item. No knickknacks, candles, or low-hanging pictures. All three of them wore only diapers.

"Bethel?" Young Sarah Yoder, also known as Sissy to her siblings and extended family, smiled as she came up the staircase from the basement. "What are you doing here?"

"We thought we might come check on you," Sissy said. The original Sissy.

"What's happened here?" Bethel demanded.

Clearly nothing by way of cleaning and straightening.

"She's bossy." Sheba, Sarah-Sissy's fraternal twin, barreled up the basement stairs behind her and pushed past her sister. "She thinks she can tell everyone in the house what to do since Emma's gone, but it's not her place."

"Just because you are twelve and a half minutes older than me doesn't mean that you get to be in charge. I have better leadership skills."

Sissy looked around at the disaster that was a once neat-as-a-pin Amish home. "Apparently not."

Bethel glanced at the battery-operated clock hanging over the sink. "Where is Priscilla?"

Given the time, Sissy supposed that the middle daughters in the Yoder household were still at school, or perhaps just now on their way home. That would be good timing.

"Out in the barn, I think," Sarah-Sissy said. "She said she would rather take care of the horses than do housework."

With these two around, Sissy could see why.

"And your *dat?*" Bethel continued.

"In the field." Sheba waved away the words as if Bethel should have known all along. Yet, Sissy supposed, with the mess that they had walked in on, nothing was a given anymore.

"Get in here and do up these dishes." Bethel pinned a look on Sarah-Sissy.

"It's not my turn," Sarah-Sissy said.

"It is too." Sheba crossed her arms in a huff. "You keep telling me that so you won't have to do them. I washed them three days in a row," she proclaimed. "Three days in a row. It's your turn."

"Sheba, enough." The word was spoken quietly, but there was a thread of steel inside. Cousin

Bethel wasn't playing around. "Sarah, wash the dishes. Sheba, you start picking up all the toys and sweeping the floor. When your brothers and sisters get home, they can step up and help. I want this house spic-and-span by the time we're done."

Famous last words, Sissy supposed. It took over two hours to get the house in order. The dishes all washed, the floors all swept and mopped. It took so much time and effort that no one really had an opportunity to fuss about the cleanup. Or perhaps they knew that it was time to follow through.

Playtime was over.

"I'm leaving you in charge of it now," Bethel told the twins. "You two need to work together instead of against each other. Make Emma proud."

Tears welled up in Sheba's eyes. "I'm sorry." The words were directed at her sisters, but included the two of them as well. "It's just so hard without her here."

Bethel nodded. "I know. But the Lord willing, we'll have her back home soon."

They said goodbye to the family and walked out to where Sissy had parked her car.

"How are we going to do that?" Sissy asked. "Bring Emma back home?"

Bethel sighed as she climbed into Sissy's car. "Your guess is as good as mine."

"How do I get myself into these things?" Sissy turned from the mirror to see if Duke had any answers.

He just squirmed in place, burrowing down a little deeper into the coverlet on the bed before resting his chin on his paws and giving her that innocent-puppy look.

"You're no help," she told him, switching back to the mirror and deciding what makeup she should wear to care for a four-year-old. Truthfully, she shouldn't be worrying about that at all. Said four-year-old wouldn't care one way or another, she figured, but she was also dealing with two adult male cousins, and somehow she had the feeling both of them would notice.

The idea was probably laughable, but she imagined that if she put on too much of a face, Gavin would think that she was trying to impress Declan. If she didn't put on enough of one, she might never be seen by Declan as more than a potential babysitter.

She studied herself for a moment, she shook her head. She wasn't in Declan's league. He was all champagne and black Mercedes, and she was beer and rodeos. Neither one was right or wrong; they were simply different.

She gave herself a thin application of eyeliner, a touch of mascara, and a quick swipe of lip balm, and she was ready. Or was she?

Duke was on his feet and barking out a warning a mere heartbeat before a knock sounded at her door.

"Coming," she called. She shot Duke a pointed look. "We have guests tonight, and I expect you to be on your best behavior."

He barked again and wagged that little stump of a tail as if he knew exactly what she was saying. Sometimes, she truly believed that he did.

She opened the door to find Declan there, in a

suit, his dark hair swept back off his forehead and his smile as bright and spectacular as ever. It was almost enough to take her breath away, so instead she turned her attention to the little girl at his side. "Hi, there," she said with a big smile. "You must be Hayley."

The little girl nodded. "Is your name really Sissy?"

"It really is. When I was born, they were going to name me Elizabeth something or another, but my dad said that, since I had an older brother, everyone would just call me Sissy, so that should be my name. So I became Sissy Elizabeth."

Hayley looked up, her eyes wide with surprise. "My other name is Elizabeth too!" She seemed delighted that they had something so basic in common.

"Hayley Elizabeth?" Sissy asked. "That is a gorgeous name."

Hayley Elizabeth Jones was a miniature female version of her father. Half of her thick, dark hair was pulled into a ponytail at the crown of her head. The rest hung down her back nearly to her waist. Her eyes were that impossible blue and her smile as dazzling, with a dimple on one side. It was just a little bit crooked as well. Charming.

"You have a puppy?" Hayley stepped into the room hesitantly, but Sissy could tell that she wanted to rush over to the bed. Only good manners kept her feet in place. "He's so cute."

"He's actually a grown-up dog," Sissy explained. "He's just a small breed. Come on in. You can pet him, if you'd like."

She looked up at her dad, who nodded, and the

girl rushed into the room to meet the dog. "What's his name?" she asked.

"Duke," Sissy answered. "And he loves to be scratched behind his ears."

Declan mouthed the words "Thank you," though Sissy couldn't figure out what his gratitude was for. Being kind to his child? How could she not be?

"Hi, I'm Gavin. Not sure if we've met." Gavin gently brushed past his cousin and into the one-room apartment. He took the pizza box over to the kitchen area and set it on the two-burner stove-top.

"I've never been in here before," Declan said. "It's . . . cozy."

Again, she got the feeling that he was way out of her league. Not that he was condescending, but she could just feel the differences between the two of them. Differences she wasn't sure they could overcome, and it had nothing to do with the fact that she hadn't even known that he'd been married. And divorced.

No, she decided. He had to be widowed. What sort of woman would have left a man like Declan Jones? None. That's what kind.

"Thanks," Sissy murmured wondering what else to say to his observation. Even that felt strange.

"Okay, Hay." Declan squatted down to be on Hayley's level. "I'll be back in a little bit. You're going to stay with Uncle Gavin and Miss Sissy."

Whoa. Going to have to do something about that.

"Just Sissy is fine," she countered, not really wanting to interrupt father-daughter time, but not wanting to hear lisping Miss Sissy all evening either.

"Can we play games?" Hayley asked.

"Of course," Declan said, then he looked up at Sissy. "Do you have any games?"

"I, uh . . . have a deck of cards," she said apologetically. It wasn't like she had a bunch of visitors of any kind, much less ones under the age of ten. Or room to store such items.

"Great," Gavin said, opening up the fridge and pulling out the carton of grape juice she'd bought yesterday afternoon. "We'll teach her how to play poker."

Declan stood and shook his head. "Thanks," he told Sissy again. "There's a list of numbers in her backpack, in case you need anything. Otherwise, I shouldn't be more than three or four hours."

Four hours? What was she going to do with a child for four hours? She didn't even have a television!

And on top of that, what was she going to do with Gavin for four hours?

Sigh. She supposed she would figure out something. She always did.

CHAPTER SEVENTEEN

*Keep your words soft and sweet, in case you have to
eat them.*
—Aunt Bess

Sissy closed the door behind Declan and turned
back to the small child standing by her bed. She
was rubbing Duke's silky ear between her little fingers much the same way that Sissy herself did.
Duke was in heaven, eyes closed and breathing
steady.

"So," Sissy said, clapping her hands together.
She wished she hadn't. The sound was way too
loud in the tiny space. "What should we do first?"

"Eat," Gavin said. He was still standing in the
kitchen, the pizza box perched on the stove on
front of him.

"Sound good to you, Hayley?" Sissy focused her
attention on the little girl.

Hayley nodded, her dark hair bouncing. "Can
Duke eat with us?"

"Duke doesn't eat pizza," Sissy explained gently. "But he can sit next to us while we eat."

That seemed to satisfy the young girl.

"Just don't give him a bite, no matter how much he begs for it. He's just a little dog, and he has no idea what's really good for him."

Hayley giggled. "Okay. I won't."

Except there was no good place for all three of them to eat in the tiny space.

"Picnic time," Sissy said, making her way over to the closet.

"A picnic?" Hayley asked. "Are we going outside?" Her expression was one of hope.

"Inside picnic," Sissy corrected.

Haley's face wrinkled into an incredulous frown. "I've never had an inside picnic."

"Then you are in for a treat," Sissy said. "Your very first inside picnic."

"What do you want me to do?" Gavin asked, finally moving away from the pizza box.

"Come over here and help me spread out this quilt for us to sit on," Sissy instructed.

"Me too!" Hayley called. "I want to help too."

"You too." Sissy waved her over.

Somehow, with all three of them working together—actually, Gavin and Sissy were working together, while Hayley pulled the blanket at odd angles in an attempt to help—they managed to get the quilt spread onto the concrete floor at the end of the bed.

"Now what?" Hayley asked.

"Pizza!" Gavin cried.

"Yay!"

And so the evening went.

Hayley was a fun child, excited about life and being "out" for an evening.

Duke was more than content to have someone new to adore him.

Sissy still wasn't sure how she got wrangled into babysitting for a man she barely knew. When she said as much as they were playing Go Fish with the deck of cards Sissy had somehow thought to bring along when she moved to Yoder, Gavin just smiled and shook his head.

"My cousin has a way of getting people to do things for him."

"Maybe I should have him talk to Earl Berry about releasing Emma from jail."

"Jail?" Hayley's sweet face puckered into a frown. "There's a jail in this game?"

"No, sweetie," Sissy replied. "Do you have any threes?"

Hayley shook her head. "Go fish."

That's what it felt like trying to solve this murder and get Emma free. A game of Go Fish.

The week chugged slowly along, like a train on broken tracks. Sissy hadn't seen Declan since he had picked Hayley up on Tuesday evening. He had tried to pay her, but she waved away his money. It was bad enough to have the hots for a man and then have him treat her like the teen around the corner. There was no way she was going to solidify the relationship by taking his money. No, this way it was a friend helping a friend.

"I tell you," someone at the counter said on Friday morning. "It's a sad day when you can't trust a man to sell you the product he promised."

Sissy was going around refilling everyone's coffee and making sure that any other drinks were topped off, and the conversation was pretty much the same the café over. From the stools at the counter to the farthest booth, the talk was the same: Everyone was grumbling over Walt Summers's Special Blend and how it had changed.

"Last year and the year before, it was hit or miss," Delaney Talbot said. Delaney was a farmer from way back, according to Lottie, and the man looked to be older than the dirt he used to grow his crops. Deep wrinkles outlined his eyes, nose, and mouth. The grooves across his forehead were hidden from view when he was out on the street, covered by the brim of his large straw hat. It was the same kind the Amish men in the area wore, though Delaney was *Englisch* through and through. He was also a gentleman and pulled his hat off upon entering a building of any sort. Lottie joked that he probably took his hat off in the outhouse. It was funny, but Sissy figured she might be spot-on.

"That's right," the first man said. After refilling all the coffee and heading back to the waitress station, Sissy could see that it was Harvey Glick talking.

Harvey was Amish, though she figured that, given a small push, the man would go over to the dark side without hesitation. He straddled the line between Amish and *Englisch* and only stepped back firmly into his community when forced to do

Amy Lillard

so. Harvey liked to push the envelope on the *Ordnung* until it was bursting at the seams.

The *Ordnung*, as Sissy had learned since moving to Yoder, was a list of rules, some written, others merely understood, that the Amish community followed. It seemed the rules changed from community to community and maybe even church district to church district, but they were always in place. Harvey liked to see how many of those rules he could break or at least bend out of shape until he got his way on something or was forced to stop. More often than not, she felt like he should go back and change those ways, but she was only repeating gossip when she said that.

Yep. That was one thing her job afforded her. Her café job, that was. She was able to keep her finger on the pulse of Yoder. If there was a story to be told, it was relayed in the café.

"I guess it was nigh on three years ago when the mixture started to change," Harvey lamented.

"Four," someone countered. Les Detweiler, an ex-Amish farmer who shocked the community six years ago by leaving his church and converting his house to run electricity. Some say he wanted to use the internet to improve his farming knowledge, while others claimed it was a beef with the bishop that caused the break. Sissy figured the latter idea was right, seeing as how the man could have used the computers at the library over in Hutchinson to access the internet and not taken such drastic measures. And there was the small matter that the bishop was Detweiler's next-door neighbor. Thankfully for the both of them, *next-door* was a relative term in rural Kansas.

"Four then," Harvey conceded. Word around town was that Harvey felt that Les had sold out by "jumping the fence." That was a term that *Englisch* people thought the Amish people used to signify that they had left the church, though to her knowledge, Sissy had never heard one Amish person actually use the phrase. As far as Les and Harvey and their relationship . . . that part, at least, seemed to be holding true. "Four years, and there's been a steady decline in results."

A murmuring chorus of agreements rose around the immediate vicinity.

"Ain't nothing we can do about it now," someone called out. Sissy missed who said the words, but it was a fair bet that it was one of the farmers in attendance. And there were plenty of farmers in that morning. Not one of them was wearing their muck boots—Sissy had looked. Such was her luck. Or maybe word had gotten around town that a shoe print had been found at the scene of the crime and everyone was erring on the side of caution in the matter of town-acceptable footwear.

The farmers continued to grumble about the Special Blend, how it had lost its magic, how it really didn't matter any longer, seeing as Walt Summers was dead and wouldn't be making any more, and it was doubtful that anyone would be willing to use the buckets of stuff that he had left.

Sissy remembered the blue pickle-bucket-looking containers that lined the edge of his growing shed. There were certainly enough of them to go around, but after they were used, that would be the end of Walt's Special Blend.

"What we should do is take a bucket of it over to

the community college and have them analyze the contents. Then they can make some more," another voice piped up.

"Not this stuff. It's crap," Les said. His pun garnered him a few chuckles, but clearly not as many as he had been expecting.

"I have an old bucket," Jimmy Joe Bartlett rapped his knuckles on the table and stood, his excitement bringing a couple of farmers close to him to their feet as well. "It's not full, but it's got a little in it."

"Enough to test?" Someone called out from across the room.

"Yeah. I think so."

"What are we waiting for?" another man called out.

"Is this really happening?" Sissy asked Lottie.

The woman shook her head and handed back the non-farmer customer his change. "Thank you," she told him, then turned to Sissy once again. "Yup. They do something like this every so often." She checked her watch. "Maybe not about the same thing, but the principle, you know. I give it three more minutes before it settles down and everyone goes about their regular day."

Sissy looked out to the muttering crowd, which was growing more and more mob-like as each second passed. She did not have Lottie's confidence that all would be well in a few short minutes. But Lottie certainly knew the town better than Sissy did.

Still, when three minutes had passed, the line to pay was out the door. The farmers had used those precious minutes to scarf down the rest of their food, guzzle their coffee, and grab their order tickets to pay.

"What was that you were saying?" Sissy asked as Lottie did her best to ring everyone up and get them on their way.

"Hush, girl," Lottie said. "I'm trying to think."

Sissy chuckled and moved over to allow the older woman more room to perform her task. The farmers might be on a tear at the moment, but she fully believed Lottie was correct. They would settle down. Especially when they found out there would be a wait at the community college before they would know what was in the Special Blend of five years ago.

Still it might be interesting to know if there really was a difference in the soil. Then again, no one had made mention of comparing the two, only discovering what was in the soil additive of a few years back. Something to think about. All the farmers wanted now was to copy it for the future; they apparently did not care to see why the current Special Blend wasn't as effective.

Lottie rang up the last farmer, who trudged out the door behind all the others.

"You really think they'll go all the way over to the community college to have the soil tested?" Sissy asked as she watched the man leave.

Lottie closed the till drawer with a metallic jingle and a sharp click. "Girl, I don't think half of them know how to get there, and the other half will calm down once their food settles a bit."

"But it would be interesting to know what made the additive so successful."

Lottie propped her hands on her hips and shook her head. "You thinking about taking up farming?"

Sissy laughed. "Hardly. But it seems like it's all they can talk about. Maybe someone should compare the two."

"Land sakes, girl! Don't go giving them any ideas."

Sissy started to hand Gavin the bottle of beer but pulled it back at the last minute. "You won't get in trouble for drinking and riding, will you?" After he'd gotten off work, he had walked his bike the short distance between the *Sunflower Express* office and the Chicken Coop.

"Har har." He took the bottle from her and sat back against the foot of her bed. It was pretty much the same space he had taken up when they'd had their indoor picnic earlier in the week, but that time together wasn't something she wanted to bring up again. Mainly because she felt a little foolish, having thought that Declan might want to go out with her when he only needed a babysitter. Of course, Gavin had no idea that's how it all went down, but every time he looked at her, she felt like it was written on her face for all the world to see, including him.

Ridiculous.

"So where are you going again?"

Sissy perched on the edge of the futon and tried not to feel as impatient as she felt. For some reason, she didn't want to invite Gavin to the Yoders' Friday-night family supper. She wouldn't want him to get the wrong idea.

"To my aunt's house. We have a Friday-night supper."

He nodded and took a swig of his beer. "That sounds like fun. And you do this every Friday?"

Sissy nodded. "Every Friday."

He took another long draught of the beer, then pushed to his feet. "I don't want to keep you," he said. "I just thought I'd come by and see if you wanted to get something to eat. But if you already have plans . . ."

Something in his voice . . . that tone that said, *I didn't think you'd be doing anything tonight.* Something made her feel like she had betrayed him in some way. Which was crazy.

"You wanna come?" Who said that? Why was she inviting Gavin to supper? Just because he turned those puppy-dog sad eyes on her and—

And nothing. She was a softie, and that was all there was to it.

He hesitated for a split second, then shook his head. "Nah. I wouldn't want to intrude on a family event. Plus, I'm not exactly dressed for the occasion." He gestured toward his spandex cycling wear.

She waved away his concern, all the while telling herself that she needed to accept his excuse and stop trying to talk him into coming with her. "It's very casual. I mean, no one else will be wearing—" She gestured toward him. "But no one will care that you're wearing it."

"Your aunt is a good cook," he finally said.

"Yes."

"And I like your family."

"They are likable," she returned.

"And it would be good to see Lizzie again."

She had forgotten that the two of them knew each other.

"Sure," he finally said. "I'll do it."

Sissy nodded. "Okay, then. Let's go."

"Tell me again how it came to be that you brought a guest," Lizzie asked sometime later. "And a male guest at that."

Sissy had felt that all eyes were on her as she and Gavin walked into her aunt's house, carrying two containers of deviled eggs—Sissy's contribution to the meal.

"Yes," Lottie said. "I want to hear this again too." She waited expectantly for Sissy to continue.

"Y'all." Sissy drawled out the word until it would have reached from there back home to Tulsa. "It's nothing."

"He's cute," Lizzie said. "I never noticed it before, but he's kind of cute."

"Hush," Sissy admonished. "You're Amish. You're not supposed to care about such things."

"I only care about it for you," she sassed back. "So it doesn't count."

"You say he just showed up at your house and you invited him to come out here with you tonight?" Lottie's eyes twinkled.

"It's nothing," Sissy said again. She glanced over to where Gavin stood, drinking a glass of tea and talking to Daniel and another of their cousins, Thomas Byler. At least, he wasn't wearing all that skin-tight cycle gear. Gavin, not Thomas. Thomas had on his typical blue shirt and broadfall pants. Gavin had managed to talk her into following him to his house and allowing him to change into something more appropriate than his cycling wear.

Reluctantly, she had agreed, wishing instead she could take back the invitation for the very reason she was suffering though at the moment—her family was making too big a deal out of his presence.

"I've been trying to tell you," Lottie continued. "That boy's got it bad."

"He doesn't," Sissy said emphatically. She and Gavin were nothing but friends. And would never be anything more. They were pals. Chums.

Lottie just looked at her, and Sissy resisted the urge to get into a staring contest with the woman. First of all, Sissy wouldn't win. Too many staring contests with her brother had taught her that lesson. And second, it wouldn't prove anything. Lottie was going to think what Lottie was going to think, and that was all there was to it. Same thing for Lizzie.

"Whatever," Sissy said with a slight roll of her eyes. It was so refreshing that she could be such a mature adult about things.

But, thankfully, someone called them to eat, and the moment passed.

"I didn't realize that Emma was your cousin," Gavin said after they had filled their plates and gathered around Lizzie to eat.

Duke, of course, was stretched out across Lizzie's enormous belly and whined for small morsels. Sissy had asked for them not to feed him from the table, but she was fairly certain Lizzie had slipped him a couple of bites when she wasn't looking.

"She's a second or third." Sissy shrugged. "I can never keep those things straight."

Gavin laughed. "Yeah. Too many Yoders in Yoder."

Everyone chuckled, then went back to their meal.

"No wonder you want to find out who really killed Walt Summers," Gavin continued.

Sissy swallowed her bite of Lottie's almost famous mac and cheese, mentally counting up the astronomical number of calories she was taking in. "But it's proving to be an impossible task."

"Nothing's impossible," Gavin said, a determined light shining in his eyes.

"Last time we went to visit her, she admitted that she didn't kill Walt Summers," she told them.

"What?" Lizzie's screech was so loud everyone turned in her direction. Duke jumped off her belly and cowered in the corner of the couch near her feet. Daniel came rushing over, his plate dropped to the floor in his haste to see about his wife.

"I'm fine. I'm fine." Lizzie waved everyone away, but Sissy supposed it would be a good day or two before Daniel got all of the color back in his face.

"Please," he said, the words earnest and heartfelt. He didn't have to finish. *Please don't do that to me again.*

Lizzie settled back down on the couch, nodding the whole while. "I'm sorry," she told everyone. "I didn't mean to scare you. False alarm," she called. "Go back to eating your supper."

Daniel eyed her warily, as if she might be telling him what he wanted to hear instead of the truth, then made his way back to where he was talking with Lottie's son Jason and cousin Thomas.

Thomas had cleaned up the mess Daniel's plate had caused when it hit the floor, and someone else had made him another.

"Why didn't you say anything?" Lizzie hissed. Everyone had indeed gone back to their meal, though every now and again someone would look over just to make sure that Lizzie was still resting comfortably.

Sissy shrugged. "It doesn't change anything."

"It changes *everything*," Lizzie said. "It has to."

Gavin shook his head sadly. "Sissy's right. The deputy doesn't care because he's got a signed confession. The DA feels that it's a slam dunk and wants to go ahead with the sentencing as soon as possible."

"How can they do that?" Lizzie asked. "Doesn't she get a trial and everything?"

"Not if she pleads guilty," Gavin explained. "They'll just go to the sentencing."

"I thought these trials took years." Lizzie looked a little perplexed and a lot worried. "I thought we had more time than this."

Sissy wondered if Lizzie had been planning on joining the quest to find the real killer, even though she would soon have two newborns to take care of.

"Usually." Gavin shrugged again. "But not this time."

Lizzie turned to Sissy and clutched at her arm. "You have to do something," she said. "We can't just leave her in there to face this. You said she admitted that she hadn't killed him. Maybe get her to write it down too, then it can cancel out the other one."

Sissy shot her cousin a wan smile. "I'm not sure it works that way."

"It doesn't," Gavin said bluntly.

"Well, it should." Lizzie's tone was bordering on petulant. She turned to Sissy. "What are we doing to do?" she asked.

"*We're* not going to do a thing," she said emphatically. "You're going to lie there and grow babies, and I'm going to cut us all a slice of the refrigerator lime pie."

"Will you be serious?" Lizzie returned.

"I am being serious. You are too busy to help anyone get out of anywhere."

"But you'll do it," Lizzie wanted confirmation.

"I've been trying." Sissy stood and gathered up everyone's empty plates.

Lizzie grabbed her arm, holding in her place before she could make her way into the kitchen, where the desserts waited on the long wooden table situated there. "Promise me, Sissy." Lizzie's eyes blazed with intensity. "Promise me you'll do better than that."

CHAPTER EIGHTEEN

The man who rows the boat rarely has time to rock it.
—Aunt Bess

What could she do but promise Lizzie that she would do everything in her power to get their cousin out of jail?

"What are you going to do?" Gavin asked as they drove toward his house. The rest of the evening went as it usually did—good-natured ribbing, lots of conversation, dessert, and talk of farming and farming-related issues.

"I don't know yet."

They rode in silence for a few moments.

"Thanks for taking me with you," Gavin finally said. "I like your family."

"They're something, aren't they?" But she smiled when she said it.

Once again, silence descended into the space between them.

"I guess I never realized how many people have

a problem with Walt Summers. *Had* a problem," he corrected himself.

"It seems like half the town," she replied, then added, "Why? What happened?"

"Nothing. I was just listening to the talk. I guess your cousin Sally Jane Yoder married one of the Brubachers," he said. "I mean, I guess I knew that, but I just never made the connection. Anyway, Melvin Brubacher was telling us how their dairy farm sold their manure to Walt Summers. Then he just up and stopped buying it. The dad—I think his name is Laverne—went over to talk to Walt, but he said he'd found a different supplier.

"None of the Brubachers could figure out who it could be. No one local, since they are the largest dairy farm in the county. They would have more manure than, say, a regular ol' farm."

"I suppose," Sissy said, not quite following his story. What was he trying to tell her?

"That's why they started to sell their manure."

Suddenly, she remembered all the signs she had seen up at the dairy store, along with directions for how to pick up manure. She hadn't given it much thought because she wasn't in the market for manure. Not now and, most probably, not ever. So she hadn't looked at it that closely.

"That must have been a chunk out of their business," Sissy said. She turned onto the lane where Gavin's tiny house was situated.

It was a small neighborhood, like everything else in Yoder, just a handful of houses situated behind the Blue Roof Antiques Store across from the Quiki-Mart.

"Worse than that," Gavin said, "according to

Melvin. They had manure stacking up everywhere and no place to store it."

Sissy pulled the car into Gavin's driveway and turned slightly so she could face him in the dark interior of the car. Outside, a security light spread a glow around, but all it did was create shadows over each of their faces. "I don't understand," she said. "Why would you store manure?"

Even in the dimness, she could see the look he gave her. City girl, it said. "You can't just put manure straight on your garden or fields," he started. "I mean, you do know that people use manure to fertilize?"

"Of course I do." She resisted the urge to roll her eyes at him.

"Okay, so once you collect it from the barn or wherever, it takes about nine months or so before it can cure enough to be helpful."

"Like having a baby," Sissy quipped.

"Sure," Gavin agreed, though she was certain he only did so to keep her quiet while he finished his explanation. "But unlike a baby, there's no manure womb—"

"Ew," she said.

"You started it," he zapped back, then continued on. "Once Summers stopped taking their manure, they didn't have a place to put it. So they made some sort of deal with the horse farm across the road. They use horse manure in conjunction with the cow manure and store it on one of the horse farm's fields, where it's allowed to cure."

"So that's why there are all those signs in the dairy store about manure."

"Yes."

And that was just one more family that had a reason to want to harm Walt Summers.

"And I suppose they lost a ton of money in the process," Sissy said. Such a small town, and yet one man had so many enemies.

"Actually, no," Gavin said. "Turns out that not long after that, Walt's Special Blend changed, and people started looking for other fertilizers to use."

"Wouldn't that have put him out of business?"

Gavin shrugged. "Something like that would take a while. People have to get dissatisfied. Then they have to realize that the product is not going to change back and is not going to work properly ever again before they completely switch. Things move slowly in a small town."

Sissy nodded. "Well, thanks for the manure lesson that no one really wanted. I learned a lot."

"Cheeky," he said. He reached up onto the dash, where he had set his foil-covered plate when she pulled up in front of his house. Lizzie had insisted that, since he liked the refrigerator lime pie so much, he should have the rest of it. Gavin, being a bachelor as well as a known pie lover, couldn't refuse. "I just thought maybe it might help you in your quest to free Emma."

Sissy frowned. "Why would it?"

Gavin shrugged. "I don't know. Reporter's instinct." He shrugged again.

Then he stopped. Then everything seemed to stop. The moment seemed suspended. They were sitting there in the dark, so close together in her tiny car. She could smell the sweetness of the pie as well as the soap on his skin. Those two smells mixed with the detergent on his clothes and the light scent of clean sweat. And for a moment, just barely one moment, she thought he was going to kiss her.

It was beyond outlandish. Why would he kiss her?

And, in a flash, she remembered the kiss they had shared only a few weeks ago, standing on the sidewalk in the middle of town. He had kissed her and told her that it was to hide them both from a Mafia dude who turned out to be an insurance agent. Or maybe it was the insurance agent who turned out to be a member of the Mafia. Either way, it didn't matter, but the kiss. That was something she remembered.

"Good night," he whispered into the space between them; then he was opening the door and getting out of the car.

Sissy watched him walk up to his front porch with feelings of both relief and longing.

She really needed to get ahold of herself, she scolded the following day. She didn't say the words where anyone could hear them. She didn't want to have to explain what she was talking about, nor did she want to see the looks that deemed her way off-balance in an off-balance town.

But Gavin? Uh, no.

She must be spending too much time with just herself and a dog and Aunt Bess for company. Speaking of which, she had two columns to write tonight when she got off work. Last week had been something of a whirlwind, and she still couldn't figure out how. It wasn't like she'd done anything other than work and walk Duke.

Oh, and then try to save her cousin from the electric chair.

She shook her head at herself as she settled down on the futon to write.

She didn't even know if Kansas had the death penalty.

Even though Sissy had been in Yoder for a couple of months now, she still hadn't found her optimum writing venue. She was just one of those writers. The kind that a writer like Gavin might scoff at. She had a feeling he could write anywhere that he landed—like in a car or in a house or on a train or on a mouse. Or something like that. More places than she could, for sure. And she had yet to find her best place to write in the itty-bitty Chicken Coop.

She sighed and turned to the side, hoping to get more comfortable and find her muse in the same motion. All she managed to do was disturb Duke, who didn't have the same problems finding a place to nap as she did to write.

It was just that she couldn't stop thinking about the manure talk she and Gavin had had the night before. Not that she particularly enjoyed talking about excrement and turning it into compost. But there was something about the whole conversation that had a niggling memory tickling at her brain.

Maybe something that someone else had said sometime before. Maybe her father? Probably not. He had quit farming years ago. But maybe he had said something about his garden?

She sighed and put her computer aside. She swung her legs back to the floor and reached for her phone. She was having more than her share of trouble concentrating, and she knew better than to fight it. It was best to call her father, get it out of her system, then start again in a bit.

"Hey, puss," her father greeted her when he answered. "What are you doing calling your old man on a Saturday night?"

"Oh, not so old," she said in return. "And you know what Saturday nights are like in Yoder."

He chuckled. "Yes, I do."

They shared a moment of laughter, then Sissy got down to business. "Do you remember a couple of years ago, something about manure compost?"

"You want to be a little more specific?"

"Do you really have that many conversations about manure?" she asked.

"Welcome to adulthood," he quipped.

"Okay," she said. "Let me see. You or someone you know had a problem with their garden, and they traced it back to something to do with the compost."

"Yeah," he said. "It was Gary Anderson at the end of the block. He grows roses, you know."

She didn't, but saying so would only prolong an unnecessary conversation about Gary and his roses. "Right," she said. Not a lie and enough prompt for her father to continue.

"He bought what was supposed to have been some organic soil supplement for his garden. Rose and tomatoes."

"Uh-huh."

"I guess he used it because he came down and

said that his roses and his tomatoes both were twisting and growing strangely. He couldn't figure out what it was and what had caused it. He had planted the roses years ago. And the tomatoes were from his own seeds, and they hadn't grown that way before. The only difference was the soil additive."

"So did he ever figure out what caused it?" she asked. She thought about Jimmy Joe Bartlett's stunted sunflowers. Not exactly the same problem, but maybe related.

"He traced it back to a farmer who used a pesticide on his hay and then fed it to the cows."

"The same cows he took manure from to make the additive?"

"Right. But it seems that the pesticide can continue being effective even through three stomachs and—"

"Got it," Sissy cut him off.

"Why are you asking all this?" he wanted to know. "Are you working on a story about gardening?"

"No." She was working on a story about online dating and sharing recipes with people at parties. Okay, not a story, but a letter of advice on not taking everything posted on an online dating site at face value and the stubbornness of some people who refused to share recipes with others at dinner parties.

"Uh-huh . . ." He waited for her to continue.

"Emma Yoder," Sissy started. "Amos's daughter," she clarified, since Emma had been born long after James Yoder had left the small Kansas town.

"Yeah, Amos," he said.

Sissy went on to tell her father the entire story about Emma and Walt Summers. She hadn't mentioned anything about Kevin the milkman, but at the time, she hadn't wanted to worry her family. Especially her mother, who would have sent her brother, Owen, up to bring her home. She wasn't ready to start her new life yet, and Yoder was proving to be the perfect place to hide out.

Well, almost perfect. Random murder aside.

But the story in itself might be enough to convince Mary Yoder that her heartbroken daughter ought to return to Oklahoma.

"Don't say anything to Mom," Sissy finished. "I don't want her to worry."

"Of course not." But her father's voice sounded a little choked.

"She already knows," Sissy guessed.

"Well, maybe," James Yoder returned.

"I'm on speaker phone."

"Yes," James admitted.

"Sissy," her mother's voice grew louder as she apparently approached the phone itself. "Now, don't you worry. You just pack a bag and come on home. We'll take care of the rest of your stuff next weekend."

"I'm not coming home, Mom. Lizzie is going to have those babies any day, and I want to be here to help."

"Now, sweetie, I'm so glad you're up there, reconnecting with your family. But you can't run away from your problems."

Wanna bet?

"I'm not running away," Sissy said instead.

"You need to get back home, where you belong,

and start looking for a job. Café work is honor-
able," Mary continued, "but you have a degree in
journalism that's just collecting dust."

But Sissy heard what her mother really said—we
left Yoder to give our children better lives. How
can you live better if you move back there?

And then, of course, she heard it: Owen is the
best. Owen never gives us any trouble. You need to
be more like Owen.

Sissy sighed. "I gotta go," she said. "Someone's
at the door. Bye."

"Sweetie, even in a town like Yoder, you shouldn't
answer the door this late—" But Sissy had hung up
the phone and cut off whatever it was her mother
was saying. Like Sissy hadn't heard it all before.

But, at least, she had cleared her head about the
manure issue. Now she just had to tackle online
dating. Yeah, piece of cake.

CHAPTER NINETEEN

He who has never done anything wrong has never done anything right.
—Aunt Bess

Sunday in a small town like Yoder ought to be a quiet day. A relaxing, on the porch swing with a cool glass of lemonade kind of day. Except Sissy didn't have a porch swing. Or a porch, for that matter. And she didn't drink lemonade that often. But she was looking forward to a slowdown. It felt like she had been zooming around all week. She supposed she had, but with no new clues on the horizon, she was looking forward to relaxing a bit. Catching up on some work and cleaning the Chicken Coop. Truthfully, as a city girl, that last part was really fun to say.

By lunchtime, she'd only had to dodge fifteen calls from her mother instead of the thirty that she had been expecting. Okay, so maybe not fifteen, but after seven Sissy had lost count, focusing instead on her Aunt Bess column instead of a lecture from her mother that she neither wanted nor needed.

No place was perfect, and there was plenty of violence in Tulsa. She was staying right where she was for a myriad of reasons, the first being she was right where she wanted to be.

That's right. She wanted to be in Yoder. The little town with its Amish vibe and its quirky residents was growing on her. She wanted to be there when her cousin had her babies, when Emma got out of jail—because Emma was getting out of jail—and she wanted to be around to see what might happen after that. Help her aunt find someone to take over her job. Maybe even start that book she kept saying she was going to write but had never managed to sit down and actually begin.

But, for now, she was content doing her Aunt Bess thing. Sissy might not have a front porch, a relaxing swing, or a glass of lemonade, but she did have an Adirondack chair, a small front yard, and a Diet Coke. It was all good.

Her phone buzzed again.

Sissy looked up from her computer screen to see who had called. It was more of a knee-jerk reaction than anything. She knew who it was: her mother. Because Mary Yoder hadn't managed to talk her daughter back home, and she wasn't giving up yet.

But the name on the phone screen read: BETHEL.

Sissy about dropped her computer onto the ground as she scrambled to answer it. "Is it the babies?" Her voice was breathless, her excitement palpable.

"Hello to you too," her aunt drawled.

Her voice was too calm, too even. Sissy forced herself to relax. Bethel wouldn't be that relaxed if Lizzie had gone into labor.

"What's going on?" she asked instead.

"I think we should go check on Amos and the kids."

"Today?" She looked back to her computer. In her haste to stand, she had closed it and placed it on the packed-dirt drive to one side of her chair. She still had a few things that she needed to finish up. But it wouldn't take too long.

But since she had spent the morning writing and dodging her mother's calls, she hadn't managed to clean any of the Coop.

It was a tiny space, and a tiny space was easier to keep up, right? Wrong. A tiny space got cluttered quicker than a wink, and since there was less space when a person came in from outside, there was less space for leaves and grass and such to be dispersed. Her little haven was starting to show the wear of her everyday trips and investigation into Walt Summers's murder and doing what she could to get the innocent Emma out of jail.

"*Jah*, today."

"But I thought you couldn't do things like that on a Sunday."

"Check on a family member?"

"Clean someone's house."

Bethel almost chuckled. At least, that's what it sounded like. Sissy pulled the phone away from her ear and stared at the screen for a moment, just to make sure she still had her aunt on the line. Yep. BETHEL.

"I'm not going to clean the house. I'm going to make a list of everything that needs to be done and leave it for the girls to execute."

"Good plan," Sissy said. "But wouldn't it be better to do that tomorrow afternoon on our way home?"

"I want to go by and see what's happening at the Summerses' farm," her aunt admitted.

"Why didn't you just say that?"

She could almost hear her aunt shrug. "I wasn't sure you'd go for it."

"Of course," Sissy said. She started to pick up her stuff from the chair. She still had work to do, but writing outside had proven to be more distracting than she had anticipated.

"I've heard word that there's been some new construction next door. I just want to see what those two are up to."

"Those two?" Sissy asked. Surely she wasn't talking about Walt and Justice. Surely not. Because Walt was dead.

"Mary Ann and Sally," her aunt clarified.

"They're up to something?" Sissy asked.

Bethel sighed, the sound heavy as it traveled the phone line. "Get here and get me, and we'll find out together."

Seriously, she was starting to feel like her aunt's pet. First, Bethel didn't like riding in her car. Now

Sissy supposed her aunt had gotten used to it because she was constantly coming up with places for the two of them to go.

Not that she minded picking up her aunt on a whim. Not when it got her out of housework, allowed her to get Duke out of the house, and wasn't keeping her from meeting a deadline. Check. Check. And check.

But there was no such thing as a quick trip to her aunt's. First, she had to stop and go in. She had to visit with Lizzie and let Lizzie visit with Duke. Sissy didn't mind, truly. She only hoped that, if she ever found herself on some type of bed rest, someone would do the same for her.

Finally, after forty minutes of petting, smooches, and half-truths about where they were going, Bethel and Sissy set out.

"Wait," Sissy said once they had driven to the end of the lane. "Isn't it against the *Ordnung* to ride in a car on Sunday?" She had heard that somewhere. But where? Someone had told her maybe. Or a documentary. Or maybe the internet. Wherever it had come from, it had decided to make itself known once again.

"You can if it's an emergency," Bethel said.

"This is an emergency?" She paused, her foot on the brake and her hand on the gear shift, just waiting to shift into reverse and take her aunt back home.

"It is if I say it is." Bethel crossed her arms and appeared to dare Sissy to counter her words. When she didn't, her aunt gave a self-satisfied nod. "Now drive."

Bethel only ducked out of sight once, and that was when they passed the discount market. Weird, because it was closed on Sunday. But when Sissy looked over to see who her aunt was hiding from, she saw Tammy Elliott standing in the parking lot, as if waiting for a ride.

"What are the chances?" Bethel grumbled as she hunkered down in her seat.

"Not sure."

"I mean of all people, the biggest gossip in Yoder—*Englisch* or Amish."

Tammy was exactly the kind of person who would see it as her duty to inform the bishop about any wayward activities of his flock.

Sissy secretly suspected that Tammy wished she was Amish. Strange how some people saw the charm in Amish life, a life they weren't destined to live, while others who were born into the fold found their joy outside of it. Regardless of what was presented in the movies and the ridiculous reality television shows and even the plethora of romance novels concerning the Plain people, it wasn't easy to become Amish if you weren't born Amish. Not impossible, but very, very difficult. Tammy was the kind of person who understood that difficulty and lived her life on the fringes. She dressed fairly plain, wearing only solid color shirts and long denim or khaki skirts. And Sissy meant long, like to-the-ground long. She had never cut her hair that anyone in town had heard of, and she covered her wound bun with a bandana. She owned a car, but more often than not caught a ride with someone else when she wanted to go anywhere. If that made her happy, then Sissy was all for it.

Still, she knew that Tammy's busybody ways were something of a challenge for the Amish people in the area, if only because they couldn't bend any rules and get away with it. Not if Tammy was around. And she always seemed to be around.

"She can't see you now," Sissy said, checking the rearview mirror. They were off the main road, headed back into the farmland, but she looked to make certain.

"Whew." Bethel straightened back up in her seat and pulled down the mirror to check her reflection. She had flung herself nearly onto the floorboard in order to hide from Miss Nosy and had knocked her prayer *kapp* askew. She straightened the covering, then flipped the tiny mirror back into place.

"Emergency, huh?" Sissy teased.

Bethel raised her chin at that stubborn angle she seemed to prefer for most everyday occasions. "It is if I say it is."

Sissy managed to hold in her chuckles and merely shook her head at her aunt's antics.

"Well, it looks like they got the septic tank in." Bethel gestured toward the Justices' house on the corner. It was a beautiful property, with trees lining one side and separating it from the road. It was a winding trip to snake back to the house, but Sissy was certain it afforded the Justices a bit more privacy than if it had not been set up that way. "Pull over."

"Like right here?"

"*Jah.* Right here."

Okay, so when her aunt had said that she wanted to see what Sally Justice and Mary Ann Summers were up to, she hadn't thought that her aunt meant really what they were up to. Sissy had imagined a buzz through the area on their way to Amos's house to see if much had changed. Sissy's car was bright enough and very noticeable without pulling over and parking for all the world to see.

From the back side, where they were, the houses looked still and quiet. But it was a Sunday. The little wooden stand where Walt Summers had sold his tomatoes was gone. Surely the To Die for Tomatoes weren't a thing of the past. But if Walt wasn't there to grow them, who would?

Maybe Justice?

Sissy pulled to the side of the road, opposite where the houses were.

Her aunt glared a bit as she unfastened her seat belt. "Could you have gotten farther away?"

"I was trying not to be seen."

Bethel harrumphed and got out of the car. "Like there's any hope of that."

Sissy decided to let that go and instead cut the engine and got out as well. She unhooked Duke from his car seat. He barked happily, then licked her face as she hushed him. "We're going on a bear hunt," she told him.

Her aunt looked at her as if she had lost her mind.

"It's from a song." A children's song, but she didn't have to tell Bethel that.

"Come on." Her aunt hooked one arm over her shoulder and motioned for Sissy to follow.

"What are we looking for?" Sissy asked, as Duke trotted along beside her.

"I just want to look at where they put that new tank in."

"Because?" she asked.

"I don't know. Just wondering about it. Have been for a while."

"I know it's a small town, but really? You don't have anything better to do than worry about someone else's septic tank?"

Bethel ignored that. She pointed to the yard where the plumbing company had been digging the week before. "See all the dirt there around the edges?"

Sissy nodded. There was a good foot of dirt between where the tank had gone in and where they had replaced the sod in the center of the space. "What does it mean?"

"Not sure, except that's a big hole to dig to put in a smaller tank."

Sissy stopped and studied the scene before her. "Who said they put in a smaller tank?"

"One of the guys from the plumbing company."

"Why'd they put in a smaller tank?" Sissy asked.

"Your guess is as good as mine," Bethel replied. "And what's that there?" She pointed to a mounded line of dirt that stretched all the way from Weaver Justice's yard clear into that of Mary Ann Summers.

"Wait . . . we saw that McDaniel fellow in the Carriage House the other day. He said that they had run into some problems," Sissy exclaimed, suddenly remembering the conversation between Gavin and Vern McDaniel.

"What sort of problems cause that?" her aunt asked.

"Gas line?" Sissy guessed. "Maybe they hit some sort of gas line and had to dig all of it up. I know they are always talking on the radio about calling before you dig and that sort of thing."

Bethel shot her a look. "I don't think they were talking to the plumbing companies. Besides, see that line of yellow flags?" She pointed toward the shin-high markers that stretched from just this side of Weaver's storage shed to the road behind them. "That's where the gas line is."

"I don't know then," Sissy admitted. "Honestly, I've never had to deal with anything like that. Dad has sometimes, when he's gardening. I remember when he put in that apple tree in our backyard, he called someone then."

"And Yoder Pumps and Pipes would have called someone too."

Sissy gazed around the yard, doing her best to take in all the details, to look at it as if she had never seen it before. But all she could think about was the digging it took to replace a septic tank and whatever else they had to fix that caused the trail of mounding dirt from one yard to another.

"Come on," Bethel said. "Let's go on to Amos's."

"You sure?" Sissy turned back to face her aunt.

Duke had dragged Sissy over to the edge of Walt's property as if he remembered that it was a place of great importance. He sniffed around as they had been talking, and now she tugged on her end of his leash to disinterest him in whatever was

left there. But he resisted. "Come on, Dukes," she
urged. He gave her an annoyed look as if she were
ruining all his fun. Then he peed on a clump of
grass and trotted merrily back over to where she
was waiting.

"I'm sure. Let's go."

Sissy secured Duke back into his seat, even
though it was a very short drive from the Justices'
place to Amos's. Then she got into the driver's seat
next to her aunt.

"Why would anyone take out one septic tank to
put in a smaller one?" Sissy asked as she started the
car.

Bethel shook her head. "That's not the strange
part."

"It's not?

"No," she said. "The weirdest part is that the old
septic tank hadn't been in the ground more than
four years."

"How do you know this?"

Bethel shrugged. "Yoder's a small town."

"I'll say. I don't even know if my neighbors *have*
a septic tank, much less when they put it in."

"Some of the guys were talking about it at the
café," Bethel admitted.

Sissy rolled her eyes and started the car. And she
thought she was a chronic eavesdropper. Truthfully, she was more of a talker. She asked questions,
delved into the heart of the matter. At least, that's
how she saw herself. Her aunt, on the other hand,
was quiet and observant. That's why they made
such a good team.

But if her aunt had known this all along, why
was she just now bringing it up?

"Because I just now remembered it," Bethel said as if reading her thoughts.

"What are y'all doing out here?"

They turned as an angry Mary Ann Summers came charging out of her house.

"I told you people to stay away."

That's when Sissy noticed the NO TRESPASSING signs that had been strategically placed in the Summerses' yard. There were enough of the signs that Sissy had to believe the concept meant a lot to the person who had placed them there: Mary Ann Summers. "There's no more tomatoes. I don't have a statement to give, and I don't want Girl Scout cookies!"

"Step on it," Bethel cried.

Sissy shoved the car into gear, throwing up dirt and gravel as she spun the tires before getting traction. The car lurched forward, but the motor caught. She stomped on the gas pedal and zoomed way in a cloud of dust.

She had the mental image of Mary Ann Summers standing in the middle of the road waving a hand in front of her face as the pair of them motored away. In truth, she couldn't see two feet behind them due to the clouds of dirt, but the image was satisfying.

"That was close," Bethel said. She looked back at the road behind them.

Sissy nodded. "Something's wrong with that woman."

Bethel dipped her own chin in agreement. "*Jah.* Who doesn't want Girl Scout cookies?"

If the situation hadn't been so tense, Sissy might have laughed. Instead, she cracked a tiny smile and navigated the narrow road down to Amos Yoder's house.

They had no sooner pulled into the drive when Sissy's phone rang. She cut the engine and checked the screen. BETHEL.

But, of course, Bethel was sitting right beside her. And the contact was actually the number belonging to the phone shanty at the end of the drive in front of Bethel's house. For the most part, the Amish in Yoder weren't allowed to have phones in their houses or barns, so instead they installed them in tiny sheds near the road.

Which could only mean . . .

She swiped the phone to answer it, and the panicked, yet happy voice belonging to Daniel's sister filled the car. "Sissy, it's Janet. Lizzie went into labor. We're on our way to the hospital. You and Bethel meet us there."

CHAPTER TWENTY

Life is what happens when you're making other plans.
—Aunt Bess

"And everything's going okay?" Sissy asked the woman at the counter. She was like a bulldog. Not in looks, but definitely in attitude. She wasn't letting anyone in who hadn't been properly sterilized, aka doused in a chemical bath and sprayed with disinfectant.

When she and Bethel had arrived at the hospital in Hutchinson, they had rushed up to the maternity ward to find Janet pacing the floor and wringing her hands. Daniel and Lizzie had gone back into the OR. It seemed that the babies'—or one of the baby's, Sissy wasn't sure which—heart rate had started to fall, and they were taking Lizzie in for an emergency C-section.

Of course, the couple was terrified, praying and hoping for the best, but terrified, nonetheless. Janet had been visiting with Lizzie when she had gone into labor and had made the trip to the hospital with them, mainly so Daniel could give all his attention to his wife and his wife could give all her attention to having babies. Janet had called them, arranged for a driver, and made sure Lizzie's hospital suitcase wasn't left behind.

But Sissy could tell, Janet was a little strung out because she could do no more. Like her, she wanted to do something—anything—to help the situation, but all they could do was wait.

"Will you come sit down?" Bethel asked. Her tone had taken on a sharp edge. Well, sharper than usual, and Sissy knew that her impatience was bothering her aunt. Probably because the more she asked what was going on, the longer it seemed like they had been waiting. And they had been waiting for-ev-er. Or at least forty-five minutes.

Before Bulldog Nurse could answer, a smiling Daniel came through the swishing doors to her left. He looked about ready to cry, despite his ear-to-ear grin. And he also looked a little green around the gills. Or maybe that was the lighting.

"She's fine," Daniel said. He was wearing green hospital scrubs and a fabric shower cap over his hair. He pulled the cap off and wadded it in his hands. "The babies are fine. Everything's fine."

Sissy slumped in relief, but not before she saw her aunt turn her gaze heavenward. Sissy knew she was sending up a prayer of thanks. She did the same as Janet grabbed her brother's arm.

"When can we see them?" Janet asked.

"In a few minutes. They're getting her settled into a room. Then they'll bring the babies in for their first feeding." He was still grinning like a crazy loon, and Sissy couldn't blame him. Even Bethel had stood in her excitement and was smiling like Sissy had never seen before.

She supposed that babies could do that to even the sternest of dispositions.

Monday, and all anyone could talk about at the Sunflower was Lizzie and the babies. Were they doing okay? How was Bethel taking being a new *grossmammi*? When would they get to come home? What were their names? And how much did they weigh?

Of course, Lottie had erased the chalkboard that listed the daily specials and printed all the pertinent info for every diner to read for themselves, but people still asked anything and everything that was listed and not listed.

Joshua Albert, three pounds ten ounces, and Maudie Rose, three pounds two ounces, were both doing fine. Right along with their *mamm*. They would have to stay in the hospital in incubators until they reached four pounds, and the doctors would decide then when they would get to go home. Until that time, Mamm and Dat would be staying close, which meant a hotel in Hutchinson after Lizzie was released. Lottie had also taken an old mayonnaise jar, one of those one-gallon jobs, and made a donation station for the new family. Already, it was filled with ones and change and a couple of fives. The generosity of the town never stopped amazing Sissy.

"When's Bethel coming back again?" Josie asked

just after they had closed and locked the doors for the day.

"She said she'd be back tomorrow," Sissy told her. Bethel and Daniel were going to take turns staying with Lizzie and the babies. Daniel needed to work all he could now, since the babies were here and piling up hospital bills, so he had asked for her help. When Bethel had said as much to Sissy, she just smiled and told her aunt, "That's why I'm here."

And it was. She wanted to help her family. And she had fallen in love with the little town. Café work not so much, but, at least, it gave her a good cover for how she paid her bills without having to explain her secret "day job."

"I suppose Emma will still be in jail when Lizzie and the babies come home." Lottie picked up one of the chairs and placed it seat down on the table-top. "I was sure hoping we could get that girl home before now."

"I know," Sissy said. She ran a pot of vinegar and water mix through the coffeepot, then went to stand closer to the dining area to avoid the smell. "But we've tried and tried to get her to tell the truth. Well, tell it to someone other than the two of us, and that is one stubborn girl."

Lottie slid another chair onto the top of the table and moved around to the next. "It's so obvious that she's not the one. I just can't see why Earl Berry can't recognize that too. That girl doesn't have a deceitful bone in her body."

Sissy shook her head and poured the hot vinegar water down the pop machine's drain. She started a clean water brew, then turned back to Lottie. "I'm going to have to disagree with you on that one. She's managed to fool Earl Berry all this time."

Lottie scoffed. "Like that's hard to do."

They finished the closing and all walked out together—Lottie, Josie, and Sissy.

"I'm going up to see Lizzie tonight. Anyone want to ride along?"

Josie shook her head. "I have a meeting." The four words sounded like a threat, and Sissy decided to not ask what sort of meeting she had. Some things she had decided—at least, where Josie was concerned—she was better off not knowing.

"Lottie?"

"Honey, I'd love to, but I ain't riding in that itty-bitty car of yours." She chuckled when she said it, but her words brooked no argument. "When are you going? You want to ride with me?"

"I thought I'd go up now." She had been thinking about it during the slow times of the day. She wanted to get some flowers and maybe a balloon or two, something bright and cheerful for Lizzie's room. She wanted her cousin surrounded by happiness. The babies were doing fine, but Sissy couldn't imagine what it would be like to have two babies and not be allowed to hold either one.

"You go on ahead," Lottie said, unlocking her sedan, her roomy, roomy sedan. "Maybe I'll see you up there."

Sissy nodded and hopped into her own car. She needed to let Duke out for a bit before heading to Hutchinson. But, first stop, flowers.

The florist shop had gone through a lot of changes since she had arrived in Yoder. The owner had moved away and sold the business to his sister and brother-in-law. Candy and Nathan Silvers were a great couple. Happy and seemingly happy to be providing the town with beautiful flowers and gifts for any occasion. Sissy bet that most of the flowers at Walt Summers's funeral had passed through Coming Up Roses, the new name Candy and Nathan had given to the place, though Sissy felt that Candy was probably responsible for the cutesy-cute name.

She parked in front of the shop, which sat off the highway right next to the Quiki-Mart, and went inside. The shop itself wasn't much different than it had been under the previous owners—a bank of floral coolers sat on one side, a collection of bows in every color imaginable tacked to the opposite wall, and a well-worn counter in the middle of it all. The place smelled of roses, carnations, and what she could only describe as the color green.

"Hi!" Candy greeted her with a smile worthy of the Miss Kansas pageant. "I wondered when I was going to see you today."

"Oh yeah?" Sissy asked. "Why's that?"

"A little bird told me that your cousin had her babies. I figured you'd be in to get her a little something."

"And you'd be right."

Candy's husband picked that time to come in from the back. "Hi, Sissy."

"Hey, Nathan."

"Look." Candy motioned for Sissy to follow her over to the set of coolers. "What do you think about this?" She opened one of the large glass doors and removed a bright bouquet of big full sunflowers, bright red Gerbera daisies, and dark purple tulips. "Now I know that it's not very 'Welcome, babies,' but I thought you would appreciate it."

"It's gorgeous." It was more than gorgeous; it was perfect.

"And then there's this." She set the flower arrangement on the counter and moved toward the entrance to the shop's back room. "Give me just a minute." She disappeared, and Nathan rolled his eyes good-naturedly.

"She's been working on this all morning for you."

"For me?" Sissy asked.

"She wanted you to have something special to take Lizzie. I asked her what she was going to do if you didn't like it, and she said she would just take it to Lizzie herself."

Sissy shook her head. "That's really sweet of her, but I'm sure I'll like it."

He smiled. "I think you will too."

About that time, Candy came out of the back with a dual set of scruffy brown teddy bears, one wearing a pink ribbon and the other wearing baby blue. They were bound together and were weighing down a balloon bouquet of various colors of pink and blue. Baby, but sweet. She loved it.

"Candy, it's perfect. I can't believe you did all this for me."

Candy blushed and playfully smacked her husband's hand. "You weren't supposed to tell her that."

Nathan just shrugged.

"I'm glad he did. And I love it all. It's just amazing that you did all this without me calling."

It was Candy's turn to shrug. "That's what a good businessperson should do: anticipate their customer's needs before they even know what they are. And in a town like Yoder, it's not as hard to do as it sounds."

Sissy nodded. "That makes sense." After all, it was a close-knit town, a sweet town where most everyone looked after their neighbors. There was a grapevine that would rival anything Marvin Gaye could come up with, but it kept everyone in touch with friends as well as enemies. It seemed Candy had decided to tap that knowledge to further her business. Smart and savvy. "I'll take them both."

The bell on the door behind her jingled. She took out her debit card to pay for her purchases and half-turned to see who had come in.

Declan Jones.

She almost dropped her entire purse on the floor. "Hey," she said. Truthfully, she didn't know what to say, not after she had practically made a fool of herself over this man. And she couldn't help but wonder if he was taking advantage of her schoolgirl crush or if he was oblivious to the effect he was having on her. At least, her greeting came out steady and strong.

"Hi, Sissy. Fancy meeting you here."

"I think I could say the same."

He gave her that killer smile. "My secretary's birthday is tomorrow. Candy here is going to deliver some flowers to her."

Sissy wondered if it might not be easier to have

flowers delivered from a florist in Hutchinson, but she wasn't about to take business away from the couple.

Then Declan continued. "Candy makes the best arrangements, so it's not hard to pay that extra to have them delivered in Hutchison."

"Thank you." Candy's color deepened at the compliment. She handed Sissy her receipt. "Do you need some help to the car?"

Sissy looked to the two arrangements. It might be tricky to balance them both and unlock the car. "No biggie. I can make two trips."

Candy opened her mouth to protest, but Declan cut her off. "I'll help you. Give me one minute." He took out his credit card and waited for Candy to ring up his secretary's birthday flower arrangement. Once he had the receipt, he thanked them, grabbed the balloon bouquet, and headed for the door. Sissy took up the flowers and followed behind.

"I take it you're going somewhere tonight?" he asked as she unlocked the Fiat.

"My cousin had her babies."

"Twins, I take it," he said, eyeing the colors of the balloons.

"Yes."

"Oh. So you're busy."

Why did he sound disappointed? Was he disappointed? How was she supposed to know? Had he been about to ask her to go somewhere that evening?

She mentally shook those thoughts away and looked from the balloons to her tiny back seat.

"How are you going to get all these in there?" he asked, as if he was repeating her own thoughts.

"I don't know." The trunk wasn't much better. She just hadn't thought of this when she had bought the large gifts. Or maybe it was the small car. A combination of both?

He snapped his fingers. "I've got an idea."

"Yeah?" She was up for about anything right at the moment if it would get her and the beautiful, whimsical gifts to the hospital. "What's that?"

"We take my car."

"What?" Had he really just said that?

"My trunk will hold all the balloons; the flowers will easily fit in the back seat with us in the front."

"You want to drive me to the hospital? In Hutchinson."

He shrugged in that nonchalant-yet-uber-confident way of his. "I wanted to take you to dinner, but this will have to do, I suppose."

She almost dropped the flowers at that. Thankfully, she managed to keep hold of them. He wanted to take her to dinner? And here she just thought she was his babysitter-in-a-pinch.

"You wanted to take me to dinner?"

"I want to, sure. To say thank you for helping me out the other night."

So she was just his babysitter. But the way he'd said take her to dinner . . .

But now he wasn't taking her to eat. No dinner, just a quick trip to see her cousin. What was wrong with that?

Nothing. Not one thing.

* * *

Declan went over to his mother's house while she saw to Duke, then took a quick shower. Then she pulled the first thing she could lay her hands on out of the closet and put it on. She wasn't going to read any more into this than necessary. Maybe even less. He wanted to thank her for babysitting. Those were his words. It wasn't like he was dying to share a meal with her. She had to get a handle on her feelings while she still could.

They talked about nothing and everything on the way to the hospital. As he had assured her, the balloon bouquet fit nicely in his trunk and left his rearview vision unobstructed. She had put the flowers in a box and set them on the back seat.

The more they talked, though, the more she started to look for the likenesses and the differences between Gavin and Declan. A full-on comparison was grossly unfair. Declan looked like an ad in *Maxim*, while Gavin was the poster child for Geeks 'R' Us. But not in a bad way.

Still she couldn't help but look at Declan and see if there was any Gavin there at all. What she discovered was, at a certain angle, their smiles were the same, And something in the way that Declan tilted his head when he laughed brought Gavin to mind. In fact, that's what had started the entire exercise.

They arrived at the hospital, and Sissy was grateful to have Declan's help taking everything in.

They decided to stop by the nursery and take a quick look at the babies, but since the newborns were in the NICU, they had a special room and couldn't be seen. So, on they trekked to Lizzie's room.

She was sitting up in her hospital bed when the two of them walked in. Bethel had most likely gone home for the day, and Daniel was dozing in a nearby chair.

"Hi," Lizzie said, looking from Declan to Sissy, unasked questions floating around like pesky gnats.

Declan reached out a hand and shook hers. "Declan Jones," he said in that confident way he had. Not quite James Bond-y, but close.

"Lizzie Schrock," she said in return. "Sissy's cousin."

He smiled, that quirk of the lips that was reminiscent of Gavin. "I've seen you around town."

Her eyebrows shot up so far Sissy thought they might get caught in her hair. "You live in Yoder?"

"My mother does."

Lizzie nodded, and Sissy could almost see her trying to remember if she'd gone to school with Declan. How could she forget a face like that?

"I went to school in Hutchinson. My mother moved into my grandmother's house when she passed."

Lizzie nodded, not at all ashamed that he had read her mind and answered without the question even being asked. "That's why I don't remember you."

There came that smile again. "I wasn't very memorable back then."

Sissy didn't believe that for a second.

At the sound of their voices, Daniel stirred,

wiped the sleep from his eyes, then shook Declan's hand as well.

"How are you feeling?" Sissy asked, her words cut in half by a loud buzzing noise.

Declan pulled his phone from his pocket and grimaced as he looked at the screen. "I've got to take this."

Lizzie waved him away. "Of course," she said.

Sissy just watched him go, still amazed that he had brought her to the hospital in the first place.

"So," Lizzie said, turning a bit in the bed and wincing as she did so. "They don't tell you that they're going to sew your belly to your knees after they take the babies."

"That bad, huh?"

Lizzie smiled, that secretive loving smile of a new mother. "Have you seen them?"

Sissy shook her head. "They have them in a special room away from the other babies."

"They're so tiny," she said.

"But perfect," Daniel countered lovingly.

"We're so blessed."

Sissy took Lizzie's hand and squeezed her fingers. "That's true."

Daniel just smiled, happy that his family was fine and whole. Thankful for their good fortune and blessings from above.

"So what about?" Lizzie inclined her head toward the hospital room door. "Are you going out?"

Sissy shook her head. She wasn't about to tell Lizzie about the babysitting fiasco. And how she continually seemed to misread Declan.

"What about Gavin?" Lizzie asked.

And, of course, Declan picked that moment to walk back in. "What about Gavin?" he asked.

Lizzie didn't miss a beat. "He's supposed to write the birth announcement for the paper."

"I'd be happy to give him all the details," Declan graciously offered.

"Thank you." Lizzie beamed while Sissy wanted to sink into a hole in the floor. But, of course, there wasn't one. Dang it.

"So how do you know Gavin?" Lizzie asked.

"He's my cousin," Declan explained.

Once again, Lizzie's brows shot north. "Oh, I see."

No, you don't! You don't see anything. Because there is nothing to see. But Sissy managed to keep those words to herself.

"Keep it in the family," Lizzie muttered.

But thankfully, Declan didn't hear.

CHAPTER TWENTY-ONE

If you know what you're doing, you're not learning a thing.
—Aunt Bess

"I didn't know I'd find a crowd here."

Sissy spun around as the hospital room door opened and Gavin stepped inside, carrying a bouquet of yellow balloons tied to a bouquet of daisies and roses.

Great. Just what she needed, the cousins together at the same time in the small confines of a hospital room. And then there was the small fact that she had driven here with Declan.

"Gavin!" Lizzie smiled, obviously enjoying the moment. Sissy would like to have said that her cousin was soaking up the attention, but she seemed much more interested in Sissy's reaction to the male cousins who had come to visit. "We were just talking about you."

"You were?" He passed by Declan with barely a

nod in his direction and took the arrangement
he'd brought and set it in the deep windowsill with
the growing number of offerings on display there.
He stopped briefly to give Daniel a quick nod and
congratulations before turning back to Lizzie.

She smiled a little too widely for someone who
had been through all that she had endured over
the last couple of days. "We were. I was telling Declan here that you had offered to write the birth announcement for the paper."

"I did." This time, he acknowledged his cousin
with a nod. It was formal and stiff, more of a jerk
than anything. "Declan. Sissy."

"I told her that I would give her all the pertinent
information, but now that you're here, I suppose
you can get it yourself." Declan's words held no
malice and yet sounded a little dismissive all the
same.

A knock sounded behind them, and a nurse
entered shortly thereafter. "Feeding time, Mrs.
Schrock. Are you ready?"

"I am." Lizzie's smile turned from cunning to
sweet. It was the one time she was allowed to hold
her precious babies. "Sorry, folks. I'm needed else-
where."

"No worries," Declan said. "I need to be getting
home anyway." He turned to Gavin. "Speaking of
which . . . now that you're here, would you mind
giving Sissy a ride back to Yoder? I really should be
getting Hayley from the sitter's, and it'll save me a
trip to and from."

Gavin cut his gaze to Sissy, and she felt her face
begin to burn.

She didn't know why she felt so on the spot, but she did.

"You drove here with Declan?"

"I rode more than anything." She gave a shrug. This was all she needed: Gavin acting weird over time she spent with his cousin.

Behind him, Lizzie mouthed, "I told you." But Sissy couldn't acknowledge the self-satisfied grin.

"The balloons I bought wouldn't fit in my car . . ." Sissy started.

"So I gave her a ride." Declan shrugged as if he had carted her two blocks instead of ten miles.

The nurse cleared her throat, a clear indication that they weren't moving fast enough. After all, there were babies to feed, and they were holding up the chow line.

"Right." Gavin's expression was unreadable, his eyes blank behind his dark-framed glasses. "Sure. No problem."

But now Sissy wasn't so sure that she wanted to ride back to Yoder with Gavin. That ten miles might stretch into an eternity.

The sun was just starting to set when they started back to Yoder. They had waved goodbye to Declan in the parking lot, then Sissy turned to Gavin.

"Wait. You don't have a car."

He shrugged. "I don't think Declan even considered it." He said the words as if that should prove some kind of point.

"How are we getting home?"

He smiled at her. "You're in luck. I brought my extra bike."

She frowned. "No, really. How are we getting home?"

She thought for a moment that he might say something more, but whatever it was fizzled out as a small SUV pulled up to the curb. The driver rolled down the passenger side window and leaned over toward them. "Gavin?"

"Arnold?" he said in return. He checked his phone for the picture of the driver as Sissy noted the sticker in the window.

"Lyft," she muttered under her breath, a bit relieved. "Of course." But that, of course, meant she wouldn't be totally alone with Gavin on the way back to Yoder. Surely, that would defuse the situation she felt brewing. Or maybe she was just imagining things.

They climbed into the back seat, and the driver offered them chargers for their phones and water to drink, and asked what music, if any, they preferred. Gavin opted for none, and Sissy cringed a little inside. No music meant more time to talk.

"So," Gavin started, just as they pulled out of the hospital parking lot. "You and Declan."

Sissy shook her head. "It's not what you think at all."

"I'm happy for you," he said. "For you both. Declan's been through a lot."

"It's not what you think," Sissy said again. "We're not seeing each other."

"You don't have to hide it from me," Gavin said. She couldn't quite read his tone. "You babysit for him. He brings you to the hospital to see Lizzie."

She opened her mouth to tell him that she hadn't been expecting to babysit for Declan, but explaining that would also reveal that she had thought for a moment that she and Declan were going on a date. And to talk more about the whys of him bringing her to the hospital tonight could possibly lead to her telling Gavin that Declan had said he wanted to take her to dinner tonight. "It's not what you think at all," she said again.

"So you say."

"So it is," she retorted so maturely. "I mean, I'm not going out with Declan. There's nothing going on between us, and if there was, why wouldn't I tell you?"

"Women have their reasons. Not that I understand them."

Sissy sighed. "I just got out of a . . . challenging relationship. That's why I came to Yoder."

"I thought you came to help your aunt and cousin."

Sissy wagged her head from side to side. "Does it matter?"

"And this challenging relationship—"

She held up one hand. "I am not talking about this right now. Just be advised that I am not in the market for a new relationship right now."

"Casual hookup?" Gavin asked.

She shot him a look. "Nor that."

"Just checking." He shrugged. "It's just that Declan is more of the casual hookup kind of guy these days."

"Why would you say that?" She half-turned in the seat to read his expression. "He doesn't strike me that way at all." Though she had gotten such mixed signals from him she wasn't sure if she was coming or going.

"There's only room for one lady in his life right now, and that's Hayley."

"Nothing wrong with that."

"I just don't want you to get your heart broken. Again," he added.

"That's sweet of you," she said, then searched for something . . . anything . . . to change the subject. "Why would someone who was putting in a septic tank dig a trench like fifty yards long and practically into another person's yard?"

"What?" Gavin shook his head, no doubt jarred by the quick change of subject matter.

Sissy wasn't sure why that was the first thing that popped into her head to talk about instead of Declan, only that maybe it had been lurking in her mind all along. "Why would someone—"

"I heard all that," Gavin said. "I just don't know why you're asking that."

"When Bethel and I were looking around at the Summerses' place, we happened to notice that the Justices—next door—had put in a new septic tank. But they had also dug some sort of ditch that led right up to the greenhouse over on Walt Summers's property."

"They dug it?"

"Whoever put in the tank did, I suppose. Whoever dug it, it's there."

"And it's open?"

Sissy shook her head. "It's closed up, but it's like a mound of dirt stretching between the two houses. You know, like when the gopher digs a hole in Winnie the Pooh."

He shot her a look.

"So much for male sensitivity," she grumbled.

"A mound of dirt," he repeated.

Sissy shook her head, then scooted onto the edge of her seat as far as her seat belt would allow. "Albert," she started.

"Arnold," the driver corrected.

"Right. Umm, Arnold, can you turn up here? On the left."

He shook his head. "The app tells me where I need to go."

"I know," she said. "But if you would stop for me, I will make it worth your while with a nice fat tip." She reached into her wallet. The smallest thing she had was a twenty. Whoever heard of a waitress without a pocketful of ones? In for a penny, in for a twenty, she supposed. Except she didn't have a penny either.

She pulled out the twenty-dollar bill, and Arnold just about started salivating on himself. "We can't stop for long," he said, then reached behind him to snatch the bill from her hands.

He slammed on his brakes and careened into the turn he had almost passed while she had been devising her plan.

"Now take the next left up here," Sissy told him.

"Where are we going?" Gavin asked.

The sun was dropping lower and lower in the sky, but it wouldn't be completely dark for a couple more hours.

"I want you to see what the dirt looks like over at Walt Summers's place," she told him.

"Okay, I know what the trail looks like when the gopher goes digging around on Winnie the Pooh. I was just being a tough guy and pretending like I didn't know."

"Well, we're already on our way." And she had already paid twenty bucks for this little detour. So he was looking at it.

He shook his head. "Fine."

They pulled around the back side of the fields. They hooked another left, which took them away from Amos's house and right up to the backyard of the Summerses' place.

Sissy pointed out the window, but the dirt trails weren't as mounded up as they had been before. In fact, from where she was sitting, she couldn't see it at all. Nor the place where the new septic tank had gone in.

"Not very gopher-looking," Gavin commented.

"I think they put down sod," Sissy said as Gavin opened his door and got out of the SUV.

"Where are you going?" Arnold and Sissy asked at the same time.

"I just want to get a better look at it." With any luck, that meant he believed her. At least, she was hopeful that he did.

Sissy looked at Arnold. She gave him her sternest, meanest stare, then pointed a menacing finger at him. Well, she tried to, anyway. "Don't go anywhere. We'll be right back."

He saluted her, and Sissy squinted her eyes one last time just for good measure before hopping out and walking toward the Justices' place.

"The dirt was humped up before," she said, as she got out and approached Gavin. He was inching his way toward the dividing line between the Justices' and the Summerses'.

"There's not even flat dirt," he said. But he was

following a line of sod. It zigged and zagged a bit, but it was still almost a straight line from the middle of Weaver Justice's all the way to where they stood now.

Instead of going to where the septic tank was planted, Gavin had turned and followed the trail of new grass all the way to the greenhouse.

The growing shed looked so different now than it had when she had seen it on that fateful day. And even in the times since. It almost appeared sad and dejected, as if it knew it would never be used again.

"What's that smell?" Gavin pulled the neck of his T-shirt over his mouth. "It smells like—well, I don't want to say what it smells like, but you know."

"I don't smell anyth—ugh! What is that?" As soon as Sissy got a little closer to the shed she could smell it. "It reeks like a . . . a . . . porta potty!"

"It smells worse than any porta potty I've ever been in."

She pulled the collar of her own shirt over her nose and mouth and shook her head. "Obviously you've never been to a rodeo and had to go really, really bad."

"That's it," he said. "I feel like there's more than one feces smell here."

She glared at him, still keeping her shirt pulled up to just under her eyes. "What are you? Some kind of a poop expert?"

"No, but animal poop and human poop have different odors, right?"

She took a step back, and then another, if only to get a whiff of fresh air, but she hadn't gone back far enough. "I suppose, yeah."

"Well, this smells like manure and regular human poop."

She really hadn't smelled it long enough to decide if he was right or not, and she certainly wasn't willing to uncover her nose and mouth to test his observation. "So?"

He shrugged. "I don't know. It just seems strange."

"Maybe we're getting one smell from one place and the other from another."

He looked at her patiently and waited without a word for her to continue.

"Maybe the poop smell is coming from whatever this line here is and the manure smell is coming from the barrels of Walt's Special Blend." There were still buckets upon buckets stacked up along the far wall of the growing shed.

Gavin shook his head and ventured a little farther into the shed.

Sissy lost sight of him and winced, and she realized the only way to see him would be to follow behind him into the thick of the smell. "The things I do," she grumbled and reluctantly started after him.

"What are you doing here?"

Sissy turned as Bethel came striding up. She had left her tractor parked just behind where Arnold waited in his SUV. He caught Sissy's gaze when she looked out and tapped his wrist where a watch would be if he had been wearing one. But she knew what he meant. They had been there a long time. And they really should be going. But there were still so many questions that needed answering.

"Gavin is—" Sissy started, but Bethel had come close enough to smell whatever problem was located at the growing shed.

"What's that smell?"

Gavin came back out of the shed just long enough to quip, "I told her not to eat that second burrito." Then he ducked back inside, out of sight.

"Burrito?" Bethel asked.

"Ignore him," Sissy stated with a frown. "Doesn't matter."

"What are you doing in there?" Bethel came forward, raising the hem of her apron to serve as some sort of air filter as she peeked inside.

The smell was bad enough that she didn't want to take one step closer.

A honk sounded from the street. Apparently, Arnold thought she should be ready to go. After all, she wasn't moving forward, but she was not willing to sacrifice her lungs for curiosity's sake.

"Be careful," she heard Bethel say. Sissy could only see her back, as she blocked the doorway of the shed. It seemed that was as far as her aunt was willing to go.

From the street, another honk sounded. Sissy turned to wave for Arnold to stop, but he figured since he had her attention, then maybe she should come back and they could get going again. He laid on the horn, pressing down for one long wail of noise.

Added to that was the slam of the back door she barely registered over the din of the car horn.

"What are y'all doing back here?" Mary Ann Summers came storming from the house. She had a mop in one hand and a scowl on her face. "I've already told everyone in town. No more Special Blend."

Sissy's ears began to ring as silence filled the air. Arnold had taken a small break, it seemed.

"I'm talking to you." This from Mary Ann.

"What's going on?" She was joined by Sally Justice, who was striding across her own yard, though, Sissy noticed, she was careful not to step on the new grass that had just been laid.

Sissy scrambled to think of a reason for her to be standing in someone else's yard, when she heard her aunt call out. "Look out!"

A strangled yelp.

And then a splash.

CHAPTER TWENTY-TWO

If it looks like poo and smells like poo, don't go swimming in it.
—Aunt Bess

"Gavin?" Sissy called, then started toward the entrance of the growing shed.

Arnold honked three more times, perhaps for good measure.

"Hey, there!" Mary Ann shouted. "Stop!"

"You!" Sally added.

Sissy stopped. She turned to Arnold. "Stop." Then to Mary Ann and Sally. "Stop! Stop! Just stop!"

She must have summoned her *listen to me or else* voice because everyone did as she said. She sucked in a deep breath, hoping to calm herself—it didn't work—then started for the door of the shed once again.

Her aunt was backing out as she was trying to

get in. She could hear Gavin splashing around. No, that wasn't quite right. It was more of a squelching sound. Like getting your rainboots caught in the mud, then trying to coax them free.

"Is he okay?" she asked her aunt.

Bethel shook her head. "I mean, I think so. Gavin, are you okay?"

Sissy thought she'd stick her head into the building, just to see that he was alive and well for herself, but the smell coming from inside had doubled. And here she'd thought it couldn't get any worse.

"I . . . do you need help?" she asked. He was her friend, and if he needed help, then she would get him some. She pulled her cell phone from her pocket, ready and poised to call 9-1-1. "Do you need me to call the fire department?"

"Maybe you ought to call the police." At least, that was what it sounded like he'd said.

"What?" She took another step toward the doorway, then two back. Ugh! "Did you say call the police?"

"Call the police?" Mary Ann and Sally screeched.

Gavin said something else, but it was lost in the cacophony of noise coming from behind her. Arnold had started honking again and yelling into the fray something that sounded like, "Twenty bucks isn't enough to put up with this."

A slam like a gunshot exploded behind her, and Sissy turned to see Weaver Justice stalking out of the house, carrying a shogun in one hand, one gallus of his overalls hanging loose and dragging on the ground.

"What's going on here?" he asked. At least, she thought that was what he said as he stalked toward them.

"The police," Gavin said again. "It looks like Walt has been stealing Justice's . . ." The last word he said was impossible to make out.

"Stealing his what?"

"I ain't stole nothing!" Weaver Justice stormed up, brandishing his gun like a madman.

"I'm calling the police," Sissy announced. Dumb move. Every time that happened in a movie, she was all scornful that the person was letting their intentions be known, and now here she was doing the same thing in real life.

"Nobody's calling nobody." He pointed the gun at Sissy, leveled it right at her heart. At least, she thought it was pointed straight at her heart. At any rate, it was close enough to be too close. She immediately dropped her phone. Arnold was gone, and it was two against three. It might have been three against three, but she assumed it was two against three if Gavin was where she had begun to suspect he was. Down a rabbit hole . . . of sorts. That left her and Bethel against Weaver, Sally, and Mary Ann.

"Nobody's calling nobody," Sissy repeated.

The sun glinted off the oiled barrel of Weaver's rifle.

Briefly, so briefly, she wondered if she might be able to kick her phone over to her aunt and have her call 9-1-1, but knowing her luck as of late, the plan would fail miserably in some dismal way. Like she would crack her screen, break her toe, *and* get shot, all in one smooth move.

The strangest part of all was that she still didn't know why she was being held at gunpoint.

"You don't have to point that at me," she told Weaver in her calmest voice. "I had nothing to do with any of this."

"You've done nothing but cause trouble since day one, coming out here and snooping around. Knocking on doors and running down clues. You should have left well enough alone." He spat, and to Sissy the action looked a little closer to off-kilter than she would have normally preferred.

"Emma Yoder is innocent," she said the words softly, with a small lilt of quiet understanding in her voice. She was definitely channeling her mother, for it was what Mary Yoder called her first day of class teacher's voice.

"Girl, you think I don't know that?"

It took a moment for the words to truly sink in. If he knew that Emma was innocent, then that meant he knew who the killer was. And if he knew for a fact who the killer was then—oh . . .

"You killed him?" She hadn't meant to say the words out loud. But there they were.

"What?" Mary Ann and Sally turned to Weaver, as if they were only now seeing him for the first time.

"You killed Walt?" Mary Ann blinked at her longtime neighbor.

"I suspected as much." Sally Justice shook her head.

"You did?" Mary Ann turned toward her friend.

"You did?" Weaver turned to his wife.

"Wait," Sissy called. "Why?"

"Well, he'd been acting funny for a week or

so—" Sally started with an offhand shrug as if they were talking about the weather and not a man's life.

"No." Sissy turned to Weaver. "Why did you kill Walt Summers?"

He grinned at her. Or maybe it was a grimace. "I never said I did."

Gavin picked that moment to come out of the growing shed. "Because Walt had been stealing your sewage out of your septic tank without your knowledge."

"It may have just been shit, but it was my shit."

O-kay.

Sissy looked to Gavin. He was covered from the chest down in dark, stinky sludge.

"Is that—"

He shook his head. "Don't ask."

Right.

A shot rang out, loud and reverberating.

Sissy stuck her fingers in her ears and turned back to Weaver. "What are you doing? Trying to make us all deaf?"

"I said, it may have just been sh—"

"We heard what you said." Sally slipped one arm around Mary Ann's shoulders and pulled her into a sideways hug. "And you're not going to get away with this."

Sissy gently kicked her phone in her aunt's direction, but Bethel was closely watching the scene that was playing out before her.

Weaver dropped his still smoking rifle, butt end down on the ground next to him. "What do you mean? That man cannot get away with stealing my shi—"

"Yes, yes, we hear you," Mary Ann said. "But you can't kill a man for that. I mean, he was a lousy husband, but he was the only one I had." Apparently, there was no love lost between the two.

Sissy looked to her aunt and cocked her head to one side. Again. And again. And again.

Finally, she got her attention. Sissy rolled her eyes in the direction of the phone.

Bethel pointed to herself, *Who me?* written clearly in her expression. Sissy knew that it wasn't taking the chance to grab the device that had her aunt questioning, but her lack of *Englisch* phone skills.

Sissy nodded.

Bethel hesitated.

Sissy jerked her head in the direction of the phone once again. *Now*, she mouthed. *Hurry!*

"You can only have one husband," Weaver said. "So why would you want a lousy one?"

"Why indeed?" Sally shot her husband a pointed look.

"Me?" Weaver said. He was so distracted by this new development that he didn't see Bethel inch out of place and pick up the phone.

Now if her aunt could just figure out how to work it.

"I've done nothing but provide for my family."

"And fight over tomato plants and now sh—"

"That was worth fighting for." Weaver lifted his chin. "The indignities."

His hold on the rifle was loose, and Sissy wondered if she could dart out and snatch it from his grasp before he could tighten it. She wasn't sure that Weaver was a kill-'em-all kind of guy, and that's what he would have to do. Plus, he only had one shell left. At least, she thought that was how it worked. So he would only be able to shoot one of them. And at the rate they were going, even in spite of Sissy's rotten luck lately, that someone would most likely be his wife.

She weighed her options, then turned to look at her aunt once more. Bethel was staring at the phone screen, her face scrunched up into a frown of thought.

If Bethel couldn't figure out how to use the thing, then Sissy had no choice.

It was do-or-die time.

She lunged forward and took hold of the wooden part of the gun. Not the stock but the other part. But Weaver was quicker than he looked and tightened his grip as well. She couldn't let him have it. He might be able to only shoot one of them, but he could bludgeon them all with the stock part, if he so chose. And if he'd killed Walt Summers with one blow, none of them stood a chance.

Sissy dug in her heels and pulled hard.

A loud boom invaded the air as the smell of gunpowder assaulted her nostrils. The barrel touched her arm. It was as hot as an iron, and she let go of the gun, stumbling backward.

She turned to make sure all was well. Mary Ann. Sally, Gavin. Beth—as if in slow motion, her aunt crumpled to the ground.

CHAPTER TWENTY-THREE

A man's life is only as good as the woman he marries.
—Aunt Bess

"You shot a hole straight through my prayer covering, Weaver Justice." Bethel glared at him from her place in the business part of the ambulance.

The man didn't acknowledge her words as the deputy loaded him, handcuffed and forlorn, into the back of a patrol car.

Just after the second shot rang out, Deputy Earl Berry had pulled up, lights flashing. He whooped the siren only once, but it was enough to stop everyone in their tracks. For a moment, at least, then Weaver took off running toward his house, and Sissy headed to her aunt.

By the time she had gotten to her side, completely convinced that her aunt was bleeding profusely from some ghastly wound, Bethel was struggling to sit up, madder than a wet hen, as Sissy's mother always said.

Earl Berry caught up with Weaver before he could make it to the house. The man could actually run—Berry, not Weaver—which was surprising for someone who ate pie every day at ten-thirty a.m.

Now Gavin had changed into some sort of coveralls, and his clothes and shoes had been placed in a bio-hazard bag. Barefoot, he had given his statement to Berry, and he was now waiting for someone to take him home.

"I would drive you," Arnold said. "But—" He waved a hand around at Gavin, not willing to say the reason out loud.

Arnold, the Lyft driver, had sped off, felt bad about deserting them, then stopped when he saw Berry parked in the Carriage House parking lot. He had told the deputy what he had seen and that perhaps the people he had left there were in trouble. Berry, more than a little upset that once again Sissy was invading his investigation, had hurried over. That was how he had gotten there so quickly. Actually, the reason he had gotten there at all. Bethel was not good with a cell phone.

Sissy made a mental note to teach her aunt her pass code and how to dial a 9-1-1 call from someone else's phone. Just in case.

Gavin nodded understandingly. "One of the deputies will. I hope." He might have wiped off most of the sludge that he had fallen into, but that didn't mean he was entirely free of it. A few speckles still stuck to the sides of his glasses, and the smell . . . well, Sissy figured that would hang around long after the actual . . . *stuff* had been washed away with clean water and a ton of soap.

He turned back to his notes. He had been writing steadily since he had gotten out of his stinky clothes. For Yoder, this was the crime of the century—a murder and a conspiracy Sissy was pretty sure Gavin would dub PoopGate.

Mary Ann and Sally were huddled together, each soaking up the other's strength and comfort. They were also waiting for their individual turns to be questioned by the police. That didn't take long. Earl Berry was convinced that at least one of them was a co-conspirator in what Sissy was certain Gavin was already writing about.

"So you mean to tell me that, all this time, you didn't know that your husband was stealing your neighbors' . . . sewage and using it for fertilizer? I find that hard to believe."

"There are a lot of things that are hard to believe," Mary Ann shot back.

You got that right, sister.

"I sort of suspected," Sally admitted. "Just a hint here and there."

"Like?" Berry waited, his stub of a pencil poised above the little notebook he carried around in his right breast pocket.

"Well, when Vern and his crew came out to clean the tank it was empty."

"Vern McDaniel?" Berry asked. "From Pumps and Pipes?"

Sally nodded. "Weaver was so mad. Carrying on about how the only charge was for the actual service visit for them to come out. Then he stormed out with the invoice."

"Where did he go?"

"I didn't ask him," she said. "But he didn't go far. He was only gone for a few minutes. When he came back inside the house, he was shaking and carrying on. And he didn't have the invoice any longer."

"That was when he killed Walt." Berry nodded in a self-sure way that made Sissy want to shake her head.

His investigative skills were impeccable.

"Why would he do such a thing?" Tears welled in Sally's eyes, and she turned to Mary Ann. "I mean, he killed your husband."

"Hush," Mary Ann told her and pressed Sally's head down onto her shoulder. "It's all over now."

The whole town was buzzing the following day. The Sunflower Café was packed all morning, residents lingering over their grits and coffee to talk about the events that had transpired the day before.

"It must be a little depressing to have to wait a whole week to get the story out in the paper," Sissy said to Gavin. He had just arrived, and she had found him a table before someone else could grab it.

"Nah," he said with a flick of his hand. "It sweetens the pot. Gives me time to talk to more people, interview witnesses, and get a more complete perspective on the whole situation."

"It's killing you, admit it."

"I'm dying inside," Gavin said with a chuckle. "But, at least, I have an exclusive since I was there."

Like it mattered. Only three other people worked at the *Sunflower Express*. The chances of him getting the story were great, even without having to fall in a vat of—

Well, you know.

She set the water glass in front of him. "The usual?"

He nodded and pulled out his computer as she went off to place his order.

She returned a moment or two later and glanced around the dining area. The place was full, but everyone was slow to leave. Lottie had a fresh pot of coffee and was going around refilling the cups of the diners who were still chatting about the big happenings the day before. Sissy supposed that no one knew yet that it was she and Gavin and Bethel who had been involved or they would have been bombarded with questions.

But until then, she slid into the booth opposite Gavin.

"Tell me again what happened," she said, propping her elbow on the table and cupping her chin in her palm.

"I walked into the shed and saw a depression at the edge of the potting table. So I pushed it aside—"

"The potting table," she clarified, even though she had made him tell her this story countless times since it had happened.

"And then—" He stopped and shot her a look.

"You fell in." She tried not to laugh. Really, she did. But Aunt Bess said it right: Everything's funny as long as it's happening to someone else.

"I smelled it all night. Even after three showers." He made a face.

"Maybe you should bathe in tomato juice."

He shook his head. "That only works if you've been sprayed by a skunk."

She shrugged. "You'll never know until you try."

"I think it's psychosomatic."

"Yeah, or just psycho." She grinned at her friend. "So what's going to happen to Weaver now?"

"The usual. You can't go around killing your neighbor even if he's stealing the contents of your sewage tank."

"I'm still not sure how he did it."

Gavin lifted one shoulder and let it drop. "When I was talking with Berry after the arrest, we figured that when Summers helped Justice install that last septic tank four years ago, he put another one for himself under his growing shed and ran a line between the two."

"And when Weaver discovered the deception and pulled the line out, that caused the stink hole in the growing shed."

"Sink hole?"

"Stink hole, sink hole. Basically, it's all the same in this case," she said.

He laughed. At least, he could see the humor in it. Well, some of it, it seemed.

"If he did this four years ago . . ." Sissy started.

"That appears to coincide with the change in his Special Blend. But we won't know for certain until the results come back from the lab."

Sissy wrinkled up her nose. "I read something about this in *The Budget*," she said. "About whether

or not it's okay to use human waste to fertilize consumption crops."

"Look at you, reading the Amish paper. We'll
made a Yoderarian of you after all."

If she wanted to admit, and she didn't, the
truth? She was closer than he knew to making this
a permanent move.

"So what did the article say?" he asked.

"Just that there were a lot of factors to it. How
the different habits of the human sources could
change the effectiveness of the fertilizer."

"Which may be the case here."

"Maybe," she agreed. "But more than anything,
I gathered that the big argument was whether or
not to label the crops as to how they had been fertilized."

"I could agree with that," he said. "One hundred percent."

She looked up as Bethel came out of the
kitchen. Her aunt motioned for Sissy to join her.
"Gotta go," she said and rose from the booth.

Bethel propped both hands on her hips and
waited for Sissy to make her way to the waitress station. Her aunt's expression was the same as usual,
frowny and unreadable, so it was impossible to tell
what she wanted until she actually spoke.

"Amos is around back," she said. "He wants to
talk to you."

"Amos Yoder?"

Bethel nodded, then shooed her into the kitchen and through to the back door.

Amos waited by the sink, his hat in one hand, a
small blue sack in the other. "Hi," he greeted as
she drew near.

Sissy nodded in return. "Bethel said you wanted to see me."

"*Jah.*" He held out the sack. "This is from the children. They wanted to thank you for helping bring their sister back home."

"So they've released Emma?" Sissy asked, taking the bag from him. It was the kind with handles, like a gift bag, but plain. It was hefty, and when she glanced down inside, she could see bags of what looked like fudge and practically every color of construction paper known to man.

"She's on her way home now. The *kinner* worked on this all evening long before bed."

"Thank you," she said. "But you guys didn't have to do anything for me."

"We did. Without you—" He broke off, obviously choked up over the events of the last couple of weeks. "We just wanted to say *danki.*"

"I wasn't the only one," she told him. "But I do appreciate the sentiment."

"It's good you've come back, Sissy Yoder." He donned his hat and made his way out the back door and into the morning sunshine.

She didn't have the heart to tell him that she wasn't *back*. She may have visited Yoder when she was young, but she had never lived there a day in her life. Until now.

Amos left, and she turned back toward the door that led to the dining room. Gavin and her aunt had helped as well. She didn't deserve all the praise.

But as she came through to the dining area, she saw that both Bethel and Gavin had their own bags. So she wouldn't have to share the fudge after all. Nice.

Gavin's order came up, and Sissy ran it to his table.

"Thanks," he said, reaching for the pepper shaker. She had never seen him add salt to anything. "How about a bike ride tonight?"

She grimaced. "How about we sit on the front porch, drink a beer, and talk about bike riding?"

"Sounds like a plan."

The Friday-night Yoder family supper was packed. For two reasons. One, Lizzie and Daniel had just brought the babies home from the hospital. It seemed little Joshua Albert and Maudie Rose were very adept at gaining weight. For the time being, that was a really good thing. And second, Emma was home with her family. The entire Amos Yoder clan had shown, along with half the aunts, uncles, and cousins who lived in the area. To anyone driving by, it looked like an Amish wedding on a Friday night.

Tractors were parked all over the yard, in addition to several buggies, whose horses were happily munching grass in the side pasture with Bethel's own buggy mare. Daniel and one of his brothers moved a long wooden worktable to the yard. Sissy had covered it with a plastic tablecloth, and the women had piled it high with the food offerings. It was a BYOLC event—Bring Your Own Lawn Chair. Everyone could fix their plate and then head off to talk and visit and otherwise enjoy the family—

the new additions and the fact that Emma had been released from jail.

"I still can't believe you did that," Sissy said, biting into one of the chicken wings that Virgil's wife, Sarah, had made for the occasion.

Then the thought struck her—Amos's wife had been Sarah Yoder. His daughter was Sarah Yoder, and Virgil's wife was Sarah Yoder as well. And she wondered . . . just how many Sarah Yoders lived in Yoder? And how did they keep them all straight?

Emma shrugged. "It just looked so much like Dat could have done it."

They were sitting on the back porch, watching her young siblings play a version of kickball that was quickly turning into quite a competition.

"Did he say anything about that? The fact that you basically thought he was a murderer?"

Emma's eyes grew wide. "I never—no, I mean—"

Such was the disposition of her Amish kin. So unassuming, so forgiving, so loving.

Sissy laid the back of her hand on Emma's knee. Her fingers were still sticky from the wings, and she didn't want to get anything on Emma's dress or apron. But she wanted her to know she was sincere. "That's the most selfless thing I have ever seen anyone do for their siblings."

Emma smiled, but tears filled her blue, blue eyes. "I love them."

Emma was willing to go to prison for the rest of her life in order to make sure her family was cared for. There had been times when Sissy's brother wouldn't spit on her if she was on fire.

Okay, that was harsh, but she and Owen definitely didn't see eye to eye on everything. Much at all. Practically nothing. He was the successful one, or so it seemed. Not that she was bitter or anything. It wasn't like she could brag about her position as a syndicated newspaper columnist without telling the whole world she was Aunt Bess. And that wasn't happening.

Suck it up, buttercup. There were worse things than having your mom call each week and ask if you needed money. But, just once, she wanted to be the golden one.

But looking at Emma and seeing what she was willing to sacrifice made that dream seem garish and unworthy.

"Have you tried these wings?" Gavin sauntered up, sauce in both corners of his mouth. He had a wing in one hand and his plate in the other, so he couldn't readily access his napkin. Sissy had a feeling that it was the least of his concerns at the moment.

"Yes," she said, as Emma nodded as well.

"They're amazing. Whoever made these could open a food truck and sell these all over the place."

"I think I'm going to join the game," Emma said. She set her plate aside and stood.

"Go get 'em," Sissy called. "I'll be right here cheering you on."

Emma smiled, and Sissy could see the joy in her expression and in her sparkling eyes.

Gavin settled down into the spot next to her. "I'm serious about the food truck."

Sissy shook her head. "Virgil's wife made them."

"Virgil is Bethel's son," he confirmed.

"Yep. And he's the reason I'm here."

"Really?" Gavin said, his brows rising in surprise.

"Yup. He put the ad in the paper that my mother saw. Then she called Lizzie and found out all that was going on, and now here I am."

"So I have two things to thank him for—getting you to Yoder and marrying the world's best maker of chicken wings."

Sissy just laughed and shook her head. "So the big story comes out Sunday," she said.

He nodded. "Breaking news."

"And how are you ever going to top that story?"

"I've got an idea." He tossed down the chicken bone and managed to get most of the sauce off his fingers and face. "A series of articles about the differences between the Amish people who live here and those who live in other communities."

She stopped for a second. Not exactly what she'd imagined he'd say. Not anywhere close. In fact, for a moment, she imagined that he might do some sort of ode to chicken wings. "I think that is a great idea."

"I might need your help with it, though. You know. Maybe open a few Amish doors."

"I'm sure I can help with that."

He nodded. "And if I get it, then I might have to travel a little."

"And maybe even buy a car?" she asked.

He shot her a look. "Don't get crazy."

She laughed. "You're always Gavin."

His face scrunched into a frown. "What's that supposed to mean?"

"Nothing. But I think you should wait until after the big scavenger hunt before you go traipsing off to Lancaster."

"Who said anything about Lancaster? There's plenty of Amish over in Missouri."

She nodded. "I knew that."

The look on his face said he wasn't buying it for a second.

"Come play with us." Ruth and Esther, two of Emma's sisters, came to pull them into the fray of the game.

"I'm eating," Gavin protested.

"You can eat tomorrow," Sissy said. "It's going to be dark soon."

And dark in Amish country was darker than most people had ever seen. Once the sun went down, the festivities would fizzle to a close, and that would be that, as Aunt Bess would say.

"I'm going to have to cycle twice as far tomorrow in order to work off all these wings." He laughed and set his plate aside before allowing the girls to pull them into the game.

He was still licking his fingers as he took his place as the first baseman.

Sissy watched him in the waning light, the pink and purple sky behind him giving him a surreal look, as if he were in some sci-fi movie on another planet than Earth.

She shook her head at her fanciful thoughts. But she also couldn't help noticing that, in the softening light of the approaching dusk, when he turned his head a certain way, he was sort of handsome. Not like Declan, but in his own right. Handsome or not, she was not in the market for a relationship. Though she could use a friend. And that's exactly what she had found in Gavin Wainwright. A friend in him and a new life in the small town of Yoder, Kansas.